Prom Dates from Hell

MAGGIE QUINN: GIRL VS. EVIL

Prom Dates from Hell

a novel by

Rosemary Clement-Moore

DELACORTE PRESS

Published by Delacorte Press
an imprint of Random House Children's Books
a division of Random House, Inc.
New York

Visit us on the Web! www.randomhouse.com/teens

Educators and librarians, for a variety of teaching tools, visit us at
www.randomhouse.com/teachers

The Library of Congress has cataloged the hardcover edition of this work as follows:
Clement-Moore, Rosemary.
Prom dates from Hell / Rosemary Clement-Moore.
p. cm.
Summary: High school senior and yearbook photographer Maggie thought she
would rather die than go to prom, but when a classmate summons a revenge-
seeking demon, she has no choice but to buy herself a dress and prepare to face
jocks, cheerleaders, and Evil Incarnate.
ISBN: 978-0-385-73412-7 (trade) — ISBN: 978-0-385-90428-5 (glb)
[1. Demonology–Fiction. 2. High schools–Fiction. 3. Schools–Fiction. 4. Horror
stories.]   I. Title.
Pz7.C59117Pro 2007
[Fic]–dc22
2006011015

ISBN: 978-0-385-73413-4 (tr. pbk.)

The text of this book is set in 12-point Filosofia.

Printed in the United States of America

Book design by Angela Carlino

10 9 8 7 6 5

First Trade Paperback Edition

To my dad, Robert Wallace Clement,

who never forgot how to tell a story

1

as an interactive horror experience, with beasts from Hell, mayhem, gore, and dismemberment, it was an impressive event. As a high school prom, however, the evening was marginally less successful.

I should start at the beginning, but I'm not entirely certain when that is, so I'll start with the day I realized that despite my most determined efforts, I was not going to be able to ignore the prom entirely.

The end of April, and a rabid satin and tulle frenzy had attached to every double X chromosome in the senior class. All available wall space—hallway, cafeteria, even the bathrooms—sprouted signage in the most obnoxious colors possible. I was assaulted by flyers in the courtyard, and harassed by thrice-daily announcements. Had I gotten my tickets yet? Had I voted for the class song? Had I voted for the King and Queen? No, no, and Hell no, because voting for royalty was not just moronic, it was oxymoronic.

No one was safe from the Prom Plague. When dog-eared copies of *Seventeen* magazine started circulating through AP English, I knew I'd soon have to fall back to the band hall and call the CDC from there.

Then one day my neutrality was over. My indifference punctured. Stanley Dozer asked me to be his date.

Stanley Dozer was even lower on the high school food chain than I was, and I was in the journalism club. Sometimes I think God must have a kind of divine craps table; every once in a while He shoots snake eyes and the next baby born is screwed from the jump. I mean, "Stanley Dozer," for starters. Maybe he could have aesthetically overcome this name, but the guy was about six foot five, pale and bony as a corpse, with hair the color of spiderwebs. His ankles and wrists shot out of his too short jeans and the sleeves of his plaid button-down shirt. I sympathized with the sizing problems, but I had to wonder at the complete inattention to fashion. And by fashion I mean "camouflage."

Back on the middle school Serengeti I learned that, lacking a certain killer instinct, my best bet was to avoid standing out from the herd and making myself a target for the apex social predators, at least until I'd built up a tough skin. Now I'm sort of like the spiny anteater. Small and prickly, trundling along, a threat to no one. Except ants, I guess, which is where the metaphor runs out.

Back to Stanley's ambush. On the second-story breeze-way that overlooked the courtyard below, the Spanish Club was selling candy to raise money for their Guatemalan sponsor child and I was taking their picture. Privately I thought little Juanita would benefit a lot faster if they sold tequila shots instead. Not that I advocate underage alcohol, but I bet there were a few teachers who could use a drink this time of year.

"Hi, Maggie!" Stanley's voice startled me.

I spun around, narrowly missing hitting him in his bony chest with my camera. I'm used to looking up, but with Stanley I had to crane my neck and squint. "Oh. Hi, Stanley."

Behind me, the Spanish Club giggled. What was Español for "Bite me"?

"How are you?" he asked, hefting his book bag onto his shoulder. The canvas bag bore the logo of the natural history museum. High on the geek quotient, but worlds better than the briefcase he'd carried freshman year.

"I'm taking some pictures for the yearbook." I hinted broadly that I was busy. After all, the next box of Chiclets might be the one that sent little Juanita to college.

"I saw you up here, and I thought . . . Well, you know how the prom is coming up?"

"Is it really?" I mumbled, messing with the settings on my camera. "I had no idea."

Sarcasm sailed over his head, which was a trick considering his height. He shuffled from foot to foot, giving the unfortunate appearance of a dancing skeleton. "Well, I was thinking you could go with me. We could, you know, go together."

The words entered my ears, but my brain rejected them.

3

Stanley Dozer was *not* asking me to the prom. Words failed me, and that's just not something that happens. Ever. I'd known Stanley since his paste-eating days, and had always tried to be nice to him. I was the spoilsport who pulled the KICK ME sign off his back, or helped him pick up his books after he'd been tripped—either by his own overlong legs or someone else's. I guess if I were a better person I'd have befriended him more thoroughly. I felt bad about that, but not that bad.

"Wow. The prom." I stalled as the rest of the school continued normal operations, electric bells calling students to class, kids buffeting us as they passed on the breezeway, calling to the people below. "I really wasn't planning to go," I said honestly. "I might have to take pictures, but I'd kind of be working."

"Yeah, but if you have to go anyway . . ."

"Oh, you wouldn't have fun that way." I flipped through my mental student files, clinging to the notion that there is somebody for everyone. "What about Karen Foley? Weren't you guys in Mathletes together?"

"Until she blew our answer in the district semifinal round," Stanley sneered. "She's not nearly as smart as everyone thinks she is."

"Oh-kay. That was a little harsh."

"Yeah, well, Karen Foley is a dork."

And *that* was unkind and rather nasty. Also, Mr. Glass House didn't have any business throwing stones. But before I could react, someone grabbed Stanley from behind. Amid laughter and alarmed squeals, the breezeway cleared of traffic as Biff the Jock bent poor Stanley over for a noogie.

4

Biff wasn't his name, but he reminded me of the bully in *Back to the Future,* so that was the name my brain supplied. Though Stanley had half a foot of height on him, the football player was muscular, so watching Biff rough up the poor dweeb was like watching an English mastiff pin an Afghan hound.

"Hey, Bulldozer! Trying to get a date?" I willed Stanley to fight back; he should have leverage to his advantage if nothing else. But his spindly arms and legs just flailed around as the pack of jocks and cheerleaders jeered.

"Leave him alone," I said, not much more effectively.

"Awww." Biff wrapped a meaty arm around Stanley's neck and baby-talked, "Does oo haff a widdle girlfriend, Dozer?" His friends roared at this example of their leader's wit. Stanley's face was turning purple with what I hoped was rage and not asphyxiation.

"I said, leave him alone. Go find another Mack truck to pick on."

Biff's girlfriend—whose name, like half of the cheer squad, was Jessica—got up in my face. "That's so cute! I think she likes him back."

"How sweet." Biff and his friend pushed poor Stanley to the edge of the breezeway, pretending they were going to launch him over the brick barrier onto the courtyard below. "You going to *fall* for her, Bulldozer?"

Stanley didn't answer; he looked paralyzed by terror. The jocks might have been pretending, but the horror on Stanley's face was very real. I raised the best weapon at my disposal and clicked off a rapid-fire series of pictures on my camera. It got Cheerleader Barbie's attention.

"What are you doing!" Yell-leading had definitely developed her lungs. Her shriek made my right eye twitch, but I replied calmly.

"I'm documenting the event. Maybe for the principal. Maybe just for the school paper. Maybe for an insert, right next to the ballot for prom queen."

"You can't do that!" My eardrum gave a seismic shudder. "I've worked for four years. My mom already bought my dress. It's *all planned*, you hag." My camera clicked in her livid, bug-eyed face. It is probably all that saved me from her claws. Instead she turned to her boyfriend. "Let him go, Brandon! You and your stupid sense of humor."

Brandon. That was his real name. He and his buddies let poor Stanley go, and the geek collapsed onto the concrete in a jumble of bony elbows and knees as Brandon turned on me. "You are nothing but a snitch and a tattletale, Quinn."

"It's called investigative journalism, asshole. The next time I even hear about you attacking someone, I'll e-mail these pictures to the principal, the local paper, and the admissions board of every school with a Division One football team."

Brandon took a threatening step toward me, but restrained himself when I raised the camera. He gestured to his knuckle-cracking goon squad and they lumbered off, followed by Jessica, Jessica, and Jessica, who each gave me the death eye before they flipped their hair and flounced after them. I wondered if they worked on that synchronized hair flip during cheer practice.

When they'd gone, the Spanish Club and their customers emerged from behind the table where they'd been hunkered, and began to applaud. I pshawed and, with a sense of whimsy, dropped a deep curtsy that probably looked silly in my jeans and Doc Martens.

"You bitch." The depth of venom in the word prickled the skin on the back of my neck. The faces of the Spanish Club changed as well, like villagers in a werewolf movie, when their kindly town grocer suddenly turns into a slavering beast.

I whirled, but saw only Stanley. He was a mess; his colorless hair stood up in limp spikes, and his clothes were askew, so that even his skin didn't seem to fit quite right. The sight should have been comically pathetic. But his eyes blazed at me from his thin face, so poisonous that I took an instinctive step back. "I don't need your help handling those asswipes. I don't need anyone's help!"

"Of course you don't." I made my voice soothing, the way they talk to crazy people on TV. I wanted to tell him to get over himself, but the malice in him stopped my tongue. I was fighting the urge to cross myself, like Granny Quinn did when she talked about the evil eye, or bad news, or my mother's cooking.

"You don't believe me." He brushed by, bumping me aside, stomping past the Mexican candy table. We all watched him, maybe afraid to look away, in case he sprouted another head or something. It didn't seem impossible. "You'll see. I don't need anyone's protection. You'll all be sorry."

Still muttering, he flung open the glass door and went in. I heard the Spanish Club exhale their pent-up breath, and someone laughed nervously. I didn't blame her. Talk about your B-movie dialogue. It was ridiculous to feel anything but sorry for the guy.

That's what I told myself as I rubbed my arm where Stanley's bony elbow had hit me, hard enough to leave a bruise.

2

avalon High was the older of the town's two public second-
ary schools. The oldest building on our campus had been
around since World War II, and I was pretty sure my civics
teacher had been on the faculty then.

Mr. Wells lectured straight from a series of overhead
transparencies that dated back to the Reagan administration. I wasn't sure if the material was that outdated, or if
the government process was that stagnant, but it meant
that as long as you copied down the information from the
overhead (or got the transcription later), you could pretty
much do whatever you wanted and the slightly deaf Wells

would keep droning on, like the little bald-headed engine that could.

This, and the fact that I had D&D Lisa to share my misery, kept me from skipping too much, despite it being the last class of the day.

Lisa had been D&D Lisa since the seventh grade. When she'd moved into the district midterm, there was already a Lisa in our class. Asked to "stand up and tell the students something about yourself," the new Lisa said shamelessly, "I like to play Dungeons and Dragons."

We laughed, of course, but she repeated this introduction in each new class period, with the same result. Finally I asked her, "Why do you say that, when you know everyone's going to laugh?" She told me it was the quickest way to separate friend from foe: one laughs *with* her, the other laughs *at* her. "And when I take over the world," she had said, with a very straight face, "I will know who to embrace into the fold, and who to feed to my undead zombie minions."

That was Lisa. She said outrageous things, and you could never tell if she was being sarcastic or not. Geeky pretty, like that Goth girl on the TV show *NCIS*, and wicked smart, she didn't even need fashion camouflage. She had the armadillo plating of unflappable self-confidence, and nothing she said, no matter how droll, seemed impossible.

Since I had no desire to be Zombie Chow, I resolved to stay on her good side. Eventually, I got over my intimidation and we became good friends, despite our obvious differences. Though she gave up the spikes and black nail polish in tenth grade, Lisa still had a way of throwing together vintage-store finds—things that should never go together—

and somehow making it work. When I do that, I just look like I dressed in the dark.

Maybe it helped that she had a tall and naturally slender physique, with chestnut hair that fell in a smooth curtain around her face. I'm short, but otherwise average, which means that I wish my butt were smaller, but I don't wish it enough to actually exercise. My dark hair is cut in a bob, which is supposed to look like Velma Kelly in the movie *Chicago*. Only it never works out that way. My hair has a mind of its own, so with my round face and pointed chin, I mostly look like that crazy girl in *Fight Club,* only without the chain smoking and the, you know, crazy part.

Maybe I'm just saving the chain smoking, binge drinking, and crazy wild sex until I go off to college. But at the moment, my major vice is sarcasm, with a side of caffeine addiction.

Anyway, Lisa had the Geek Chic thing working for her, was the front-runner for valedictorian, and though she was in no way popular, she knew people in every subgroup in the school and had her finger on the pulse of the student body in a way that even I—plucky girl reporter—could only envy.

"I heard you took on the Jocks and Jessicas this morning," she said as we sat in civics class that afternoon. The hum of the overhead projector covered our conversation easily. "When I am an evil overlord, you may be my minister of disinformation."

"Thanks. I'll need a job after you dissolve the free press."

"Of course you will."

Mr. Wells changed the transparency and we copied

down the overview of the judicial system. Test questions came word for word from the notes, making rote memorization the path of least effort. "I heard Stanley Dozer totally wigged out."

I made bored curlicues out of the bottoms of my *g*'s, *p*'s, and *y*'s. "Who could blame him after the meatheads roughed him up?"

"Did he really call you a bitch?" I nodded and she made an annoyed sound. "That's gratitude for you."

"The fragile male ego makes no exceptions for nerds, I guess." Finished copying the page, I slumped back down until the next installment, and rubbed the bruise on my arm. "You think he might climb the clock tower with an assault weapon one day?"

"Dozer? He's in the Chess Club, for crying out loud." She chewed the end of her pen. "Besides, we don't have a clock tower."

"You know what I mean." No one really talked about Columbine High School anymore, but when I was in middle school we had three drills: fire, tornado, and one that involved locking the doors and huddling together as far away from the windows as possible. They told us this was an "extreme-weather drill," for when there wasn't time to move to safety. But it didn't take a genius to figure out that nobody locked a door against a tornado.

"I'll make you a deal," Lisa mumbled around the pen in her mouth. "If Dozer comes to school in a black trench coat, we'll ditch the rest of the day."

"We can take my Jeep."

Wells changed the transparency again, and we had to

shut up because the plastic was yellowed to the point where deciphering the print took all our concentration.

✳ ✳ ✳

"There's no coffee." At five-thirty the next morning I stood in our kitchen in my pajamas and ratty old bathrobe and stared at the coffeemaker stupidly. "Why is there no coffee?"

My father continued to eat his cereal, showing not nearly enough concern for this crisis. "Write it on the grocery list." He gestured with his spoon to the scrap of paper that was stuck to the fridge with a Disneyland magnet. "Your mom is going to the store this afternoon."

"I don't need coffee in the afternoon. I need it now." I was whining, but I didn't care. I needed caffeine.

"Have some tea."

Grumbling, I opened the fridge. There was no Coke, either. This day was shot to Hell already. I scuffed my bunny slippers to the breakfast table and sat, head in hands, moaning piteously until he noticed my misery.

"What's the matter, Magpie? You're up early."

"I had a nightmare." I laid my cheek on the table. "I couldn't go back to sleep, so I figured I'd get up."

"You're not nervous about your exams, are you?"

"No." True, I was a little swamped at the moment. But the nightmare that rattled me wasn't a brain dream, where my anxieties ran around in my skull like ADD gerbils. It was what, when I was little, I used to call "gut dreams," after the "gut instincts" I still sometimes get. Those flashes were easier to filter than the dreams they sparked, because my defenses were down while I slept.

I 3

This nightmare was little more than disjointed images, but I'd awoken in a sweat, certain that something was very wrong somewhere. I had stumbled downstairs to try and chase the shadows away, but without my usual morning stimulant, the unease simply would not fade.

"Is Mom all right?" I asked.

Dad set down his spoon; his bowl was empty except for three Cheerios clinging together like tiny lifesavers in an ocean of milk. "She's delicately snoring away." He paused, then gave me a verbal nudge. "Did you dream about your mom?"

"No. It was really vague." I frowned, doubting myself. "Probably just random stuff."

"Tell me. Maybe you'll feel better."

Eyes fixed on those three little oat rings, I let my thoughts drift back to the dream, which always worked better than trying to purposefully remember details.

"I was somewhere really hot," I began haltingly. "As hot as that blast of air when you open the oven door. There was fire, and really foul smelling smoke." My brows knotted. "Or maybe I only thought there were flames, because of the heat and the smoke. It was more the *impression* of fire, of trying to leash a force of nature."

He nodded. I saw the motion in the corner of my eye as I let my mind float with the Cheerios. "And smoke?"

"All around me, burning my eyes and my throat. The smell was horrible, like a Dumpster on a hot day. Rotten eggs, spoiled meat, and something like gunpowder." The images played before my unfocused eyes and I went on describing them in a droning voice. "In the center, the smoke thickened. Not solid, but with substance. Viscous, maybe."

I wasn't sure that was the right word. I remembered the toy slime I'd had as a kid, and the way the goo would slide through your hands, and squish through your fingers. The stuff also made a comical farting noise when you pushed it into the jar, but there was nothing funny about the formed yet formless darkness in my dream.

"What else happened?" Dad leaned on his elbows, eyes alive with an academic interest.

"A voice was calling out a list of names. Gibberish or another language, but definitely a roll call of some kind. I knew they were names of people. And I knew which name was mine."

The images slipped away now, faster and faster the more I tried to grasp them. Then Dad bumped the bowl; the Cheerio rings broke apart, and with them my concentration. I breathed deep, and scrubbed my hands over my face.

"That's all I remember." My fingers speared through my thick mop of hair, worsening a raging case of bedhead. Dad watched me carefully, and I dredged up a sheepish sort of smile. "The whole thing doesn't sound that scary when I say it aloud."

He rose, gathering his breakfast dishes, and gave my shoulder an encouraging squeeze. "Isn't that the point?"

"I guess." I rubbed a little crust of sleep from my eye and asked, as casually as I could "What do you suppose the dream means?"

"I don't know, Magpie. What do you think?"

"I think it means I'm going to Hell."

His dishes clattered in the sink. "What in God's name makes you say that?"

"Come on, Dad. Fire? Brimstone? And that roll call, like

Gabriel, only on the crispy end of things." I did feel better voicing the fear. Things lose a lot of power once you name them. "I'm probably going to Hell for telling Stanley I wouldn't go to the prom with him."

"Professor Dozer's son?" Dad taught history in the same department where Stanley's mom taught anthropology.

"Yeah. He asked me yesterday."

"Heh."

That was the support I got from my loving parent. "Heh." I also noticed that he didn't deny I might be Hellbound. I was *so* glad we'd had this little heart-to-heart.

I got up and shuffled toward the hall. "I'm going upstairs to get dressed. I'll grab some coffee on the way to school."

"You need to eat some breakfast."

"Yes, *Mom*."

"Maggie?" I turned at the door, my hand resting on the jamb. "If you want, you can talk to your granny about the dream." Despite the length of the kitchen between us, he spoke softly, in case Mom was awake. There are certain things that make Mom give this *sigh*, a sort of forced exhalation of see-what-I-have-to-put-up-with martyrdom. Granny Quinn's "superstitions" rank somewhere between not eating breakfast and Dad's insistence, every year, that there is nothing wrong with leaving the Christmas lights on the roof until Valentine's Day, as long as you don't turn them on.

"Thanks, Dad. But it's no big deal. Probably just graduation anxiety. I mean, we've got eight bazillion seniors. That ceremony is bound to be hellishly long if nothing else."

He smiled, I smiled, and then I turned to go. With all

that smiling, you'd think at least one of us would be reassured.

∗   ∗   ∗

I climbed the stairs without my usual caffeinated zip. A few years ago Mom had been hinting about a new house, but Dad didn't want to move. He has tenure at the university, and he can walk from home if he wants. All the shiny new subdivisions are all the way on the outskirts of town, near the state highway that leads to the big city. Plus they have no trees.

To compromise, my parents remodeled our raised ranch-style house so that it looked less like the Brady Bunch lived here. Among other things, they'd moved me upstairs into what used to be the game room, and my old room became Mom's home office. I think the plan was to encourage me to stay home and go to school here. It isn't that I don't like Avalon. It's a college town, with an idealized retro feel. We didn't even have a Starbucks until a year ago. People love it or hate it here. I love it, but it's not really on my road to the Pulitzer Prize.

In the meantime, I had a pretty nice setup: the whole loft for myself, with bedroom stuff on one side of the room, a study area on the other. The decorating scheme, though, was Early American Disaster Zone. I had to wade through the clothes on the floor. My computer equipment took up the entire desk and had started to spill onto the adjoining table. Every surface was covered with books, paper, binders, disks, and CDs.

But who had time to clean? Besides the Dance-That-Shall-Not-Be-Named, there were pep rallies and games, the

Big Spring Musical and end-of-the-year band concerts, field trips, service projects—not to mention term papers and final exams. School spirit is not my thing, but I was on both the school paper and the yearbook staff. The night before I'd taken pictures at the basketball game, then written an essay on *Julius Caesar* before going to bed to be tied in knots by my subconscious.

I was down to my last clean pair of underwear, but a search unearthed some jeans that didn't yet stand up by themselves. At the back of the closet was a shirt from Aunt Joyce that I'd never worn because it was a little too Woodstock: kind of gauzy, with a tiny floral print, belled sleeves, and a square neck trimmed with thinly crocheted lace.

Any port in a storm, I groused. Then I felt guilty because of little Juanita in Guatemala; they could clothe her village with what lay unwashed on my floor.

Stress and guilt. The longer I was awake, the easier it was to believe that the nightmare was just that. I kept trying to put a rational face on things, even when my instincts said otherwise.

When I was little, I loved Granny Quinn's tales of the fair folk, will-o'-the-wisps, and *bain sidhe*. My dreams seemed part of that at first, more fairy stories and make-believe. Nobody took them seriously, until one morning at breakfast I asked how long until Aunt Joyce had her baby. Mom told me not to be ridiculous. That afternoon, her sister called and said she was pregnant.

After that, Mom started getting a pinched expression when I talked about my dreams, even as Gran and Dad took them as a matter of course. Then one night—was it eight years ago already?—I woke up screaming, babbling about glass and metal and blood, hysterical with fear. Mom was still quieting my tears when the phone rang.

No good news ever comes in the middle of the night. While Mom listened on the phone, I stood beside her in my Little Mermaid pajamas, and slipped my small hand into her icy one. Her face was a mask, but her eyes were snapshots of grief. Dad, awakened by the phone, stumbled out of their bedroom and froze at the sight of us.

"There was a terrible crash," I told him, trying to be strong for Mom, trying to be grown up. "Nana and Pop are dead."

He held her hand while she listened to the police officer on the line. She made the appropriate responses as tears coursed down her face. Then she hung up, and drew me in tight. Tight between them, like she was afraid I'd be lost to her, too. She clutched at us both and we held her up while she wept for her parents, gone in the swift, bloody instant that I'd seen in my dream.

✳ ✳ ✳

I blinked, coming out of the dark room of memory into the morning light. I had been thoroughly immersed in the past. I guess that was what made last night's dream so hard to dismiss. The rather vague nightmare had somehow stirred the pot of my psyche, and old, hibernating parts of me now creaked awake.

I looked around the room; my hands had been busy while my mind had been wandering, sorting laundry into reasonably contained heaps. Likewise, the flurry of paper that had blanketed the carpet of the study area now sat in neat stacks on the desk. The books were either back on the shelves or waiting tidily by the computer. The lair that time forgot hadn't been this neat since middle school.

Something glinted at me from the carpet, and I picked up the thin gold chain that held the crucifix Gran had given me at my first communion. I wondered why it wasn't where I'd left it, but since I couldn't remember where that was, I didn't linger on the thought, or on why it seemed natural to drop it on top of the pile of clothes I was going to wear that day.

What a weird morning. My brain hurt from thinking so much while in a state of caffeine deprivation. I was headed toward the shower when my cell phone rang. I fished it out of my schoolbag, not entirely surprised to see Granny Quinn's number on the caller ID.

"Hey, Gran. I was just thinking about you."

"I know you were, dear." Her voice was brighter than anyone's had a right to be while the sun still moved upward. I could hear the background whirr of her treadmill, which explained her slight breathlessness. "That's why I called."

Why couldn't I have inherited the chipper genes instead of the spooky ones?

3

You wouldn't think that a day could go downhill after dreaming you were on the roll call for Hell. But it did.

"Have you voted for the class song yet?" A student council drone shoved a half-sheet of paper in my face. Astrobright Orange is painful at any time of day, but at seven-thirty a.m. it was vomit inducing. Also, the only thing perky I want in front of me at that hour is a coffeemaker. Since the drive-thru line at Take-Your-Bucks had stretched to Canada, I was still severely caffeine deprived.

I voiced my preference in the life-and-death matter of Gwen versus Ashley by wadding up the ballot and throwing it over my shoulder on the way to the Coke machine. "You don't have to *litter!*" yelled Student Council Sally. "The recycle bin is right *over there*."

My response to that was equally nonverbal.

"Maggie Quinn!"

I knew that tone. Mr. Halloran, the assistant principal, must have looked up the word *stentorian* in the dictionary on his first day at work, and practiced in the shower until he got the voice just right.

Busted, a scant twenty feet from the Coke machine. So close, and yet so far.

"Yes, Mr. Halloran?" I Goody Two-shoed. "May I help you?"

The administrator stood by the doors leading from the courtyard to the front hall. He was fairly tall, with a full head of suspiciously thick brown hair. He was the type of stocky that comes when gravity turns linebacker shoulders into a desk-job gut. I would lay down money that he'd been a Biff in high school. "I'd like to see you in my office."

"Ooooooooo," said the kids in the courtyard—either a taunt or the buzzing of their hive mind.

I followed the assistant principal inside, not quite meekly. Student Council Sally smirked as I went by.

I waved at the secretaries managing attendance and they waved back through the chaos. Halloran waited at his office door like a prison warden. I entered and stood until he closed the door and gestured for me to sit. The office windows made sure we were properly chaperoned by all the staff. Everything was correct and polite and did nothing to explain why my hair wanted to crawl off my head.

"So, Miss Quinn. I hear you were involved in a hazing incident yesterday."

"Nobody hazed me yesterday, Mr. Halloran."

"Don't get smart with me, Quinn."

This seemed like an odd thing for a school administrator to say, but since he was glaring down at me, hands on his hips, I kept my opinion to myself.

"I have a reliable report," he continued, "that you were witness to some students bullying a classmate."

By "reliable report," I assumed he meant "rumor." I still hadn't had any caffeine, my head was feeling funny, and baiting the assistant principal could hold my interest only so long. "Then I don't see why I'm here. If there was a witness to my alleged witnessing, then you don't need me to tell you what happened."

He settled on the corner of the desk in an aren't-we-buddies way. "I understand you took some photos."

Irritation jabbed me; I couldn't imagine who had gone tattling to Halloran. Stanley? The Spanish Club? I guess I'd been overestimating the intelligence of the general populace. Blackmail has power only as long as it remains secret.

I considered Stanley, and his desire for revenge. But he'd been adamant that he didn't need my help, so I didn't think he would tell Halloran that I had pictures of his humiliation.

"I don't know what photos you are talking about," I lied. I was already on the list for Hell—what did one falsehood matter?

"The photos of the hazing incident," he said, getting a little red in the face.

"I don't have any photos of a hazing incident." This was less of a lie. "Hazing" was making freshmen wear stupid hats. Pretending you were going to drop someone off a balcony was not "hazing." It was "terrorizing."

"Then you won't mind if I look at your camera."

I had to clamp my teeth on some choice words that would get me expelled. I was offended for the entire fourth estate. As a journalist, I wanted to tell him to get some sort of court order and then we'd talk. As a high school student still five weeks and three days from graduation, I knew there was nothing I could do to stop him.

Furiously mute, I dug into the backpack at my feet and handed over the camera. Halloran turned it over, his big thumbs pressing tiny buttons as he reviewed the pictures on the memory card. Pictures of the Spanish Club's fundraising table, with its rows of gum and candy, and last night's basketball game, including a stellar shot of Eric Munoz nailing an NBA-worthy jump shot.

But no Biff, a.k.a. Brandon. No bug-eyed Jessica. No terror-stricken Stanley.

Halloran grunted with frustration, started to say something, then thrust the camera at me. "Get out of here, Quinn. And don't be late for first period, because I'm not giving you a pass."

I didn't have to be told twice. Despite the big windows, the office felt claustrophobic. Maybe it was Halloran and his power trip. Maybe it was the wall behind his desk, filled with pictures of past sports triumphs—not the school's, his own. The thought that this was what bullies grew into, minor tyrants who took jobs where they could relive their glory days by continuing to terrorize students, made my head ache.

I felt immediately better when I left the office, as if the air were somehow cleaner. My granny might say something about the Quinn ability to sense things unseen, but more likely it was the evil power of Halloran's aftershave.

The warning bell clanged directly over my head. I had five minutes to find a caffeine infusion before English, which was on the other side of the building from the nearest Coke machine. (I had them all plotted on a sort of mental MapQuest.) I could make it if I ran. But pairing my graceless jog with a hurriedly gulped-down soft drink seemed like a recipe for disaster.

So I went to class, sans soda.

In English, we turned in our homework assignments, and were given the rest of the time to work on our term papers, due in a week. My theme concerned Jonathan Swift and the use of sarcasm in social commentary, and Lisa was flipping through my notes.

"I could get behind a guy who proposed that eating Irish children would solve both the famine and the population problem. I'm going to remember that when my despotic plans come to fruition."

"He was being satirical, Lisa."

"Maybe I am, too. Maybe not." She wiggled her eyebrows maniacally. Lisa had finished her paper a week ago. Her subject? Machiavelli. Sometimes I thought my friend was one of the drollest people I knew. Other times I thought she was one of the scariest.

"What did Halloran want?" she asked.

"Are there *no* secrets in this school?"

"My spies are everywhere."

"Girls!" We jumped guiltily as Ms. Vincent called from her desk. Well, *I* jumped. Lisa merely turned complacently. "Are you working on your papers, or are you gossiping?"

My compatriot replied with a composed lie, "I'm helping Maggie, Ms. Vincent. She needs advice on solidifying her argument."

The teacher accepted this with insulting ease. "Why can't *I* be helping *you*?" I hissed at Lisa as we pretended to get back to work. "I'm the future Pulitzer Prize winner. You're just the future Lord High Poobah of the World."

"You can be helping me next time." She brushed a glossy lock of hair over her shoulder and asked again, "What did Halloran want?"

"The pictures I took of yesterday's bully-o-rama."

Her brows lifted. "You got actual dirt on Brandon Rogers?"

"Yeah. Snapped a really unflattering picture of the prom queen front-runner, too."

"You didn't hand them over, did you?"

"No. I deleted them from the camera last night after I downloaded them onto my computer."

"Smart thinking. The camera is school property, like the lockers, with no expectation of privacy. Well done, my Padawan apprentice."

I tucked my hair behind my ears and tried to get back to work. I wasn't very successful, because I was now thinking about Halloran and bullies instead of Swift and Lilliputians.

"Why do you suppose Halloran wanted the pictures?" I mused aloud. "He likes good ol' Biff. Why would he want incriminating evidence on him?"

"To take it away from you, of course, and make sure it never sees the light."

"But I have copies."

"You ought to put them in an envelope marked 'Open in the event of my mysterious death or disappearance.'"

"Gee thanks, Lisa. I would never have thought of that. How handy to have a criminal mastermind as a friend."

"I prefer Evil Genius. And you're welcome." The class began gathering their books. There was no visible signal, just the action of the collective unconscious. Lisa and I rode the wave.

"See you in civics," she said as the bell rang.

✳ ✳ ✳

I had journalism next. The class was supposed to be separate from the lab where we worked on the school's weekly newspaper, but by this time of year the structure was pretty fluid. I turned in my article on the Spanish Club and gave Mr. Allison the pictures of the basketball game. He whistled when he saw the jump shot. "Great photo, Maggie! You really caught the motion."

"Thanks." Sports and action photography took a knack and a bit of luck. I think I'd been more lucky than anything else, but I was still proud. "May I have a pass?"

"Where are you going?" he asked, reaching for his pen.

I didn't think "To the Coke machine" was going to cut it, so I said, "To the auditorium. Big Spring Musical is this weekend, and I thought I'd interview the cast."

"Good idea. Phillip was saying we could use something to round out the edition. Think you can have it ready tomorrow?"

"Just a fluff piece? Sure." Phillip was the student editor and he had a gift for knowing exactly how many inches of story the edition lacked at any given moment. Mr. Allison tore the pass off the pad, I took it with a cheery "Thanks!" then grabbed my backpack and headed to C Hall where lay the Band Hall, Choir Room, auditorium, and, not coincidentally, several vending machines.

Finally! Sweet liquid ambrosia of caramel-colored, high-fructose, caffeinated bliss. With the carbonated burn coursing down my throat and the sugar rushing through my veins, interviewing the Drama Club seemed a small price to pay.

✳ ✳ ✳

Mr. Thomas, the drama teacher, was a harried-looking guy who didn't seem long out of high school himself. "All those things need to be organized on the prop tables, stage right and left. How are we coming on costumes? People! We *open* in less than three days!"

He might have been addressing the air for all I knew; there was no discernible change in the chaos in the auditorium, where there seemed to be an awful lot going on, but very little getting done. I coughed to get his attention and he turned his wild-eyed stare on me. "Hi. I'm Maggie Quinn, from the Avalon High paper. I was hoping I might interview a few of the cast members."

"Excellent! I'll introduce you to our star." He called toward the stage at a volume that made me jump. "Jessica! Have you got a minute?"

Boy, this day just kept getting better and better.

The model thin blonde who turned at her name was not, thankfully, the Queen Jessica—the Jessica Prime—though I did recognize her from the Jessica chorus in the Incident with Stanley on the Breezeway.

She joined me at the edge of the stage with a distinct air of noblesse oblige but no sign she knew who I was, other than paparazzi, and therefore a necessary inconvenience. That suited me fine. I flipped open my notebook and donned the armor of professionalism.

"Why don't you start by telling me what made you interested in Drama Club."

"First of all"—she tossed her blond hair—"it's not the Drama Club. It's the *Thespian Society*." She mistook my blank expression for a sign that said *Yes, thank you, I would love a generous helping of condescension*. "Named for the Greek god Thespis?"

I hated when people did that, went up at the end of a statement when the only question they were asking was "Don't you realize I'm smarter than you?" Especially when they didn't even know that Thespis was not a god, but just some ancient Greek whose life must have sucked so bad that he had to write a bunch of plays about it and call it "tragedy." Sort of like a preteen with a blog, only with less Avril Lavigne lyrics.

"O-kay." Professionalism, Maggie. "Why don't you tell me what made you interested in the *Thespian Society*?"

"Actually, I've been performing for a long time. Ever

since I won the Little Miss Princess Pageant when I was six years old. And maybe you've seen my television work? The commercial for Calaway's Quality Used Cars?"

"Oh really?" My response wasn't strictly necessary. Thespica was used to an audience that didn't talk back.

"Honestly, I really didn't have time for the musical this year. After all, there's cheerleading tryouts—I'm an officer, so it's a *big* responsibility, choosing the next squad—and the Prom Queen Nominating Committee. But when Mr. Thomas *begged* me to audition, I knew I had an obligation."

"Your dedication is truly awe-inspiring." Maybe I would invent a society named after the Greek goddess Sarcastica. "Talent can be such a burden."

She sighed, completely without irony. "I know. You'd be surprised how many people never realize that."

I had to leave then, or bust a gut laughing.

✳ ✳ ✳

Back in C Hall, I breathed deep of the unpretentious air outside the auditorium. I didn't feel like walking all the way back to class for the five remaining minutes, so I ducked into the nearest restroom. It wasn't entirely unjustified. I had, after all, gulped down that soda.

I took care of business and was straightening myself back out when a whiff of something half-remembered made me pause. Obviously, there are plenty of odors in the school bathrooms, none of which I wanted to investigate too closely. But the sickly sweet smell tickled the back of my throat, and brought back a not-quite-clear memory of smoke, flame, and . . .

Pot. Someone had lit up a joint in the boys' room, and the smoke was seeping through the vent.

The door to the bathroom opened, and I heard familiar voices. It was the unholy triad of the ruling class, Jessica Prime and her two most senior handmaidens—Jess Minor, and my new friend Thespica, who was briefing the others on our meeting.

"I cannot believe that Quinn actually *asked* for an interview with you." Jess Minor was the queen's permanent shadow, copying everything she did, but not quite as well. The result was a tweaked stunt-double resemblance and a slightly desperate air of tries-too-hard. "What a loser."

"It's pathetic." Jessica Prime's voice, when not shrieking like a banshee, was sugar sweet and slightly husky from years of yell practice. "Does she really think that sucking up to you is going to do anything for her social credibility?"

"Maybe she thinks I'll be her friend. You should have heard her fawning all over me."

From my hiding place, I rolled my eyes. It was wishful thinking that they would conveniently go into the other stalls and allow me to escape. I guess girls as perfect as the Jessicas never had to pee.

Instead, they planted themselves in front of the sinks, applying powder, lip gloss, and venom. They went on about me for a while, talking about what a loser I was, then numbering me among all the other people they considered geeky, poor, fat, unfashionable, or otherwise beneath contempt, and how they'd rather die than be any of the above.

As fascinating as this insight into the bitch psyche was,

the smoke was getting stronger and making me slightly nauseated. Granted, I didn't have a lot of basis for comparison, but this had to be the worst smelling weed ever.

"What is *that*?" Prime's voice held such horror, I figured she smelled it, too. "Jess, is that . . ." She seemed to be having trouble even saying it. Not the smell, then. I edged forward, peering through the gap in the stall to see Jessica Prime staring at Minor's purse as if something slimy were crawling out of it. "Is that a . . . knockoff!"

Lip gloss wand suspended in midair, the lesser Jessica looked baffled. "No. My mom bought it for me at Saks when I was staying with her on spring break."

Prime laughed, making me think about D&D Lisa, and the important distinction between laughing *with* and laughing *at*. "You didn't get that at Saks."

"I did!"

"Jess!" She grabbed the bag and pointed to the metal insignia on the front. "It says *Conch*. You didn't buy a purse, you bought a type of fritter."

Thespica peered at the name. "It does say Conch, Jess. I'm afraid you've been had."

"Did you buy it off the back of a truck or something? Maybe your mother did."

"No! She took me to the store!"

"It's okay, Jess." Prime patted her shoulder in a consoling, condescending way. "Everyone gets taken sometime."

Jess had dropped the lip gloss in the sink and grabbed her purse with both hands, reading the metal tag. "It says 'Coach.'" She sounded like a lost little girl. "You two are making fun of me."

I never thought I'd feel sorry for a Jessica; her confused hurt almost made me forget she was one of them. That was one of the most loathsome things about the breed. The pack could turn on its weakest member just as quickly as on an outsider.

Queen Jessica finished applying her makeup, pressed her lips together, then studied the effect of her pout. "Don't worry, Jess. As long as you hide that thing in your locker, we'll still let you eat lunch with us." While Jess Minor continued to examine her bag with a bewildered expression, Prime stepped back and studied her own reflection with the slightest frown. "Does this skirt make me look fat?"

"Of course not," said Thespica, completing her own toilette. "I wish I had your figure."

As far as I could tell, she did. I was so sick of their nonsense that I was ready to burst out of the stall and take my lumps. Whatever had possessed me to stay hidden in the first place? At this rate I'd be well prepared for a job with the *National Enquirer.*

Finally, they left. I barely stopped to wash my hands before I vacated the place myself. There was an intolerable stink in that bathroom, but it had nothing to do with the toilet.

4

My phone buzzed in my pocket only a moment after the bell rang. My father, according to Gran, is not eligible to have The Sight because he is a man, but Dad's timing often makes me wonder.

"Are you free for lunch?" he asked when I said hello.

"Where are you?"

"Parked out front. Come eat with us."

I didn't know who "us" was, but I wasn't going to turn down an excuse to get out of the building. We have an open campus, so I zipped out the door with the other parolees. Dad waved from beside his Saturn and I galloped down the stairs to meet him.

My steps slowed as a complete stranger unfolded himself from the shotgun seat and held the front door for me. Dad had brought a friend. A young and handsome friend, with a tall, lean build and a lopsided, Han Solo sort of smile. He wore an oxford shirt and khakis and his dark hair was cut conservatively short.

"Maggie," said my dad, "this is Justin MacCallum. He's a student in the history department. You don't mind if he comes with us, do you?"

"No problem." I was suddenly rather glad that Aunt Joyce's shirt had been the only thing clean.

I got a bit of a Boy Scout vibe from the guy, which was confirmed when he held the door for me. Dad put the car in gear and asked, "Where do you want to eat?"

"I don't care." My stomach was pretty excited about the idea of food, though, and growled loudly. I tried not to blush. "Not too heavy, though; I have P.E. right after this."

"Are you still swimming?" Dad laughed when I groaned an affirmative. "Maggie doesn't like the water," he told Justin.

"Dad!" Bad enough I was treating us to a gastric symphony. I didn't need all my idiosyncrasies trotted out for the *Embarrass Maggie Show*.

Justin looked amused in a "laughing *with* you" way, only I wasn't laughing. "Not even to drink?"

"I don't like to get *in* the water," I explained, shooting daggers at my father.

"She does take showers," said my oblivious parent, "as you can tell by the fact we don't have to roll down the windows."

"Dad!"

"That's interesting." Justin leaned his elbows on our bucket seats. "Most people love the water. It's natural, ingrained. Reminds us of the womb."

"I must have been a really seasick fetus."

That got a chuckle. Score for me.

"What's the criteria, Mags?" asked Dad. "Has to be shallow?"

"I have to be able to see the bottom."

"That's right." He glanced at Justin, who was still hanging between us. "I remember when Laura, her mother, tried to put her in a bubble bath one time. She screamed bloody murder until the bubbles went away."

There ought to be a law against naked baby stories in front of strangers. I changed the subject. "You have class with my dad, Justin?"

"Yes. I'm doing some research on folklore, actually, and Professor Quinn was nice enough to introduce me to your grandmother. I wanted to hear some of her stories from the old country."

I glanced sideways at my father. "The fairy stories?"

Dad kept his eyes on the road. "And some family history."

My eyes narrowed. "What family history?"

"You should go see your gran after school" was Dad's random answer. "If your day doesn't improve."

"Martians could invade and it would be an improvement on my day. What does that have to do with anything?" Justin and Dad exchanged glances in the rearview mirror and my suspicions flared. "All right. Cut to the chase. Why were you there? And for that matter, why are you *here*?"

Justin cleared his throat. "Your grandmother says that you—your family, that is—share a gift. She sensed that you were having a rough morning, in fact."

I stared at my father, disbelieving and betrayed. "You *told* him? You told a perfect stranger?"

He took a placating tone. "It came up in the conversation. Your grandmother is not shy with a receptive audience."

I scowled at Justin. "What, exactly, are you studying?"

"Well, my major is history, but I'm doing an independent study on the history of the occult in different cultures, from folk tales to high magic. . . ."

"Stop the car."

"Oh, Maggie," said Dad. "Don't be ridiculous."

"Stop. The. Car."

He slammed on the brakes. It was a good thing we were only going twenty-five miles an hour and everyone was wearing their seat belt.

I turned to them both. "I am not some kind of freak. I don't see things. I don't *know* things. And even if I did have . . . whatever . . . I sure don't want to be someone's research project." I opened the door and climbed out, hauling my backpack with me, which made my wrathful dignity a little harder to maintain.

Dad leaned across the gearshift. "What are you doing?"

"I'm walking back to school. It's not that far." I slammed the door. Dad argued with me through the open window for a while but I took a shortcut between two houses and left them behind.

* * *

By the time I got back to school I was still hot under the collar, but mostly from lugging my gargantuan book bag for five blocks. The angry churning in my stomach had time to die down, too, until I remembered it was time for P.E., and the pool.

It wasn't that I couldn't swim. I could keep my head above the water and move from place to place with all the grace of a Labrador retriever. I'd made it through the past five weeks by stubbornly moving down my lane in a sort of combination dog paddle/breaststroke so I could keep my eyes on the bottom of the pool, and anything that might be sneaking up on me from below.

The other problem with swimming in P.E., which had nothing to do with my fear of the water, was the difficulty of embarking on this exercise without, at some point, being completely naked in the locker room. Most of us changed in the shower stalls. But even so, to stand there in the buff, for even a transitory moment, while your classmates lurk on the other side of a very flimsy curtain was fifty kinds of vulnerable.

I had done extensive experiments in changing in stages: Remove pants. Slip suit on while shirt hides important bits. Wiggle arms out of sleeves while keeping shirt down around other bits, then contort out of bra and into remainder of suit.

Having worked up quite a sweat this way, I bundled up my clothes and bent to pick up my shoes. Gran's cross swung lightly against my collarbone as I straightened. I'd forgotten about it until then. I debated for a moment, then unclasped the chain and stuffed it into my shoe.

We made our way out of the locker room and into the cavernous aquatics gym. The administration was always telling us how lucky we were to have a pool. Only they called it a "natatorium," which is an old-fashioned term for "really expensive indoor swimming pool." I hate that word. It's too much like "crematorium" and I have enough liquid issues as it is.

Some sadist at the health department had decreed we had to shower before getting in the pool, so we trudged through the spigots then stood dripping in our swimsuits while we received instruction from the girls P.E. teacher. Coach Milner had the whipcord-lean frame of a long-distance runner. She'd competed in the Boston Marathon for ten consecutive years. Her age was difficult to determine, because her fitness regime clearly did not include the vigorous application of sunscreen.

The deal with Coach Milner was that she didn't just run marathons, she lived them. "Quitters never win," she had yelled at me as I wheezed around the track. "Never say die," she hollered up at me as I dangled from a rope trying to climb more than four feet off the mat. "Mind over matter," she cajoled as I threw up my lunch after taking a basketball to the gut. Fitness was her religion, and she preached these things like the Gospel according to Nike.

The class lined up like a multicolored, omnisize, Bizarro-world Miss America contest. Coach Milner strode in front of us, our judge, jury, and executioner.

"Congratulations, ladies. Today we move on to the diving portion of our aquatics unit. We'll be in the deep pool now, so grab your towels and—" My hand shot into the air. "What is it, Quinn?"

"I just ate," I lied. "Aren't we supposed to wait an hour before going in the water?"

"Winners never make excuses. That's an old wives' tale. Twenty minutes is sufficient." She grasped the whistle hanging around her neck and blew a rousing note, like Gideon on his trumpet. "Come on, ladies! This way."

Coach marched us from our spot beside the lap pool (good-bye, safe haven of only moderate distaste) to the diving area (hello, bottomless pit of liquid doom).

"Are you all right?" A blur of fingers broke my gaze and I dragged my eyes from the depths and focused on the concerned little moon of Karen Foley's face.

"Huh?" That was all I could manage. Behold the wordsmith.

"You look really pale." Karen was one of the nicest girls I knew, which was why, though I pitied Stanley, after his spiteful words about her, I didn't feel much sympathy for him.

I tried to rally. The champion who faced down Biff et al. should show a little gumption. "I'm always pale."

"Yeah, but I think the undertone of green is new." She touched my arm. "And you're all clammy."

A chorus of giggles made us turn. Jessica Prime and her henchbitches clustered together in a lump of malice. I usually gave the witless triplets a wide berth, but yesterday's debacle had incurred the wrath of the Jessicas. As much as I wanted to ignore them, I was now firmly on their radar.

"You're not scared of a little kiddy pool, are you, Maggie?" Prime taunted, with a toss of her blond head and a smile of parade-float insincerity.

I gave an exaggerated sigh. "Not everyone has installed personal flotation devices, Jessica."

A scarlet flush darkened her perfect tan. I knew that expression; I had a close-up of it on disk. "You'd better watch it, Quinn. No one likes a smartass."

"That must make the world a more comfortable place for you, then."

"I'm warning you! Someone is going to serve you up a big plate of comeback one of these days. And it's going to taste a lot like my foot up your butt."

"I think you mean a 'big plate of comeuppance.'"

"What?"

"Comeuppance. A 'comeback' is what John Travolta kept having in the nineties."

Jessica showed me her palm. "Whatever. You are such a loser. I should have known you'd watch disco movies."

"Let's keep the line moving, ladies!"

Holy Cheez-Its. I'd been having so much fun baiting the Barbies that I'd almost forgotten about my imminent demise.

"Steady there." Karen grabbed my elbow when my knees threatened to fail me.

It was Jessica Prime's turn. She climbed onto the board, waggled her manicured fingers at me, then with a leap as graceful as a gazelle, made a perfect arc into the water. The board applauded with the "wocka wocka wocka" of its spring.

If I didn't hate her before, I sure did now.

Jess Minor took her place with a snotty glance my way. Her dive was true to form: a knockoff of Prime's perfection.

Thespica came after, and I guess there wasn't a diving portion of the Little Miss Perfection Pageant. But her lackluster effort was still better than anything I could do.

Finally, there was no one in front of me. Just Coach Milner, her whistle, and the diving board. "You're up, Quinn."

"Uh . . ."

"Come on. You're holding up the line."

"Er . . ."

"Let's go, Quinn. Fear is the mind-killer. Get up there and just do it."

"Geez, Maggie," said Jessica Prime, fluffing her dripping hair back into shape, "it's the low board for crying out loud. It's, like, three feet above the water."

High board, low board, made no difference. It was the indigo invisibility of the water below that kept my bare feet rooted to the tile.

Coach Milner shook her head sadly, jotting a note on her clipboard. "This is going to affect your grade, Quinn. Quitters never prosper."

If she was going to humiliate me, she ought to at least get her clichés right.

"I'll go first." Karen took my place in line with a bracing smile. "After I belly flop anything you do will look like a swan dive."

My ears began to burn. Nothing that Milner said shamed me more than Karen the Mathlete climbing confidently up the two steps to the diving board, unconcerned about the water below, or the jiggle of her thighs, or the snickers of the Jessicas.

"A hippo would look like a swan after her." One's hiss was indistinguishable from the others.

"If she belly flops, there won't be any water left in the pool."

I spun around and whispered in tight, soft fury. "I swear to God, Jessica, one more word, and that picture goes up on the school Web page."

Prime's eyes flashed, but a movement over the pool caught my eye and I turned back to watch Karen, standing at the back end of the board, taking a deep breath.

The class broke out of line to watch. I drew a breath with her, and held it as she stepped out. Her stride, her placement at the end of the board, looked perfect. She gathered herself as the springboard dipped down, and then released that energy upward.

Again my eye snagged on some dark movement—her shadow on the water? I barely had time to wonder, a half-fired neuron of warning, then everything went wrong.

Karen's foot shot out from under her and her arms flung out, catching nothing but empty air as she tumbled backward toward the board. The impact echoed through the natatorium as her head smacked the fiberglass. Her limp body hit the water with a splash, and sank slowly into the stygian depths.

5

Coach Milner dove into the pool, slipping into the fathom-less water after Karen. I couldn't see how she would be able to manage the girl's limp weight without help. I edged toward the pool, not sure what I could do. Below the surface I could see them, distorted by ripples and depth. Surely some help was better than none, if I could just make myself take that step off the ledge.

"I got it." A guy's voice, someone from the boy's P.E. class that had taken our place in the lap pool. He dove in while the rest of us were still reeling.

His action shattered the horrified spell that held us in

stasis. I grabbed the girl to my right. "Get the boys' coach." The concrete-and-tile vault of the gym was so loud, it might take a while for the news to spread. Meanwhile, I ran to the wall where the life preservers hung, returning just as three heads broke the surface: Milner and the boy, with Karen hanging between them, blood trickling from under her hair.

I tossed out the life preserver. Milner caught it and draped Karen's arms over the ring, balancing her. Amanda and Sarah took up the rope and we pulled the three of them to the side of the pool.

"Watch her head." The boys' coach had arrived, with the class following behind, like curious rubberneckers on the freeway. I supported Karen's head while they lifted her out. As her stomach hit the side of the pool, water trickled out of her mouth, and she began to cough. A relieved sigh rippled outward from the ring of students.

She coughed until she retched. Coach and I turned her on her side until all the water came up and out, and with it a strange smell. You'd expect puked up pool water to smell funny. But the chlorine odor was mixed with rotten eggs and burnt toast, and my hands began to shake.

We rolled her back when she started to breathe more easily, in hoarse pants instead of asthmatic wheezes. Someone handed me a towel to put under her head, as Milner ran to call 911. I pressed a second cloth to the gash on Karen's head. Blood mixed with the water on the tile deck, so that we were awash with it, real horror movie stuff.

"I'm so sorry, Karen," I whispered, not really knowing what I was apologizing for.

Her brow squinched up and her eyes opened slightly. "For what? Did something happen?"

"Yeah, you could say that."

"My head hurts."

"I'm sorry," I repeated. I'd been trying not to press too hard on the cut because of the enormous lump that was under it. It looked like a gory Mount St. Helens.

"Get out of the way, Quinn." Coach Milner brushed me aside. "How many fingers am I holding up, Foley?"

My knees had stiffened while I knelt on the deck and I had to struggle to my feet as the paramedics arrived and took over. The tension drained quickly after that. Assistant Principal Halloran showed up to take care of anything official; I bet there was going to be some paperwork on this one. Our classes were dismissed to go change but I hung back, watching silently as the EMTs put a brace on Karen's neck before they lifted her.

As the paramedics strapped her down for the ride, I sidled up to where one of them stood writing on a big metal clipboard. "Is she going to be all right?"

"I can't really say." He glanced up from his chart and saw my face. Maybe I looked as tightly wound as I felt, because he added, "She'll definitely be needing tests and observation for a concussion, but it could be worse."

In other words, it was a lot better to have a big bump going out than a big dent going in. The EMTs gathered their stuff quickly, and after a last signature from the assistant principal, they whisked Karen away.

The air seemed eerily quiet once they were gone. The gym was pretty much empty, and the lap of the water echoed strangely on the concrete and tile.

I found myself at the edge of the pool, looking for . . . I don't know what. Another glimpse of black shadow, a whiff of something other than chlorine. I'm not sure what it would mean if I *did* smell something. That I was crazy? Or I wasn't.

My hand touched my throat. It took me a moment to realize I was unconsciously reaching for Granny's necklace.

Was it possible that my dream had somehow been a warning?

I rejected the idea almost immediately. I was too old to believe in fairies and soothsaying dreams. What I had was very good intuition, and sometimes things I picked up subconsciously play out in my dreams. That was the only logical, adult explanation.

And I never saw the future. I couldn't have warned Karen any more than I could have warned my grandparents that night. There was nothing I could have done.

"Of course there wasn't."

My heart slammed against my ribs. I jumped, too, arms windmilling to keep myself from somehow defying physics and falling into the water three feet away.

"Whoa! Careful." Big, tanned hands caught my waist. Well, where my waist would be if I wasn't wearing the World's Most Unflattering Swimsuit.

As soon as I was steady, I backed away, my heart still pounding. Mostly I was startled. But it may have had a little to do with the blue plate special of hot, athletic goodness standing in front of me.

Finally, I had a good look at Bobby Baywatch. The lifeguard patch on his well-worn swim trunks explained his quick action earlier, as well as his bronze tan, washboard stomach, and muscular shoulders. He had a great face, too—good bones, blue eyes, and a mouth that looked like it smiled more than not.

It was also a familiar face, and my brows pinched together as I made the unwelcome connection.

"Oh Hell," I said. "You're a Jock."

With a capital *J*. As in, one of the Jocks and Jessicas, a lord of the watering hole.

He didn't pretend he didn't know what I meant. "Maggie, right?" I nodded. "Look, Maggie, I'm sorry about what happened yesterday. Brandon went too far, and . . ." He faltered and finished weakly. "I'm just really sorry."

I could see plainly that he was repentant, embarrassed, and a little ashamed of himself. But that wasn't my problem. "I don't need an apology. You didn't do anything to me."

"I know. I'll apologize to Stanley, too. But I just don't want you to think I'm like those other guys."

I had to tilt my head back to look him in the eye. I'd had a craptastic day, and there was enough weird stuff going on in my life to fill an episode of the *Twilight Zone*. I didn't have the patience to coddle his guilty conscience.

"I don't know why it matters to you, but here's the deal. You may not have helped, but you stood there and did nothing while the people you call your friends demeaned and physically assaulted someone weaker than them."

He flushed guiltily and looked away. "I just didn't know what to do that wouldn't make things worse."

His whipped puppy expression made me feel guilty, too, for lecturing. "Yes, well, I don't want to be late to class, so . . ." I gestured for him to move out of my way. If he thought it was strange that I didn't go around him on the pool side he didn't say so, but just backed up to open more ground. I hadn't gone far, though, when he called, "Hey, Quinn!"

I turned back, lifting my brows in inquiry.

"It's not the same thing," he said.

"What's not?"

"Yesterday and today." He closed the gap between us, looking down at me with spectacularly blue eyes. Not that it changed my opinion of him, of course. "I heard you talking to yourself. It's true, there was nothing you could have done. If you had jumped in, we'd have had two people to pull out instead of one."

"I can swim." If your definition of swimming was broad enough.

"Swimming and rescuing are two different things." He smiled, a little ruefully. "I thought it was cool that you thought about it, though. I guess that's why I wanted to . . . make an excuse, I guess."

I understood that I'd been paid a compliment of a sort. By a Jock. The Weirdness just went on and on.

I didn't know what to say so I settled on, "Thanks. I think."

With all that had happened that day, I had much more important things to think about than how my rear end looked in my bathing suit as I walked to the locker room. But I worried about it anyway.

I had less than five minutes to change and get to my next class, on the other side of the planet from the pool. I unlocked my stuff and hauled it all into one of the shower stalls. I had no time for Victorian hang-ups about nudity, or wrestling matches with my clothing. I shucked off my suit, pulled on my panties and had just fastened my bra when the curtain flew open. Jessica Prime, head bitch of the universe, snapped my picture with her camera phone.

That's right, ladies and gentlemen, in one short day— eight short hours, actually—I'd gone from worrying that the demonic forces of the universe might be appearing in my dreams, to wondering whether, by six o'clock tonight, most of the student body would have received an e-mail attachment of me, looking like a deer in the headlights, wearing my washday underwear.

6

She text messaged me between classes: NOW I'VE GOT A PICTURE, TOO. Hello Queen of the Obvious. But I understood the implied threat. If I went public with her impression of a screaming baboon, she'd broadcast me and my Hello Kitty underwear to her entire friends list.

Chemistry lab demanded my attention, and I was glad for it. Given the choice between (1) angsting over whether Jessica Prime was petty enough to distribute the picture for the heck of it, or (2) blowing myself up in my distraction, the decision was fairly easy.

"Your experiment is set before you." Professor

Blackthorne walked through the lab benches, hands clasped behind his back. "You are to follow the instructions—to the letter, Mr. Anderson—adding Powder A to Liquid B and heating the resulting Solution C as indicated, and based on the resulting reaction, identify Product D. Understood?"

We chorused a trained "yes, sir" so hearty that you would have thought we lived to identify Product D from the reaction of Liquid B and Powder A. Truthfully, our experiments were usually interesting if not pyrotechnic. Professor Blackthorne loved a good exothermic reaction.

I should point out that on Halloween, my chemistry teacher dressed up like Professor Snape from the Harry Potter books, and he sometimes referred to his course as "Potions Class" even when it wasn't October. He had a last name out of a Brontë novel and he looked like the mad scientist from *Back to the Future*. I love Professor Blackthorne.

"Right then. Goggles on . . . Is something funny, Mr. Hobson?"

I tensed with dread as the football player tucked something under his desk. "Er, no, Professor Blackthorne."

"That's not a cell phone, is it?"

"Oh no, Professor Blackthorne." Except that it totally was.

"Good. Cell phones should always be turned off during lab experiments. Should they ring, even in silent mode, the arriving signal could cause a static charge that would ignite any volatile fumes in the air, and the user would certainly go up in a fiery ball of agonizing death." He stared down his nose at the wide receiver. "And we wouldn't want that to happen, would we, Mr. Hobson?"

I want to marry Professor Blackthorne.

"Now! Goggles on . . . and begin."

The instant the bell rang, I headed toward civics. It was pointless to dwell on what a malicious bitch Jessica Prime was and the senseless cruelties she inflicted on girls every day. But I did anyway, jumping at every chirruping cell phone, convinced my picture would be all over the school by seventh period.

It wasn't that I had some enormous popularity at stake. I occupied neutral territory—a sort of social Switzerland—nowhere near the "in crowd" but not so far out that I had to sit by myself in the cafeteria. No, the only thing at risk was my total humiliation. And the more I thought about it, the larger it loomed, until I was convinced that every laugh in the crowded hallway was aimed at me, and the Cingular airwaves were burning up with the traffic of my downfall.

New plan: Duck into the nearest bathroom and hide in a stall. I was getting good at that. It would be handy in my career as a tabloid reporter, which was the only job I would be able to get once that picture was posted on the Internet, available to anyone who Googled me.

My phone buzzed against my hip. I pulled it out and looked warily at the caller ID, then flipped it open.

"Where *are* you?" Lisa's voice blared in my ear.

"Hiding in the bathroom."

"Which one?"

"B Hall. By the computer lab."

"I'm there."

I heard her enter only a few moments later. "Get out,"

she told the freshmen primping in the mirror. I saw their little feet scurrying toward the exit, then my stall door flew open.

"Are you all right? Why are you hiding?" she demanded, one hand braced on top of the swinging door, the other on her hip, a warlike, gray-eyed Athena in vintage Gap.

"I'm having a terrible day." My voice cracked pathetically.

"I know, Mags. I heard it was awful. But you're all right?"

"*Awful*?" So she'd sent it. And even my best friend thought I looked awful with my fish-belly-white thighs and bug-eyed expression. My eyes began to sting, despite my best efforts not to cry. "Was it really that bad?"

"Well, you were there."

"I know. But I didn't think she'd really do it."

Lisa frowned, her arched brows drawing together. "You didn't think she'd really jump?"

"No. I didn't think she'd send my picture to the whole school."

She dropped the other hand to her hip. "What are you talking about?"

I stared up at her, realizing we were talking about two different things. "The picture Jessica Prime took of me mostly naked in the locker room. What are *you* talking about?"

"Karen Foley's accident." She pressed her palms to her forehead, paced away from the stall, and came back. "You mean I've been worried sick about you, about Karen, and you're in here crying about a *Jessica*?"

Jumping up, I defended myself. "I was not crying. And I think I'm entitled to five minutes of self-pity."

"Are you in the hospital? No. Are you the first person those bitches have humiliated? No."

I shoved past her, out of the stall. "You know what? You could give me a little perspective without being such a witch about it. You're supposed to be my friend."

"My friends don't hide in toilets from a little humiliation."

"Kiss off, Lisa."

"That's the spirit." She handed me my backpack. "Let's go to civics."

I grabbed the bag from her, squared my shoulders, and set my chin, daring her to give me any more grief.

"Good girl." She smoothed my hair, fluffed the sleeves of my blouse, and straightened the neck. "I'm glad you're all right."

"Afraid I'd turn into Self-Pity Girl permanently?" I asked, still sulking.

"No. I heard about the accident and worried."

My anger abated. I can never keep it up very long, especially when I'm sort of at fault, too. "I'm fine. Karen was the one hurt, not me."

"But it could have been. She took your place in line, didn't she?"

I hadn't thought about it that way, and the idea was like a punch to the gut. Was it possible I had dodged some kind of bullet of Fate?

After school, Gran was waiting with tea and sympathy. Literally.

I hadn't told her I was coming over, but by the time my Jeep Wrangler pulled into her driveway, the tea was hot in the pot and the cookies were warm on the plate. I'd resolved to be done feeling sorry for myself, but there's something about a grandmother's couch. Before I knew it, I had told her all about Jessica Prime and the picture, Halloran's ambush, Karen's accident, and even the dream that kicked it all off.

"I knew there was something going on." Gran withdrew her arm from my shoulders. "I knew this morning that you weren't being straight with me."

Self-pity time had expired, I guess. I sighed and poured myself a cup of tea. The brew was Darjeeling, but the pot and cups were Japanese, which summed Gran up pretty well. She had an icon of the Virgin and Child on one wall, and a set of Buddist temple bells hanging near the door. She looked like a red-headed Debbie Reynolds, dressed in a lavender tracksuit, completely American except for her lingering Irish lilt.

"It was just a nightmare, Gran."

"You keep telling yourself that and you may miss an important clue."

"To what? All I dreamed about was fire and smoke. That's not a lot to go on."

She lifted her steaming cup. "That's your own fault. If you had honed your ability instead of ignoring and repressing it . . ."

Surging to my feet, I paced across the small living room,

endangering a bamboo tree in my frustration. "I don't have an ability!"

"Then why are you here?"

I didn't answer her, just folded my arms with a sullen expression. Stubborn? Who, me?

"You are here because something about your dream will not allow you to ignore it." Gran set down her cup and clasped her hands together. "I can sense there are forces at work around you, Magdalena. You sense it, too, or you would not be wearing that." She pointed to the delicate gold cross around my neck.

I reached up to trace the shape. "I just found it while I was cleaning up my room, and since I hadn't worn it in a while . . ."

"Nonsense. Your subconscious recognizes the threat, the need for spiritual protection. Why don't you?" For a woman of her years, she had relatively few wrinkles, but every one of them was drawn deep with annoyance.

Pacing again, I tried to answer. "Because it's just—" Scary? Ridiculous? "—impossible."

"There are things in the world that cannot be dismissed simply because they cannot be quantified. You have a gift—"

I started to protest. "Gran, I don't—"

"Honestly, Maggie." She interrupted me, clearly at the end of her patience. "If nothing else, you have a *brain* and the obligation to use it to take a stand against Evil."

"Evil?" She had pronounced it with a capital letter.

"Yes, Evil. It doesn't take much for Evil to flourish in the world. People invite it in much more readily than they do Good. Evil is easy, effortless. Good requires action."

I flopped onto the sofa, thinking about my words to Lifeguard Jock. There was a quote from Edmund Burke that I'd spared him, but spoke now to myself. "'The only thing necessary for the triumph of evil is for good men to do nothing.'"

"Exactly." She leaned forward, catching my gaze. We have the same green eyes, and I could see my pale face reflected in hers. "It worries me that your denial may blind you, Maggie. Promise me that while you're applying your formidable brain you won't ignore your intuition."

It sounded so reasonable when she put it that way. But wasn't that why I'd come here, to be bullied into admitting what I couldn't deny any longer?

"Okay." My admission made her relief a palpable thing, as her tension uncoiled from her compact frame. "So how does this thing work?"

Her brows screwed up at the question. "It isn't that simple. It's different for everyone."

"That's not a lot of help, Gran."

"What did you expect? There isn't a magic spell. It's a skill like anything else, and it has to be practiced."

I sighed. Loudly. "That doesn't do me any good right now, though, does it?"

She refreshed her cup of tea with an astounding lack of concern. "You could stop being so stubborn, for one thing. Just let go once in awhile. Trust your instincts."

"Yes, Obi-Wan Kenobi." Gran reached over and tweaked my earlobe, hard. "Ow!"

"Don't be flippant with your elders."

I rubbed my ear. She looked so modern, I sometimes

forgot that my grandmother was old school when it came to getting an erring child's attention.

"While I'm being disrespectful, what's the big idea telling a complete stranger about me?"

"Justin MacCallum? He was so polite and curious about my stories. And so handsome, didn't you think?"

I did, but that was beside the point. "Can't you think of a better way to play matchmaker than telling him I'm a freak?"

Gran gave me an odd look, as if she couldn't believe I was so dense. "Honestly, Maggie. He's a young man who spent his morning recording an old lady's fairy tales and believed without question that The Sight runs in our blood. What makes you think *he's* entirely normal?"

7

In Gran's world, you didn't go to a sickbed empty-handed. I arrived at the hospital bearing a batch of chocolate chip cookies for Karen and for her mother, two paperbacks, a travel toothbrush, a variety of tea bags, and a bottle of aspirin.

Mrs. Foley, who probably had her daughter's friendly smile when her mouth wasn't framed by deep lines of worry, held up the pain reliever in wonder. "How did you know?"

"The Force is strong with my family," I answered. "Do you want to take a break, go down and get a drink or something? I can bore Karen until you get back."

The offer tempted her, but she glanced at her daughter

in the hospital bed. "Go," Karen said. "I'm fine, and Maggie will be here."

She wavered another moment, then said, "I'll just be a few minutes." She picked up her purse and the aspirin.

"No hurry." I turned to Karen. "You look better than the last time I saw you." It was true. Her color had returned and she wasn't covered in blood. She looked pretty good except for the goose-egg on her head. They'd had to shave some of her hair to put in stitches. Maybe she could manage a tasteful comb-over.

"Thanks." She gestured to a chair. "You want to sit down?"

I sat, mostly so she wouldn't have to strain to look up at me. "I'll bet your mom was pretty freaked."

"God. I thought she was going to come apart. But Coach kept telling her: 'Don't give up the ship, Carol. Winners stay focused. Eye on the prize.'" We laughed at her Milner impersonation, and Karen winced, holding her head.

"How about you?" I asked. "How are you feeling?"

"Well, it hurts when I laugh."

"You really scared the crap out of me. Out of all of us." I studied the Technicolor lump on her head. "Have they said when you can go home?"

"They did some X-rays and an MRI. They want to make sure no swelling develops, but it looks pretty good."

"Not on the outside, it doesn't."

"Gee, thanks." A smile told me she hadn't taken offense. "I hope I can get back to school soon. I can't let my grades slip."

I rolled my eyes. "Because a concussion wouldn't be an excuse or anything."

"I'm trailing D and D Lisa for valedictorian. I know she's your friend, but I can't let her off easy."

"No argument here. You should definitely make her work for it." I paused, trying to frame my question without influencing her. "At the pool, you couldn't remember what happened. Has any of it come back to you?"

"Let's see." She gazed at the ceiling, trying to recall. "I remember you turning chicken . . ."

"I did not!" There was a disbelieving pause. "Okay, I totally did. Please continue."

"I climbed on the low board, and heard the hags cackling. And then I started to jump, and that's all I remember."

"So you don't know what went wrong?"

Her forehead knotted, not with pain, but confusion, maybe.

"Coach Milner said I must have placed my foot wrong, not had it all the way on the board."

"Well, she would say that, wouldn't she? I mean, if you slipped, it could have been the equipment, and then the school would be in trouble."

Her brows knit more tightly. "Did I slip?"

"I couldn't really tell what happened." I tried to reassure her. She seemed upset by the hole in her memory, and who could blame her? "It doesn't really matter, does it? I'm just glad you're okay."

"I just had the strangest feeling . . ."

I waited a polite nanosecond, then prompted, "Did you remember something?"

She gave her head a very careful shake. "I don't know. I have this memory of jumping into the air and seeing my shadow underneath me, but it was moving in the wrong direction. I wonder if it's some kind of distortion from banging my head."

"Optical illusion, maybe?" I kept my voice neutral. "That's not so strange."

"That's not the weird part. There was—or I imagined there was—a horrible smell. Like food gone bad. I thought, 'No wonder Maggie doesn't want to jump in there. It smells like a sewer.'" She worried at the memory a little longer, then let it slip away. "And that's the last thing I remember."

With a slightly determined smile, she changed the subject. "I didn't do anything to help you get over your phobia, though. What do they call that? Aquaphobia?"

"I-don't-wanna-die-ophobia."

"Ow! Don't make me laugh."

"Sorry."

We talked about random, unimportant things—gossip, school, homework, college—until her mother came back. Mrs. Foley looked better for the break, and I gave up her seat.

"Here's my cell phone number." I scribbled it on the pad by the phone. "Call me if you need anything or . . . well, anything." I didn't want to say "if anything weird happens," because I wasn't even sure what was normal anymore.

For instance. You could have blown me over when five minutes later I met Stanley Dozer in the hospital lobby. I actually said "Stanley?" though there was no mistaking his pale, gangly form for any other.

"Hi, Maggie." He didn't look very pleased to see me, which, considering he'd called me a bitch the last time we'd met, wasn't really a shock.

"What are you doing here?"

"Mr. Yanachek asked me to bring Karen her math homework." He held up a folder and didn't meet my eye.

"That's nice of you." Considering that you called *her* a dork, I added silently.

"Yeah, well. No one else wanted to do it."

"You really try and spread sunshine and light wherever you go, don't you, Stanley?" He looked at me blankly. I sighed. "I'll take it up for you, so you don't pain yourself."

"No. I have to explain the problems. You'll never understand it."

"There are lots of things I'll never understand," I said as I strode past him. Then I paused. "Hey, Stanley. What did you mean when you said that everyone who picked on you was going to be sorry?"

He gave me a long, unreadable stare, then shrugged. "You know what I mean. I'll join the space program, and they'll end up like their kind always do: fat, divorced, and managing a Safeway."

Yeah, well, *there* was a fate worse than death.

I watched him go, wondering if there was something different about him, or if it was his outburst yesterday that changed my viewpoint. I didn't spend too much time on it, though. I had bigger fish to fry. It was time for some old-fashioned sleuthing. I was going to have to unleash my inner Nancy Drew.

8

Maybe Nancy Drew isn't the coolest role model. There are a lot more kick-ass heroines nowadays, like Buffy and that chick from *Alias*. But I had a retro fondness for the girl detective. I didn't know what I'd find at the pool, but I knew I had to take a closer look. If Karen caught a whiff of icky weirdness, too, then it wasn't just my freaky intuition.

The school was far from deserted when I pulled into the parking lot. The baseball and basketball teams had practice. There was a meeting of the decorating committee for the You-Know-What. There would be people still in the newspaper and yearbook offices. And of course, rehearsals for the musical would go until late.

I was worried the aquatics gym might be locked, or full of swimmers, but my timing was good. As I wove through the locker room, a bunch of dripping, broad-shouldered girls passed on the way to the showers, chattering about split times and fly strokes. I acted like I was supposed to be there, nodding to them and walking purposefully to the pool entrance.

I hung back against the wall until I saw the boys and their coach pass, leaving the gym empty. My rubber-soled shoes squeaked on the tile as I ventured in. The high dive loomed at the end of the vaulted building, the low board squatting alongside like its own little henchman.

I forced myself to the lip of the diving pool and looked down. A wave of vertigo hit me, as if I were standing on the edge of a high building. If I fell, the water would swallow me, suck me under, as whatever lurked unseen in the depths captured me with fins and tentacles and dagger-like teeth.

Get a grip, Maggie. Sweat prickled under my arms. *What would Nancy do?*

She wouldn't let her imagination defeat her, that's for sure. Taking my camera from my bag, I inspected the safe end of the low board first, working up to the hard part. No greasy spots, no loose screws. When I could put it off no longer, I hung my camera around my neck and grabbed the handrail. Nothing left to do but walk the plank.

My palms left foggy prints on the metal as I edged toward the end of the railing and stopped. My next step would be over the water. I extended my foot . . .

And retreated.

My inner chicken was firmly in control.

"All right, Mags." My voice rang in the empty gym. "Don't be ridiculous. Suck it up and just do it."

God. I sounded like my mother, gene-spliced with Coach Milner. But it had become a point of honor now.

Fists white-knuckled on the railing, I lowered myself to straddle the board. Then I scooted out, my center of gravity glued to the fiberglass. A ridiculous method of locomotion, but it worked. My feet dangled over twenty-one fathoms of water.

I reached the end with a thrill of satisfaction that quickly turned to disappointment. I'd risked my continued enjoyment of oxygen for nothing. But then I ran my finger over the textured surface and left a swath of lighter-blue behind.

A strange grimy blackness outlined the whorls of my fingerprints. It wasn't slippery, like motor oil, though there *was* an oily sort of quality. But sooty, like the stuff that collects on the chimney glass of a hurricane lamp.

Could it have caused Karen to slip? I didn't think so. I could vouch for the nonskid treatment of the board; my jeans had rasped with every scoot. Plus, no one else had fallen and the scum coated the board in a thin, complete layer.

After photographing several angles, I sat for a moment, getting the courage to unclamp my legs and move again. I knew I should appease my grandmother by looking at this with my, I don't know, instinct, inner sight, third eye, whatever you want to call it. But I didn't know how to begin. I'd been slamming shut the door of my skepticism for so long, I had no idea how to open it.

I sighed and gave up trying to make it happen. As soon as I did, I got a flash, clear as a bell: I had to get out of there. The sudden certainty of it made my stomach jump and twist.

I hurried, but not even the *The Amityville Horror* moment could make me anything less than overcautious. I scooted backward the same way I'd gone out, and as soon as I was over dry land I swung off the board, grabbed my backpack, and fled.

✳   ✳   ✳

The locker room was empty except for the drip of the showers and the musty smell of mildew and old sneakers, but the feeling didn't abate. I ducked out, and the door had just closed behind me when I saw Halloran headed down the hall, wearing a face like thunder.

"Margaret Quinn!"

First of all, my name is not Margaret. Second of all, no one could hold a candle to my mother when it came to the Invocation of the Full Name. The mere threat of Mom bellowing "Magdalena Lorraine Quinn!" had always guaranteed my unwavering obedience. All other attempts at given-name intimidation fell far short by comparison, especially when attempted by ex-Jock assistant principals who couldn't be bothered to get it right.

"What are you doing back here?" He might not know my name, but he did know that I didn't darken the door of the gym unless my graduation credits demanded it.

"I left my swimsuit in the locker room. But the door is locked, so I couldn't get it."

Eyeing me suspiciously, he tested the door. It didn't budge. No mojo there; I had heard it latch behind me. Unable to catch me out in a lie, he turned grumpy. "What are you doing at school so late?"

"I need to take some pictures of play practice." Boy, those thespians were darned handy.

"Well, I'm headed that way myself. I'll walk with you."

The auditorium was in the opposite direction from my car. But if Halloran suspected I'd been taking pictures of the diving board he'd confiscate my camera in a second, on the remotest possibility of a lawsuit.

So I let him escort me to C Hall. He watched me all the way up to the auditorium doors, where I slipped in without saying thanks.

Rehearsal was in full swing; compared to that morning, it was a marvel of organization. On the stage was a simple but artistic set and in front of it Thespica danced in a blue gingham dress, singing about chicks and ducks. Honesty forces me to admit she seemed quite good, for someone singing about farm animals.

The drama teacher saw me. I held up my camera, then pointed at the stage. He nodded and went back to scribbling notes on a legal pad. I found a good angle and took some shots of the star, then of her "Granny" as she came onstage in a frumpy outfit that *my* granny wouldn't be caught dead in. Though the same could be said of the farm, really.

When they stopped the action to work out a scene change, I slipped backstage, thinking I might grab a couple of pictures of the crew. Foolishly, I did not realize it would be pitch-dark there. The only lights were blue—either a blue bulb or a normal work light with some kind of blue plastic covering it.

"Hey," said a guy in a black T-shirt, looking officious. "You're not supposed to be back here."

"I wanted to get a look behind the scenes. At the unsung heroes, you know." Yes, shameless flattery is my friend.

"Well . . . all right. But try and stay out of the way."

"Thanks." I edged toward the wall, where a blue light illuminated a stand with a script on it. Backstage was not as big as I thought. Set pieces and actors and crew were stuffed tightly in the available space.

I think the black clothes were supposed to make the stage crew inconspicuous, but I noticed Stanley Dozer almost immediately, despite the crowded darkness. Man, that boy kept turning up like a six-foot, five-inch bad penny.

Still more interesting, he looked nothing like the sour dweeb I'd seen earlier. I watched him bend to listen to something a girl in costume said, then he gave a muted laugh.

Stanley Dozer, you fickle son of a gun. I couldn't judge if the girl returned his interest, but his infatuation was plain on his homely face.

"Dude."

It took a moment to realize that someone was talking to me. I'm not the girliest girl ever, but no one has ever mistaken me for a guy before.

"Dude." The guy at the prompting stand repeated it until I turned. "Your ass is glowing."

"What?" Definitely not something I expected to hear in the normal run of things.

"Your ass is glowing. Dude, what did you sit in?"

I craned around to look. Sure enough, in the deep violet lamplight, the seat of my jeans glowed fluorescent blue.

Great. A radioactive butt. What a topper for the wedding cake of disaster that had been my day.

9

finally, all those *CSI* reruns were going to pay off. As soon as I got out to my Jeep, I stripped off my jeans and tucked them into a plastic grocery sack, tying off the top to preserve the evidence. Of course, this meant I had to drive home in my underwear, but I had a ratty old wool picnic blanket in the back of the car. I wrapped it around my waist, and headed home.

Beltline was the most direct road, but it was the main drag through Avalon, and always clogged with traffic. The street led past the most important places in town: the red brick downtown area, the university, my school, the hospital, and if you kept going it would take you to the mall near the state highway bypass, the "new" high school (built only twenty years ago), and the treeless subdivisions where my dad refused to live. Going south you'd pass the Wal-Mart, the bars that catered to people who wanted to drink more than dance, and eventually the lumber mill and the paper plant, thankfully far enough away that it only stank when the wind was very strong from the southwest.

The upshot of this arrangement was that Beltline was the last road you'd want to take when you were bottomless in a topless Jeep.

The back way home wound through a residential area, between a park and the west side of the university campus. There was exactly one traffic light on the route. I was stopped there, mulling over the glow-in-the-dark spooge, when I heard my name.

"Maggie?" Justin MacCallum was loitering on the corner, wearing a sweat-soaked T-shirt and athletic shorts. His short hair stood up in damp spikes, which emphasized the clean, chiseled planes of his face. And the rest of him . . . Wow. Michelangelo could have sculpted those thighs.

He smiled as though I hadn't been in a total snit the last time he'd seen me. "I thought that was you."

"What are you doing here?" Not the most intelligent question, but at least I managed to drag my gaze up to his face.

"I was running in the park."

"Running from what?" The light turned green and the car behind me honked. With a gesture to Justin, I pulled through the intersection and into the tree-shaded parking lot.

I turned in the seat as he jogged over. "Actually, I have a question for you."

He looked surprised. But then, so was I. The words had sort of popped out of my mouth. My thoughts were going in a bizarre direction, and I would have rejected the idea completely, except maybe I still had my Nancy Drew thing going on, and good detectives don't eliminate things without examining them from all angles.

"Okay, shoot," he said, with a crooked sort of smile.

The afternoon was warm and humid, and the wool blanket was extremely itchy, but I tried not to scratch. "Is there really such a thing as ectoplasm?"

"Ectoplasm?" His eyebrows shot up in surprise.

"You know how in *Ghostbusters,* when the ghosts leave behind that slime when they touch something?"

"Why are you asking *me*?"

"Because you're the one getting a degree in weirdology."

He opened his mouth to argue, then shut it, mulled over a few responses, and finally settled on, "Do you think you've seen a ghost?"

"I don't know. Maybe." I'd begun thinking about phantoms when Karen told me about the shadow, even before I found the fluorescent soot. "I'm considering all possibilities."

Justin seemed intrigued; he leaned on the roll bar of the Jeep and I couldn't help thinking that he smelled awfully good for such a sweaty guy. "Okay. The way I understand it, ectoplasm is—supposedly—an ethereal substance that manifests when a spirit is present, like while a medium is channeling at a séance."

"So it's sort of like a psychic snail trail?"

His brows twitched in suppressed laughter. "I haven't heard it described in quite that way."

I thought about taking issue with his amusement, but stayed focused. "But does the stuff actually exist?"

"There was a lot of research done when that kind of spiritualism was popular at the turn of the twentieth century. But there are so many frauds, it's hard to say."

I pursed my lips, dissatisfied with the nonanswer. "What about you? Do *you* think it exists?"

"I keep an open mind." He smiled at my frustrated sound. "I have some books." A pause, while he seemed to mull something over. "That's my dorm there. Drive over and I'll get them for you."

"Sorry. I can't. I'm not wearing any pants." Now *there* was a phrase I never thought I'd say out loud.

"Oh." He glanced down, then quickly back to my face. "I just thought that was a very ugly skirt."

"Thanks." I grabbed my phone from the drink holder. "What's your number? In case I have more questions."

He rattled it off and I punched SAVE.

"What if I want to get in touch with you?" he asked.

"About my alleged psychic powers?"

"Maybe."

"Then think about me real hard, and I'll know to give you a call." I flashed a sunny smile, put the Jeep in gear, and drove away. For the first time that day, I felt as if I'd gotten the upper hand in a human interaction.

✳ ✳ ✳

I dreamed of blue fire that night, burning in a big, beaten metal bowl, with engravings scrolling around the edges.

There was liquid in the brazier, too. It didn't quench the fire, but made the clean blue flame hiss and spit and throw out thick black smoke. As the darkness rose, it didn't drift aimlessly, but pulled into the center and coalesced into a shapeless mass.

I watched, both repulsed and fascinated as the thing built itself from soot and shadow. It seethed above the flames with sentient awareness. Though it had no eyes, I knew the moment it looked back at me. Somehow, on some strange dream plane, it saw me. More than that, it *recognized* me.

A shock of fear and revulsion jolted me awake. My eyes opened but I lay frozen, afraid to move in case some *thing* was there, in the room with me. I heard nothing but the blood pounding in my ears, saw nothing in the stripes of moonlight that fell through the curtains. I forced myself to turn my head, to search the darkness, but I was alone.

Just a dream. I repeated it like a mantra.

Then I whispered it like a prayer.

✳ ✳ ✳

I woke in a lousy mood. I had washed underwear and shirts the night before, but my last marginally clean pair of jeans had been bagged and tagged. I found a casual skirt and put it on with a sunny yellow T-shirt and a pair of Converse. Mom's reaction when I reached the kitchen was predictable.

"Is that what you're wearing?"

I got my coffee cup out of the dishwasher as I answered. "No. I just put it on to annoy you."

"If you would go to bed at a decent hour, you wouldn't be so grumpy in the morning." She frowned at my extra-tall travel mug. "You wouldn't need to drink so much coffee, either."

"It's my drug of choice, Mom. Be grateful."

She sighed. "I know. I just thank God you turned out as well as you did."

I cast her a grumpy look on my way to the door. "It's nice to know you think I could have turned out worse."

Her voice followed me out. "You need to eat some breakfast!"

I scored an excellent parking spot at school, and was downing the last of my coffee when a shadow fell across me.

"Cheese and Crackers!" I screeched and mopped at the splashes on my skirt. "What is it with you and sneaking up on people?"

Bobby Baywatch smiled. "Sorry. I didn't mean to scare you."

"It's been a rough couple of days. I'm a little jumpy."

"I noticed." His hair had pale highlights from the sun, which might have looked girly on someone else. With his tan and his lifeguard physique, though, it worked.

"Can I help you carry anything?"

"Let me get out of the car, first."

I loved my Wrangler. My trusty steed was safari brown—mostly—and bore the scars of a long and useful life. But it was impossible to exit with any grace. It figured I would be wearing a skirt.

Once I'd lost my dignity but gained my feet, I handed him my books then grabbed my backpack and the plastic bag of jeans. He ignored my attempts to reclaim the heavy stack of texts, and started walking toward school. "Hey, Sir

Lancelot." I trotted after him. "Isn't there a Jessica looking for you somewhere?"

He shortened his stride; considerate of him not to make me run to keep up. "There might be, but that's her business. I'm friends with Brandon and Jeff. I don't . . . None of the girls is . . ."

"Your girlfriend?" I felt sorry for any girl who was, since he couldn't even say the word.

"Right."

"My mistake. Three guys, three girls. You always look paired off like tasty packs of snack cakes."

"Well, we're not."

We passed the tennis courts and the gym, and curiosity got the better of me. "So are you stalking me, or what?"

He stopped, and I did, too, since he had my books. "Listen, I'm sorry about what happened in the locker room yesterday."

The day had been so jam-packed with wackitude that it took me a moment to realize what he meant. As soon as I did, my heart twisted in dread. I could literally feel the blood drain from my face, like someone had pulled a plug. "The picture? She actually sent it out?"

"No." His quick reassurance didn't make me stop wishing for a bathroom to hide in. "She just showed it to the gang."

"Oh, just to the six people who hate me the most. Great. I hope you had a good laugh." The blood had rushed back to my head, making my ears burn.

"Well, *I* didn't laugh."

I groaned and covered my face with my hand. *Okay, get a*

grip, Maggie. What would D&D Lisa say? So they laughed at me. No novelty there. At least I could honestly say that nobody's opinion mattered less to me than the Jocks and Jessicas.

Bobby Baywatch was watching me like I might burst into tears. "I'm really sorry."

I glared up at him, not hysterical, just pissed. "Why do you keep apologizing for things that aren't your fault?"

His shoulders lifted in a shrug. "I guess because they're my friends, I feel responsible."

"Maybe you need to find new friends." I reached for my books, but he held them out of reach.

"Let me walk you inside. Maybe it will help."

His intention dawned on me, absurd as it was. "Are you offering me the protection of your reputation?" My sense of humor was returning along with my perspective, and I gave a short laugh at his chagrin. "Boy, you *do* feel guilty."

"I'm sure not offering because of your charming personality."

"Oh, ouch." I put out my hands. "At least let me carry my own books. This isn't *Our Town.*"

He handed them over and we walked the rest of the way into school, mostly in silence. Embarrassment aside, I didn't have a social standing to preserve, but it was a nice gesture. I didn't want to like him, but he was making it hard not to, just a little.

✳ ✳ ✳

With a half hour before the bell, I found Professor Blackthorne in his chemistry classroom, drawing molecules on the board. He heard my groan and turned.

"Not a fan of organic compounds, Miss Quinn?"

"I would say no, but I'm here to ask a favor."

"A chemistry favor?" He didn't *quite* rub his hands together in anticipation. "Have you brought me something interesting?"

"Maybe." I set the grocery sack on the lab bench and untied the handles. As the plastic bag opened, we both took a hasty step backward. A horrible odor escaped, like when you accidentally open something green and fuzzy from the very back of the fridge, only about fifty times worse.

"Good God, girl!" Blackthorne blinked his watering eyes. "Did something die wearing these trousers?"

"They didn't smell that bad last night. Maybe the fumes built up in the closed bag."

"Possible." The stench was dissipating slightly in the well-ventilated lab, but I felt sorry for the first-period class. Blackthorne put on a pair of gloves before he touched the denim. "Now, let's see what you've brought me."

"Do you have a blacklight?"

He pointed toward a cabinet where I found a handheld lamp. I turned off the overhead; even with the residual light from the windows, we could see the eerie phosphorescence under the ultraviolet glow. "I sat on something."

"Obviously." He scratched his chin. "I'm loathe to think in what sort of seedy places you've been spending your time."

"Okay, that's just . . . eiew."

"No Dumpster diving recently? Well, smells can be deceiving."

"There's a test to figure out what that stuff is, right?"

"Certainly. Gas chromatography."

"So can you work some *CSI* magic on those pants?"

"Not here. This is a high school chemistry lab. I have difficulty getting money to buy paper towels." Brow furrowed, he drummed his thumbs against the slate lab bench. "We could send it to Dr. Smyth at the university. She owes me a favor."

"Excellent!"

"They may have to take a sample from your trousers, though."

"You mean cut a hole in them?" I really liked those jeans; they made my butt look great. Honestly, the sacrifices a detective has to make. "When do you think she can do it?"

"I'll take them to her after school. She'll have to work it into her schedule, though." He bundled the jeans back up, then put the grocery sack inside a small trash bag and tied it closed. I didn't blame him for doubling up. I'd thought the stench was bad in my dream, but smelling it through my real, live nose was the difference between a cheap pair of headphones and a symphony orchestra of stink.

"Hey, Professor Blackthorne." I followed him to the chalkboard. "Is that what sulfur smells like?"

Hexagon chemical bonds had his attention again. "Hmm? No, sulfur doesn't have a smell."

"I thought it did. That whole 'stench of brimstone' thing."

"Burning sulfur gives off sulfur dioxide, which is probably what that phrase means. It's noxious and extremely irritating to the lungs." He added a few more notations to the diagram on the board. "Though you may be thinking about the thiols—the sulfhydryl group. They are quite odiferous. In fact, ethanethiol is added to natural gas so that leaks can be detected by the 'rotten egg' smell."

"So maybe that's what's on the jeans?"

"Do you want to open them back up and take a whiff, or wait for the chromatograph?"

"Um, no. I'll wait for the test."

"As you wish." I shouldered my backpack and started out. His voice stopped me at the door. "If you want my opinion, and not a scientific fact, I'd lay money that either putrescine or cadaverine will be in the mix." He went back to writing, talking more to himself than to me. "Yes. I think I'll make a bet with Dr. Smyth. See if the nose still knows."

Boy, I could have gone my whole life without knowing I'd gotten something named after a putrid cadaver on my butt. On the upside, though, I was no longer ambivalent about destroying those pants.

10

I knew that my personal humiliation had a limited comedic lifespan, but I didn't expect to have turned invisible before second period.

"What's up?" I asked Jennifer Fitzwilliam, catching up to her on the way to class. She was the most reliable source of gossip in the entire school. If someone bought someone else a Coke at lunch, five minutes later Jennifer would have the scoop on when they'd met, whether they were going out, and if they were, how many dates they'd had before going all the way.

"Jess Michaels"—translation: Jess Minor—"showed up

wearing a knockoff Donna Karan top, and Jessica Prentice"—a.k.a. Prime—"spilled the beans in front of everyone. Jess threw her Snapple in Jessica's face, and we were all set for a catfight, but Brian Kirkpatrick got between them and broke it up."

"Brian Kirkpatrick?"

"You know. Swim team, baseball team. The guy who carried your books into school today," she added with a coy look.

So that was his real name. He was Brian Baywatch, not Bobby. I had to admit, Bob would be a sad name for anyone in the lifeguard profession.

"Was it really a knockoff?" I asked.

"Seems to be. Ironic, isn't it?" We'd reached the journalism room, which was buzzing with a frantic kind of schizophrenia as students bounced from being reporters, to editors, to publishers, trying to get the paper laid out in time to send to the printer.

"What's ironic?" I dropped my backpack beside my desk.

"Well, Jess Michaels is something of a fashionista, isn't she?"

"True," I answered, but I was losing interest in the Jessicas and their drama, and I was glad when Jennifer continued to her own desk so I could get to work on more important things.

In addition to the little piece about the Big Spring Musical, I'd written a few inches about Karen and her fall. Besides being newsworthy, it gave me the excuse to look into the history of the "natatorium" to see if there was any kind of trend of suspicious accidents. The building wasn't very old, especially compared to the parts of the school that dated back to the 1940s. I found nothing in the paper's online archives, which only meant that I had to broaden my search.

"Quinn!" Phillip, the student editor, had watched too many movies with irascible newsmen bellowing for their errant reporters. All he lacked was the cigar and the beer belly. "Where's your copy!"

"On its way, Chief." I knew he'd miss the sarcasm in the title. Ghosthunting would have to wait until the paper was put to bed. I wonder if Brenda Starr ever had this problem?

✳ ✳ ✳

By lunchtime a rampant rumor was circulating that Jess Minor shopped at Wal-Mart. In P.E. the tension hung thick in the air. Jess and Jessica ignored each other with an acid deliberateness, and Thespica tried to act as though there were nothing wrong. A few hangers-on were quick to exploit this possible opening in the inner circle. When Jessica Prime snapped her fingers, one sycophant supplied a hairbrush. When she needed a nail file, another one appeared. And when she said, "I look so fat in this" (at least five times), all the toadies were quick to reassure her it wasn't so.

I ignored this, or tried to, while I searched for the Get Out of Diving Free note Dad had written. It turned out to be unnecessary. Coach Milner came in and announced:

"I want you all to know that I believe we should get right back on that horse and not give up the ship. But the administration has decided that we will finish up the aquatics unit by practicing our racing dives in the lap pool."

Oh fabulous day! No more diving board, and soon, no more swimming pool, either. Things were looking up.

* * *

Despite organic compounds in chemistry and a film in civics that was so old, Chief Justice Rehnquist was alive and well and still had a full head of hair, my good mood carried me all the way to the parking lot that afternoon. There was a cherry limeade in my future, and research in the city newspaper archives, but first . . .

But first, furious Jocks. My steps slowed warily on the asphalt as I saw a familiar threesome, the Jessica's masculine counterparts—Biff/Brandon, Brian Baywatch, and Henchman Jeff—in a taut group, the air around them blue with curses. Jeff authored most of the profanity, aimed at the rassin', frassin', son of a gun who had scratched the beautiful, cherry red, vintage Mustang. I paraphrase, of course.

The entire school knew how Jeff Espinoza lavished love and attention on that car. And he was a big guy. I had to say, that was one brave rassin' frassin' son of a gun.

"What are you looking at, Quinn?" Jeff was eager to transfer his rage to a handy target.

"Yeah," Brandon echoed. "Where's your camera? You could take a picture. It would last longer."

"Thanks, Mr. Originality. But some people I'd rather forget."

He took a menacing step forward, but Brian grabbed his arm and redirected his attention to the car, and soon they

85

were once more cursing the walking dead man who had damaged Jeff's manhood.

I left them to it and hurried to my own car. The phone rang just as the engine grumbled to life. "Hi, Gran."

"What is this about a ghost? Why do I have to hear from someone else? Have you lost my phone number? Do I have to draw you a map to my house?"

"I'm well, thank you for asking. How are you?"

"Madder than a wet hen."

"I guess Justin MacTattletale called."

"He's here now. I *knew* something otherworldly was at work near you. Come over this instant."

"I have to stop by and see my friend in the hospital."

"Are you coming over after that?"

"Yes, ma'am." This seemed to appease her. "Put the fink on the phone."

"Justin is a nice young man. You should be glad he told me what you were up to."

I plucked at my T-shirt; it was hot with the late April sun bearing down on the roofless Jeep. "Just put him on. I'll see you in an hour, tops."

She murmured dire predictions if I didn't make good on that, and a moment later I heard a baritone voice on the line. "Hello?"

"Go in the other room." I fished in the glove box for my headset so I could drive and chew him out at the same time.

"Why?"

"Because I'm going to yell at you and I don't want Gran to hear."

"If you had given me your number . . ."

"Oh, don't *even* go there. You could have just asked her for it."

"Yeah. I could have." But then he couldn't have needled me. He left that part unspoken, but I heard his amusement.

"So what do you want?"

"I brought you some books on . . ." I heard Gran banging around in the background. "On what you asked me about yesterday."

"You didn't have to do that."

"I didn't want you using *Ghostbusters* as a definitive source."

"Thanks." I pulled out of the parking lot and onto the drag. "I need to stop by to see my friend. You want to wait at Gran's, or what?"

"I'll wait. There are cookies."

"Those are *my* cookies. There had better be some left when I get there."

"No problem." His voice dropped in volume. "I think your grandmother cooks when she's worried."

"She's not worried, just irked I didn't tell her first. See you in an hour."

Was it weird that I was more pleased than pissed that he'd tracked me down through Gran? If he hadn't gotten her worked up, I wouldn't be upset at all that a college guy wanted to help me bust ghosts.

✳ ✳ ✳

Karen was alone when I tapped on the hospital door. "Boy, you must be bored if you're doing homework."

She looked up from a dog-eared copy of *Animal Farm* and grimaced. "Trying to stay caught up, remember."

"You are an inspiration."

"Not really. I can only read a little at a time before my head starts to hurt. I haven't even started the calculus homework that Stanley brought me."

"Speaking of Stanley—" Because it seemed like I was doing that a lot lately. "Has he seemed a little . . . gruff to you?"

She shrugged. "We're all ready to be done with school."

"Good point. Any word when you get to go home?"

"Maybe tomorrow. They sort of freak out when you lose consciousness, even for just a minute. And they're worried about pneumonia from inhaling pool water."

I touched her hand. "I'm so sorry, Karen."

"You keep saying that." Her smile was gently quizzical. "It's not your fault."

How weird that this morning I'd been on the other side of the exact same exchange with Brian. Maybe I was having the same kind of guilt that my inaction had somehow put Karen in harm's way. "It isn't logical. But you took my place in line and . . ." I took a deep breath. It seemed as good a time as any to ask to perform my little experiment. "And I keep thinking about your shadow. The one you mentioned yesterday."

Her eyes narrowed. "You mean the one you said was probably an optical illusion?"

"Uh, yeah. But, well, this is going to sound crazy, but . . ."

"But you don't think it was my shadow." I must have looked surprised that she said it so plainly and so calmly. She smiled ruefully. "I haven't had anything else to do but think about it, Maggie. I know my own shadow, and I know when something is . . ." She struggled for the right word. "Foreign."

I let out a pent-up breath. This was going to be easier than I'd thought. "Do you mind if I do a little experiment?"

"Nope. I'm relieved you don't think I'm off the deep end."

I dug into my backpack and took out the blacklight I'd borrowed from the chemistry lab. I did ask. I'm not sure that Blackthorne really heard me—he'd been happily explaining carbon bonds to a glassy-eyed student—but I *did* ask.

I had a distinct memory of the way Karen's leg had shot out from under her, as if it had been yanked. Flipping off the light, and feeling ridiculous, I shone the lamp on her ankle, and saw a familiar fluorescent glow.

"Oh my God." Karen stared at her own foot as if it belonged to someone else. "What is that? And why didn't it come off when I washed?"

"Honestly, I don't know." I didn't see a reason to mention putrescine or cadaverine. "I found it on the diving board, too."

"What do you think it is?" Her brown eyes searched mine, avidly curious. I still hesitated.

"It sounds kind of crazy."

"I promise I won't laugh." I gave her a narrow-eyed look and she raised her hand, as if taking an oath. "Scout's honor."

"Okay. Have you ever seen the movie *Ghostbusters*?"

11

I arrived at Gran's house with fifty-nine seconds to spare. Justin sat at the kitchen table, books spread around him. He was wearing jeans today, and another oxford shirt, untucked this time, and there was chocolate smeared at the corner of his mouth.

"How's your friend?" he asked as I came in.

"Pretty amazing, actually." I was stunned at how easily Karen had accepted the idea of the supernatural, and more to the point, how non-freaked-out she was at having been touched by it. I'd only *dreamed* about the shadow and I was kinda wigged.

"Have you ever known someone for years, and then

something happens, and all of a sudden you realize you've never really known them at all?"

"I think we've all done that." He didn't look particularly freaked out, either. Was I the only one who was dizzy from spinning back and forth between "this is real" and "this is crazy"?

I picked up one of the books: *Ghosts and Specters: An Empirical Study.* Another one was, *A History of Paranormal Experience.* And another: *The Literature of the Supernatural.*

"I thought you were a history major."

"I'm getting my bachelor's in history. I want to do graduate studies in the anthropology of myth and occult experience."

"That should open up a world of career choices for you." I set the book down. It was the size of a toaster but considerably heavier. "What made you choose an advanced degree in creepy?"

He shrugged. "I've always been interested in the theory of the supernatural. My upbringing wasn't exactly conventional."

"Do you have a nutty grandmother, too?"

Her voice came from the other room. "I hear you!"

"I love you, Gran!" I called back, then poured myself some tea and sat down near the plate of cookies. "Anything on ectoplasm?"

Justin folded his arms on the table. "Let's back up a bit. Tell me why you think you've encountered a ghost."

Gran bustled into the kitchen, carrying a load of laundry. "I want to hear this. Since it's the only way I'll know what my granddaughter is up to."

Sighing, I took a chocolate chip cookie for fortification.

While Gran folded towels and Justin made notes, I told him about my frustratingly vague dream, and the unease I couldn't shake. I described the strange awkwardness of Karen's fall, and the smell I might have just imagined. I related her glimpse of a shadow moving over the water. When I finished describing my impromptu detective work, they both stared at me.

"What?"

"I'm just stunned," said Justin. "Because yesterday you seemed very, um, resistant to the idea that you might have some extrasensory perception. And now you're tracking down a ghost."

"First of all, I don't have ESP. I don't bend spoons or see dead people, or any of that freaky stuff. I just have good intuition." From the corner of my eye I saw Gran roll hers, but she didn't say anything. "Second, I'm not tracking a ghost. I'm investigating the possibility it *might* be a ghost."

He gave me a look I was starting to recognize. It meant he thought I was funny but didn't want to piss me off by laughing. "Okay. Let's be logical about this, then. What makes you think it's a ghost?"

"Well, the shadow, I guess." The evidence seemed sparse, once I tried to lay it out. "And the spooge it leaves behind."

"Which we don't know is related." He wrote down "shadow" but not "spooge." "It could be nothing more than a strange sort of mold or mildew."

I snapped, irritated at his skepticism. "You're the Mulder here. *I'm* the Scully."

"I'm just helping you be objective." He tapped his pen on the pad. "What else?"

"The smell," I said. "There's that awful smell."

"Okay." He jotted it down. "That's good. What about a feeling of cold or dread?"

"No cold. And I was faced with a bottomless well of dark water, so I wouldn't have noticed any extra dread."

"A sense of another presence?"

"Lots of people were around when Karen fell." I thought a moment. "But I did have a weird feeling later, when I went back."

"You can't be more specific?"

I raised my hands in a shrug. "It's not like telling if the lights are on or off. It's ambiguous. I was nervous about getting caught."

Again the pen tapped, an aggravated rhythm. "Your perceptions aren't a lot of help."

"Sorry. Next time I'll bring my spectrometer."

Gran spoke up, preventing an argument. "What about history? Has there ever been another incident or accident in the pool, or even the gym?"

"I didn't find anything in the school newspaper about the pool, but the online records only go back five years. I'm going to check the city paper archives tonight, and the microfiche at the library tomorrow."

"Good plan." Justin closed his notebook and started gathering his books. "Strange that those other girls were able to dive without anything happening. Karen must have been the unlucky number."

I must have reacted to that, because he looked at me closely. "What is it?"

"Nothing." I shook my head. Gran had taken the plates to the kitchen a few feet away.

His expression said I hadn't fooled him, but he let it go. He said his polite good-byes to Gran and as she saw him to the door, I took our cups to the sink, rinsed them, and put them in the dishwasher. By the time I'd finished, Gran had returned. She put her arms around me and kissed my hair.

"I am so proud of you."

"What for?"

"For opening your mind to the possibility of things you cannot see with your eyes."

The praise embarrassed me, since I hadn't so much flung wide my mind as cracked open the door with the safety chain still firmly in place. "It's no big deal, Gran."

"It is a very big deal." She cupped my face in her hands. "You have so much potential to do good things in the world. But you be careful. Listen to that intuition and be smart."

"Yes, Gran." I hugged her back. "I will."

I told her I'd keep in touch, then grabbed my stuff and let myself out the front door. I wasn't surprised to see Justin MacCallum still outside, leaning against the fender of my car and looking serious.

"So, what happened?" he asked, in a tone that didn't allow any arguments.

"Karen switched places with me in line at the diving pool," I said, giving in without a fight. "I've been convincing myself it was just random luck."

He thought for a moment, then said, "That's probably all it was." Another considering pause. "But . . ."

I groaned. Was there any more ominous word in the English language?

"But," he continued, ignoring my drama, "you should keep your guard up. There's a theory in science that the very act of observation can influence a situation. Once you start looking closely at something, it might start looking back at you."

Last night's installment of the subconscious creepshow came slamming back into my brain so hard that I flinched. Justin didn't need any ESP to interpret it.

"Something looked back at you, didn't it." He didn't bother to make it a question. "When? At the pool?"

"Last night. I saw the fire again, but this time the smoke thing . . . It *looked* at me, just like you said." I shook my head. "It was a dream, but it feels like it really happened."

"We should assume it did."

I liked that "we." Justin had a steadiness that made me glad to have him on my side. "Maybe your vision was a warning, that the spirit has noticed you. Or maybe you met in some kind of dream plane. I don't know."

I rubbed a hand over my eyes. I'd had a sort of buzzing in the back of my brain all day and the thought of wearing a supernatural bull's-eye ratcheted it up to a head-splitting volume.

Justin's hand touched my shoulder. "You okay?" I shot him a what-do-you-think look, and he lifted his hands in surrender. "Stupid question. Sorry."

I sagged into the driver's seat, half in, half out of the car.

"Four days ago my life was simple. All I had to worry about was avoiding the prom and living through graduation."

He ignored my whining and cut to the heart of the matter. "What happened four days ago?"

"I had the nightmare." I ran my hand over the leather-wrapped steering wheel, the rough bumps and tears keeping me anchored, and away from the deep water of fear and supposition. "And something inside me . . . woke up."

"Woke up?"

"That's what it felt like. I hadn't had a dream in years. At least not one I couldn't ignore." I sighed. "They ought to come with an instruction manual."

He didn't give even a courtesy laugh. He was deep in thought. "Weird."

"That's the understatement of the century."

"No, I mean, I wonder which woke first, the spirit or your visions?"

✳   ✳   ✳

What kind of ghost-hunter has to put the spirit world on hold while she finishes her homework?

The outline for my English paper had been unfairly disapproved by my teacher. Jonathan Swift was over two hundred and fifty years dead, so unless Ms. Vincent had a direct pipeline to the afterlife, I couldn't see a reason for her to call my well-annotated suppositions bunk. Then again, if she did have the ability to communicate with the dead, maybe she could actually be of some use to my current situation, which would definitely be a novelty for Ms. Vincent.

An instant messenger window popped up while I was knee-deep in Lilliputians.

0v3rl0rdL15a: Where did you go after civics? You shot out of there before I could ask you about the English homework.

I clicked over to the IM window and typed back:

MightyQuinn: We have English homework?
0v3rl0rdL15a: Five paragraph essay question on the last Act of Julius C.
MightyQuinn: :P I didn't want to sleep tonight, anyway.

We kept the chat window open while we worked, which probably wasn't very efficient, but I felt less lonely in my room. The sound of my parents puttering around downstairs made the house seem normal and safe. Even the sheer mundane boredom of homework settled my nerves and made my fears seem a little foolish. When I finished my paragraphs on J.C., I was even able to pick up the book Justin had lent me and thumb through it with a certain detachment.

It seemed weird that I hadn't talked about all this with my closest friend. Despite the D&D thing, Lisa was a rock of unflappable logic. I'd never told her about the dreams I'd had as a kid, never talked about my intuition. I didn't want her to think I was a flake. Even though I was beginning to admit that I was, quite possibly, exactly that.

MightyQuinn: Hey Lisa . . . Hypothetical
  question.
0v3rl0rdL15a: ?
MightyQuinn: Do you believe in ghosts?

There was a long pause. Maybe she was just analyzing
Julius Caesar and not deleting my name from her address
book or marking it: "Nutjob."

0v3rl0rdL15a: You mean cold spots in a
  room, or poltergeists, or what?
MightyQuinn: I dunno. Either one.
0v3rl0rdL15a: Why do you want to know?
MightyQuinn: I'm not going to publish it
  in the paper. It's just a hypothetical
  question.

Another long pause.

0v3rl0rdL15a: Do you?

Put up or shut up time, I guess. I was surprised she
hadn't simply fired back a flippant reply. If she was entertaining an honest answer, I should offer a little trust.

MightyQuinn: Yeah. I guess I do.

What was with the pauses? Was she polishing her toe-
nails between responses?

0v3rl0rdL15a: Interesting.

MightyQuinn: Is that all? Just "Interesting"?

0v3rl0rdL15a: I'm just entering it into
my mental files.

MightyQuinn: Look. I'm reading about
ghosts, and how many people believe in
at least the possibility of a
spiritual imprint of some kind. Maybe
not stacking furniture or—

I was out of window space, but not out of steam.

0v3rl0rdL15a: Chill. I'm teasing. Why are
you reading a book about ghosts?

MightyQuinn: There's a guy.

That was honest, at least.

0v3rl0rdL15a: Not Brian Kirkpatrick.

MightyQuinn: No! O-O

0v3rl0rdL15a: Good.

MightyQuinn: B.K. is The Hotness, but
he's a Jock.

0v3rl0rdL15a: So why'd you let him carry
your books?

MightyQuinn: He's bigger than me, and I
wasn't getting them back without a fight.

0v3rl0rdL15a: lol. Okay.

I went back to work. My essay was proofread and my outline revised to Curriculum Conformity when a new window pinged open.

Ov3rl0rdL15a: I do believe in ghosts. Don't tell anyone. It would destroy my frightening reputation.
MightyQuinn: My lips are sealed.

Now what was so hard about that?

* * *

I had figured out this much about my dreams: If I wake with a sense of clarity, it was just random neuron firings, or my subconscious working out my fears or something. But if I wake with the dream still clinging to me, like I'd walked through a spiderweb and my brain was covered by sticky threads of night memory, it was more than that.

I had been dreading sleep, but when I couldn't resist my bed any longer, all I'd dreamed of was talking horses. Nightmare free was a wonderful feeling. I turned on the radio while I showered and dressed. I may have even danced around a little. When the rising sun warmed the gaps between my curtains, I flung them open to welcome the day.

The filthiness of my bedroom window startled me. The morning light had to struggle through the murky glass. It was depressing and simply *wrong* somehow. True, I wasn't the neatest person in the world, but the grime coating the window was just gross.

I opened the study curtains, and had to squint against the light. Slowly I turned back to the bedroom and realized with a sinking feeling that one window was much dirtier than the other.

Not dirty. Sooty.

Leaden feet carried me to the window. With shaking hands I flipped open the latches and raised the sash, then ran my index finger through the greasy, powdery film that coated the outside glass, leaving a streak of sunshine in the grimy shadow.

I drew my hand in and closed the window. Locked it. Then I got the little blacklight out of my backpack, went into the bathroom and closed the door.

My fingertip glowed a bright, spectral blue.

12

I arrived at school early for the third morning in a row. I had searched the online city paper archives for any news from the high school. Except for budget cuts, there wasn't much of suspicious malevolence. But there were sixty yearbooks in the school library, and a couple of decades of school newspapers archived as well. After my visitor last night, I was extremely motivated to get to the bottom of this.

Was that why I hadn't dreamed last night? Had the smoke specter decided to get a look at me in person?

Balancing an armload of textbooks and a venti vanilla

latte, extra shot, extra foam, I climbed the front steps, wondering why Brian Baywatch was nowhere around when I could actually use a hand. Then, as if the thought itself had conjured him, I saw him standing just inside the glass doors.

He broke off from his friends and opened the door for me, an act of necessity rather than chivalry; my hands were completely full. The Jocks were not the only ones loitering around the foyer. There was a mixed bag of cheerleaders, band geeks, and drama nerds. "What's going on?"

"I don't know." Brian glanced toward his buddies, who were staring at him with a kind of astonished contempt. "Jessica called Brandon and told us to get over here."

The auditorium entrance was closed. I saw no sign of any of the Jessicas—I assumed Brian meant Prime—but I caught a glimpse of the prompter from backstage and beckoned him over. "Is something happening in there?"

"I don't know, man. I heard some dude over there say they may be canceling the play."

"Why would they do that?"

The guy shrugged his slumped shoulders. "I don't know. Sure would suck, though, after all that work." He slouched off with one last "Dude" and a shake of his shaggy head.

Visions of *Phantom of the Opera* filled my head as I left Brian and elbowed my way through the crowd. I had reached the front when the doors opened and the Three Original Jessicas emerged. Thespica was crying great inconsolable tears, supported by her friends, Jessicas Prime and Minor—

their feud apparently forgotten in the crisis. They bore her limp and sobbing form toward the office.

Brian caught my eye. I shrugged, as clueless as he was. Then his pack leader beckoned and they trailed after the girls. Brandon, the alpha dog, gave me one last, long stare. It was almost territorial, which, gladiatorial subtext aside, seemed to say he thought I was a threat to his pack.

With a Nancy Drew determination to satisfy my curiosity, I ignored the closed doors and went into the auditorium.

I expected scenic carnage. Maybe not a smashed chandelier, but the state of artistic chaos seemed the same as ever. The director's hair was standing on end, as if he'd been trying to pull it out, but I think that was status quo.

"Mr. Thomas?"

He stared blankly for a moment before recognition dawned. "How did you get in here?"

"Through the door. Look, everyone outside is saying you're going to cancel the show tonight. I just wanted to get the real story."

A huge sigh rattled his chest. "I hope we won't. The female lead, Jessica Jordan"—Thespica, obviously—"has come down with laryngitis. She can't make a sound."

My brows shot up. "Really."

"Yes. No amount of tea and honey is going to fix that by tonight."

"What are you going to do?" I didn't have to fake my concern. I'd been making fun of the drama nerds, but I knew how much work they'd put into the project, how important it was to them. Even if I wasn't sympathetic to Thespica (and I wasn't, really), I felt bad for the rest of them.

Then someone called from the stage. "She's here, Mr. Thomas." The choir teacher stood alongside a vaguely familiar, very nervous-looking, brown-haired girl.

Mr. Thomas excused himself. "That's the understudy. If she's up to it, then we'll open as planned."

He scurried down the aisle. I watched him talk earnestly to the girl, then gesture to the choir teacher, who went to the piano. Understudy Girl started to sing the chicks and ducks song, and though she lacked a fraction of Thespica's confidence (and by that I mean rampant egotism), she had a pretty voice with nice inflection. It sounded like the day was saved, and the show would go on.

All praise the Greek god Thespis.

✳ ✳ ✳

"It's just like *Phantom*, isn't it?" Emily Farber gushed, turned around in her desk to chatter at Lisa and me. It was English class and we were—big surprise—working on our papers.

The understudy's name was Suzie Miller. She was in the afternoon AP English class, as well as AP Calculus with Karen and Stanley. Her ascension to stardom was seen as a score for the smart kids, and a much more interesting topic than grammar and subtext.

"Where the phantom sabotages the prima donna so that Christine could have a chance at the limelight . . ." Emily sighed. "That is *so* romantic."

"I don't get that movie." Lisa slumped in her chair. "What's so hot about a homicidal psychopath?"

"Well, those eyes, that voice, that face—the part not all melty and gross, I mean." Emily looked prepared to go on at length.

"Those shoulders," I added.

"Girls!" snapped Ms. Vincent. She really ought to set up a subroutine for that. "You're supposed to be working on your themes. They are due in a week."

Lisa groaned and slithered lower in her seat. "Wake me up when the term is over."

She had a theory that term papers were a sort of "get out of teaching free" card. From the start of the assignment to its end, anytime the teacher wanted to dodge lecturing, she could give us class time to work on our papers and expect us to be grateful.

Personally, I was grateful for any day I didn't have to listen to Ms. Vincent regurgitate the textbook analysis of literature and expect us to parrot it back without alteration.

"Hey, Lisa." I doodled on my paper to make it look like I was working. "Have you ever heard of a student dying, maybe here on campus?"

She opened an eye and gave me a monocular glare. "You're not referring to that thing we were talking about last night that we are not going to talk about at school ever, are you?"

"No. Well, not really."

She sighed, then thought about it. "I think there was some kid who killed himself about twenty years ago."

"In the gym?"

"In the band hall."

That was not particularly helpful. Then I remembered that geography didn't seem to be a real issue here.

"Are you going to the play tonight?" I asked, changing the subject.

She laid her head on her folded arms. "I wasn't. But if there's a chance Gerard Butler might show up in a tux and a half-mask, I'm there."

"Dude. Me too."

∗　∗　∗

Naturally, since I'd lost the research time that morning, my second opportunity—journalism class—was taken up by a lecture. In lab I discovered that while our high school might have four decades of archived newspapers, the index only went back one and a half.

"Curses!" I half-slammed the drawer closed. "Foiled again."

"What's the problem?" asked Mr. Allison.

I blushed slightly, having been caught in a temper tantrum. "What happened to the index before the nineties?"

"It was lost when they moved the journalism lab up here. They started again with the current year, and no one has ever had the time to replace the old one. There's not that much call for old football scores and homecoming courts."

"I guess not." I drummed my fingers on the metal cabinet.

Mr. Allison came around his desk. "Something I can help you with?"

"Maybe. I'm looking for record of any student who may have died here on campus."

"That's grim."

"It's for a research paper." I was getting too good at lying. "Someone mentioned there was a kid who killed himself, maybe in the Band Hall?"

"Oh yes. That was a shame." He shook his head sadly. "I was in school here at the time." He opened a file drawer and came out with a microfiche spool marked 1981–85. "Look through the spring of 1984."

"Thanks." I went over to the projector. I wondered if someday, when all the archives in the world were stored on computer, microfilm projectors would be extinct. Even now, it's a dying art. Like calligraphy and Morse code, and about that efficient, too.

✳   ✳   ✳

"Only one week until prom!" I'd barely set foot in the courtyard when a neon green paper fluttered before my face. "Have you voted for your Royal . . . Oh. It's you." My friend from Student Council snatched back the ballot. "I don't have enough of these for you to wad up and throw on the floor."

"We're outside," I said, very reasonably, considering the neon green was hammering spikes into my eyes, which were aching from an hour reading little bitty backlit type. "There is no floor."

"Whatever. You can't have a ballot." She tucked the stack protectively against her chest.

"Are you taking away my constitutional right to vote for a King and Queen?" I raised my voice in outrage.

"Well . . ." She wavered as people around us turned to stare.

"I demand the right to choose my own representation of all that is wrong with adolescent social hierarchy."

"Right on!" said a voice near me.

"You cannot deny me a voice in the senseless aggrandizement of those already entitled by wealth and privilege!" Encouraged by cheers and laughter, I leapt up on a bench and orated with a fervor worthy of Patrick Henry. "No! I tell you, popular is not enough! They must be royalty."

A roar went up from the crowd. I grabbed a painfully green ballot and raised it in my fist.

"For we hold these truths to be self-evident! That there is no greater embodiment of the American Way than the choosing of a leader based on their physical beauty and mediocre intelligence."

Cheers and whistles filled the courtyard. The Spanish Club shouted "¡Olé! Viva mediocridad!" from the breezeway. A Biff-like voice called out "Freak," and then, over it all, the stentorian shout of the assistant principal.

"Margaret Quinn! In my office, right now!"

And that was how I ended up in detention for inciting a riot. I hoped that Syracuse wouldn't revoke my acceptance without giving me a chance to explain.

* * *

I didn't mind spending lunch in detention, but I wish Halloran had seen fit to extend it through P.E. I would much rather have been studying chemistry than enduring the last day of swimming.

But there I was, dragging on my swimsuit and stuffing my clothes into my locker. Jessica Prime passed behind me. "You are such a freak, Quinn."

"Thank you."

"It's not a compliment, dumb ass."

Jess Minor followed, adding "Yeah, freak" as she walked by. The Jessicas seemed to have buried the hatchet. The upshot was, as Prime turned this way and that in front of the mirror, Minor was there to lavish attention on her, and the wannabes were once again pushed to the fringes of the queen's court.

Busy squeezing my fifty-pound backpack into the undersized locker, I rolled my eyes. I didn't understand this constant need for reassurance. Jessica Prime had a beauty pageant figure. Her cleavage was suspiciously full, but she was not, in any way, shape, or form, fat.

Coach Milner called time and we rushed out to the pool, all except Prime, who must have broken a nail or something. I finished the preswim shower, then realized I'd forgotten my goggles.

"Hurry up," snapped the coach. "And tell Prentice to get a move on, too."

I dashed to the locker room as fast as was prudent on the wet tile. My goggles lay on a bench, but I saw no sign of Jessica. Then I heard someone retching in one of the stalls. I thought about calling out or going for help, but before I could do either, the toilet flushed, and Jessica Prime came out.

She was startled to see me, but almost instantly had her sneer in place. "What are you looking at, freak?"

The queen didn't look any more interested in sympathy than I was, so I pretended I hadn't heard anything. "Nothing. I just came for my goggles."

With a dismissive snort she brushed past me, and my nose twitched at an all too familiar smell. Sudden fear cramped my stomach as my eyes followed her perfect, blond form. She passed the mirror, but my gaze hung there as a black shadow slipped across the surface of the glass, like oily smoke.

13

I had called Justin as soon as school was out and asked him to meet me at Froth and Java, the coffee bar by the university. He listened to me blather about Jessica Prime and the shadow, and calmly tried to restore my logic processes. "Back up a minute. Is this the first time you've seen the shadow around her? Did you smell the odor?"

I wrapped my hands around a tall mug of tea with extra sugar and nodded. "The air was thick with it in the stall where she'd been."

His fingers drummed on his own cup of coffee. "Have you ever gotten the sense that she was . . ." Trailing off, he looked embarrassed to complete the sentence. I wasn't.

"Evil? Most every day since I met her."

"Does she have a reason to hurt Karen?"

"Evil doesn't need a reason. She didn't need a reason to show my picture to the whole world, either." Okay, it was just her friends. But what was a little exaggeration when there was a point to be made.

Justin pulled his notebook closer and read what he had written. "But what about this other girl? The one in the play. I thought they were friends."

I was disgruntled at this flaw in my theory. "Jess Minor is her friend, too, but she's been telling everyone Jess's designer clothes are cheap knockoffs."

"True." The pen tapped. "It's also possible she's not doing anything intentionally. Poltergeists are said to attach themselves to adolescents and cause mischief around them."

"Putting someone in the hospital is more than mischief."

"Don't split hairs. I'm talking about the unintentional part. And . . ." He paused delicately. "You can't have missed the signs that your nemesis may be in trouble herself."

My expression solidified into a mask of I don't give a damn. "Yeah, I noticed."

He shrugged. "I'm just saying."

"So you said it. Move along."

Justin gave me a studying look, a real frog under the microscope stare, but with disapproval. I sipped my tea and looked around the room, anywhere but at him.

Froth and Java was furnished with cast-off chairs and comfy couches, usually packed with college students who came to study or just hang out. I pretended I was enormously interested in the group to our left—and absolutely refused to show any sympathy for Jessica Prime, no matter how long Justin stared at me.

Finally he sighed in defeat. "Did you ask your chemistry teacher about the test on your jeans?"

"He gave them to someone named Dr. Smyth at the university. She'll get to it when she can."

"What about the suicide you mentioned?"

I sighed, quoting the article I'd found. "A disenfranchised student, driven to a desperate act because he felt outcast. Hanged himself in the Band Hall."

"Tragic." The true sorrow in his voice made me finally look at him again. We exchanged a glance, feeling for that poor bastard, and all the others who couldn't see any other escape from their pain.

"Yeah." I dropped my gaze and shrugged. "I guess that's why I went a little bit nuts at lunch."

Justin tilted his head curiously. "What happened at lunch?"

"I led an insurrection." After that, I had to tell him the whole story. By the time I finished, he was holding his sides laughing as people at neighboring tables stared. I was laughing pretty hard, too, and God, it felt really good.

"That's great. The First Mediocrity Rebellion." He tried to catch his breath. "I'm sorry you got detention."

I shrugged. "It'll be forgotten by Monday. *Viva la revolución.*"

"Will you get in trouble with your parents?"

"Oh, Dad will laugh. Mom will be furious. Kinda the status quo around my house." I smiled sheepishly, and he grinned back. My cheeks grew warm for no good reason, except that he was handsome and smart and I'd never had a college guy smile at me that way before. Let's face it. Stanley Dozer was the best date prospect I've had . . . maybe ever.

"So what should I do now?" I asked. The question covered a lot of ground.

Justin closed his notebook. "To be on the safe side, don't make Jessica Prime angry. We can keep checking out the ghost angle, but—"

"I don't think it's a ghost."

He shook his head. "Neither do I. I'll do some research into other kinds of spirits. Luckily I have some resources."

I wished I had something else to say to keep him there. Right then, we could be any two students, studying something as normal as sociology or statistics. He handled this strangeness so academically, so reasonably, that it made me feel as if this wasn't all so strange and things were going to be just fine. "Justin?"

"Yeah?" He paused in collecting his stuff.

"Do you think this thing is like a vampire? Not with the blood sucking, but the part where it can't come into your house unless you invite it."

He gave the question his full consideration. "The boundaries of property figure strongly in a lot of traditions. Thresholds and holy ground and running water all mark territorial borders. It may not even be able to leave the school."

"I think it can." I squirmed as he gave me that patient,

no-arguments look, waiting for me to explain. "You know that residue I found on the diving board? The supernatural snail trail? It was all over my window this morning."

Justin sat back in surprise. "On your window?"

"Yeah."

He seemed to be thinking very hard, weighing options one against the other, discarding them as quickly as they came to him. "I think you should stay with your grandmother tonight."

"And leave my parents there if it comes back? Or worse, draw it over to Gran's house? No way."

"Yes, but . . ."

Hands flat on the table, I leaned forward. "See, this is why I didn't want to tell you. I knew you'd flip out."

"I'm not flipping out. I'm just worried for you."

"What you said about boundaries *feels* right. The spooge was all on the outside of the glass. I think it might be able to visit, but it can't enter."

"Maggie." Justin covered my hands with his. "You are a clairvoyant. A seer, to use your granny's word." I tried to pull my hands away, but he held fast. "I know you want to deny it, but hear me out. We don't know what this thing is, but I'll bet anything it wouldn't have to physically reach you to do harm."

I yanked my hands hard from his grasp. "Look. If I admit that I have this"—I gritted my teeth and finally said it aloud—"*Sight*. I can't just walk away because things aren't all fluffy bunnies and unicorns. Now that I See, I cannot just *do nothing*. It doesn't work that way."

Justin clenched his fists for a moment, then deliberately

relaxed. "All right." He took a deep breath. "You're right. But at least let's set up some kind of protection."

"You mean like horseshoes and holy water?"

"Something like that."

"Okay." I hid my relief. My brave words would go a lot farther if I had an Early Phantom Warning System. "Come over at six. I'll work you in between getting yelled at by my parents and going to the Big Spring Musical. It'll be loads of fun."

✳ ✳ ✳

I had seriously underestimated my mother. Not her anger at my getting detention, but her verbosity on the subject. We had gotten through "What were you thinking?" and "Better sense than that," and moved on to "Follow you for the rest of your life." She was just bringing Dad into it with "She's *your* daughter" when the doorbell rang.

Saved by the . . . well, you know. I jumped off the sofa like I had springs on my butt. "I'll get it!"

"Sit!" barked Mom.

I sat. Dad went to answer the door, but he raised a fist in solidarity as he passed behind Mom. She snapped without turning around, "I saw that, Michael Quinn!"

Boy, for someone who disavowed belief in the supernatural, Mom could be darned spooky.

With the interruption, she jumped to the closer. "I am seriously disappointed in you, young lady."

"Yes, ma'am."

"It is ridiculous for you to be making waves this late in the school year. You graduate in a month."

"I know."

"So if you could save mocking the establishment for a

time when your class standing will not be affected, I would deeply appreciate that."

"Yes, ma'am."

My complacency took the wind out of her sails. She floundered for a moment, then said in a calm voice, "All right, then. You're only grounded for the weekend."

"Grounded! You can't!" How was I supposed to fight the forces of evil if I was grounded?

"I can. You live under this roof, and you don't turn eighteen for two months—"

"Fifty-two days, Mom!"

"And you're still in school."

Dad cleared his throat in the hallway. "Maggie, Justin is here."

I saw him behind Dad, staring at the ceiling and pretending he was deaf. Mom looked questioningly at me.

"We're working on a project together. For school." I figured I wasn't really lying—keeping the campus safe from ghostly things counted.

"On a Friday night?"

"Mom!" I stretched the word to three syllables and jerked my head to where Justin lurked in Dad's shadow. She looked the young man up and down—nice frame, broad shoulders, trustworthy face.

"Oh." It would have been funny under other circumstances. She wanted to be the strict disciplinarian, but she was clearly pleased—and surprised—that I had handsome company on a Friday night. Finally, she gave in. "As long as you don't go anywhere."

I jumped up. "We'll be up in my study." She looked as if

she might protest, but I didn't give her a chance, gesturing Justin into the room and introducing him to Mom.

"Good evening, Mrs. Quinn." He extended his hand and she put hers out automatically, looking pleased at the formality. "You have a lovely home."

She smiled, finally relaxing. His air of good-natured steadiness had that effect on people. "Thank you, Justin. Maggie, you have enough sodas?"

"We're good, Mom. Thanks." I motioned for my guest to follow me up the stairs.

"Your mom seems nice," said Justin as we reached the landing and my study area.

"She is. A little tightly wound sometimes, but Dad balances her out." That summed them up pretty well, actually. Mom was conventional and rational. Dad was more like Gran—intuitive and spiritual. And there I was, smack in the middle.

Justin carried a heavy backpack with him; he set it on the hand-me-down loveseat as he looked around the loft. "This is twice the size of my dorm room."

"Yeah. I've got a pretty good thing going." I casually dropped last night's Coke cans in the trash. The desk had reverted to its wilderness state pretty quickly, but the rest still looked vaguely civilized.

"Which window was it?" he asked, getting down to business.

I led him to the bedroom half of the room and pulled back the curtain. There was enough daylight to see the dark, greasy film on the center of the three windows that covered the east wall. My skin prickled as he opened the window and ran his finger through the soot. Rubbing forefinger and thumb together, he gave a tentative sniff.

"It doesn't smell much when it's in the open," I said.

"No. But there's a whiff of something." He made a face. "It smells like death."

"Okay. I definitely don't want to think about death on my bedroom window."

"You want me to wash it off?"

"You do windows?"

My mom kept cleaning supplies under the sink in my bathroom, a blatant hint that I usually ignored. Justin and I discovered that soap and water only smeared the soot around, and even Pine-Sol didn't cut it. I ran downstairs and got some vinegar (and some strange looks from the parents) but that didn't improve matters, either. The glass was now a mass of black smears and streaks. Adding water was making the smell stronger, too, and the stink of pine-scented rotting garbage turned my stomach.

"Just close the window," I said. "We're only making it worse."

"Hold on." Justin hung out of the casement, trying to talk while holding his breath. Not an easy thing to do. "I want to try one more thing. Bring my backpack and some fresh water."

His satchel weighed almost as much as mine did. I brought it over, then dumped the old water and refilled the bucket in the tub.

When I returned with the pail, Justin threw a handful of salt into the water, soaked a clean rag in the solution, then wiped it over the grimy mess on the glass. In a few passes, the pane shone like a Windex commercial.

"Wow." I stared, amazed. It had worked like, well, magic. "We should market that. For all your home exorcism needs."

"Something like that." He swung his legs out; the roof jutted below. By balancing carefully Justin was able to clean the whole window, and give the other two a rinse for good measure.

"What else have you got in here?" I poked through his bag. No wonder it weighed a ton. In addition to the pound of salt, he had a package of nails, a couple of books, and half a forest of leaves and twigs. "What *is* all this stuff?"

He leaned in the window, setting the bucket carefully on the floor. I thought the water would stink to high heaven, but there was no odor at all. "Since we don't know what tradition the . . . whatever . . . comes from, I'm using a scattershot approach. Give me the nails."

I knew that one. Iron kept away fairies and bad luck in Celtic traditions, and like a lot of things had been adapted into Western/Christian superstition: nails equals crucifixion equals Christ's protection.

"What're these twigs?" They were covered with bright red berries. Kind of pretty, really.

"Rowan." His voice drifted in while he scattered the nails on the ledge above the window.

"Where did you get rowan twigs? Witch Depot?"

"There's a New Age herb shop near campus. Would you believe the hardest thing to find was the iron nails? They're all nickel alloy now."

"How inconvenient." I got out of the way as he climbed back in the window. He was filthy from all the window washing. We spread a thin line of salt and placed a rowan twig on every sill, then closed those curtains and went to give the study window a similar treatment.

The whole operation didn't seem nearly as silly as it should have. Maybe it was the way the saltwater had cleared the window and nothing else had. Maybe my idea of what was "normal" had taken a radical left turn.

I had just closed the window when I heard footsteps on the stairs. We exchanged panicked looks, but didn't have time to do anything other than hide the nails (Justin) and the salt (me) before Dad's head appeared at the landing.

"What the blazes are you two doing?" he demanded.

"It's a . . . chemistry experiment," I said, not guiltily at all. "Justin is helping me with a chemistry experiment."

Dad continued up, giving us the Paternal Eye. Justin actually squirmed. I think if we'd actually been doing anything illicit he might have thrown himself at my father's feet, begging his forgiveness.

As it was, when Dad held out his hand, Justin meekly gave over the package of iron nails. With resigned chagrin, I took the canister of salt from behind my back.

"Something I should know about?"

I glanced at my partner in crime. He gave a little shrug of his eyebrow as if to say it was up to me. Gran would believe us. Heck, Gran would help. Mom would wig out on so many levels, but Dad was a wild card.

"Actually," I began, choosing my truths carefully. "It's Justin's experiment with different protection superstitions, and since I'm, you know, sensitive, we're going to see if I feel more, um, protected."

The Paternal Eye pinned me with suspicion. "You know your mother would freak out if she knew about this."

Parents should not say "freak out." But I'd just been thinking that exact thing, so I simply answered, "Yes, sir."

Dad handed the nails back to Justin. "Don't worry about the doors downstairs. My mother did them when we moved in, and checks them every year." See. I was right about Gran, too. I had no trouble picturing her going around with a ladder, sprinkling iron nails over all the door frames.

"I'm taking your mom out to dinner." Dad smoothed his tie. "I convinced her that Justin is trustworthy, but she's not so sure about you."

"We're just about done, Dr. Quinn." Justin started gathering up his things.

"Right. Good to see you, Justin. We'll be home in a couple of hours, Mags."

"Don't hurry on my account."

Just as he disappeared, my phone rang. Justin gestured for me to go ahead and answer. As soon as I flipped it open, I heard Lisa's unhappy voice. "Are you coming to this thing or not?"

"The play?" I reordered my thoughts. I had not forgotten about it; I just hadn't figured out how I was going to get there, being as I was grounded and all.

"Yes, the play. I thought you were coming. I bought you a ticket. I'm out sixteen bucks here."

"I got kind of held up." Justin looked at me curiously. I made a face, not sure what it was supposed to convey beyond a general helplessness.

"Well, the damned thing is about to start. If you're not coming, then I'm not about to endure a lot of singing about chicks and ducks. Not to mention the drama triplets trying to steal Suzie Miller's limelight."

"The Jessicas are there?"

"And their Jock counterparts. The full unholy bunch. The Voiceless One is wearing sackcloth and ashes and the others are all telling her how selfless she is to be here to support the rest of the cast. I may hurl."

"Hang on, Lisa." I put the phone against my shirt while I asked Justin, "Can you drive me to the school?"

"Uh . . . I thought you were, um . . . you know."

"Yes. But I have a bad feeling."

My unease must have been obvious. I couldn't put into words the tight knot in my gut and my certainty that something was going to happen. I was more sure than ever that this was tied to Jessica Prime, maybe all the Jessicas together. If I sat in my room with this dread clawing around my insides, if I could do something and didn't, then all my fears about Nana and Pop, about Karen's accident would be real.

Justin hesitated a moment more, then nodded. "All right."

I told Lisa, "Leave the ticket for me in the front. If they won't let me in after the show starts, I'll see you at intermission."

"You'd better," she answered. "Do *not* make me suffer this alone, Magdalena Quinn."

"I'm on my way."

I grabbed some clean clothes from the closet and went

into the bathroom to change. I came out brushing my hair, thrust my feet into a pair of ballet flats, and searched for a purse.

When I found it, Justin gave me a handful of stuff. There were a few sprigs of the rowan, a couple of nails, and a Ziploc baggie full of salt. "This won't help against your mother," he warned me, "so I hope you know what you're doing."

I tucked them in my handbag, smoothed my skirt, and nodded. "It'll be all right," I said, with a certainty I didn't quite feel.

14

Murphy's Law for Ghostbusting must go like this: If you risk parental wrath by breaking your grounding and several speed limits to get to somewhere you are certain will be a hotbed of supernatural activity, then suffer through two hours of songs about ducks, not to mention a choreographed hoedown, assuredly *nothing will happen*.

"I can't believe it." I stood on the school's front steps where the "after-theatre" crowd milled peacefully, laughing and congratulating the cast.

"I know. I thought it would suck even worse." Lisa stood beside me, deeply inhaling the late April air, cooler now that the sun had gone down. "Though I think some of the laughs were unintentional. Like when Joe Cowboy dropped his partner. Or Stanley Dozer, looking like a seven-foot-tall mutant deer in the headlights when that scenery fell over." She grinned at the memory.

"No falling chandelier," I mused. "No plummeting sandbags. Nothing burst into flames."

"Yeah. I'm disappointed, too." We paused to watch Thespica swan over to Suzie Miller and graciously give her whispered congratulations. Suzie surprised us by throwing her arms around Thespica in an ingenuous hug. The Prima Donna's expression of horror and outrage sent Lisa and I into whoops of laughter.

"Hey."

I turned at the familiar monosyllable, still grinning at the Drama Queen's expense. "Hey, Brian."

Brian returned my instinctive smile with a broad one of his own. "Wow!" He put his hand over his heart, reeling back. "She actually smiles. I never thought I'd see it."

"Stranger things have happened lately." I could feel Lisa beside me, practically vibrating with displeasure. Had I always noticed those things, and never thought about it before? "Brian, this is my friend Lisa. Lisa, this is . . ."

"I know who he is."

Her tone could cut glass. "Geez, Lisa," I murmured.

Brian pretended not to notice. Maybe that was his conditioned response to unpleasantness. It explained why he did nothing when his friends acted like assholes, but then apologized for them later. Brian did not Make Waves.

"Good luck with the valedictorian thing," he told Lisa sincerely. "I saw you're the front-runner."

"By a hundredth of a point. Thanks for reminding me."

She turned to me, arms crossed tightly. "I'm going to talk to Emily. Come see me if you still need a ride."

She stalked off before I could say anything, which was probably just as well. Lisa took a certain pride in being a bitch and wouldn't appreciate me calling her on it.

"You look different tonight." Brian studied me in an exaggerated way. "I know what it is! No camera."

"It wouldn't fit in here." I patted my vintage beaded purse, hanging from its thin satin strap.

He shoved his hands in the pockets of his khakis. He looked nice, too. A lot of the kids were in jeans, but some had at least pretended it was a real theatrical experience, falling scenery aside.

"Listen. I was wondering if you might like to go out some time."

Maybe I'm not psychic after all, because I totally did not see that coming. "What, you mean on a date?"

He'd been looking at the tops of his shoes, but now he peered up at me with a wry smile that made his eyes seem incredibly blue. No, it didn't make sense.

"Yeah. On a date."

God, I was speechless. A Jock—a HenchBiff, no less— had just asked me out. I was stunned, outraged, appalled, and, on some level, illogically delighted because, well, I mentioned the hotness, right?

"That's . . . wow . . . um."

He ducked his head to search my face, his smile adorably uncertain. "Is that a yes or a no?"

"That's an 'I can't believe my ears.'"

A shrill voice shattered the Kodak moment. There was nothing wrong with Jess Minor's vocal cords, even if she was no match for her leader's cheer-honed stridency. "Brian! What's taking so long?"

Translation: What are you doing talking to that lower life form?

I folded my arms, my posture going defensive before I could check the movement.

"I'll be over in a minute, Jess." Brian was a lot nicer than I would have been, were I called to heel that way.

"Go on," I said. "You don't want to rock the boat."

"*Bri-an.*" Minor ramped up to a major fit of pique. "We're all about to leave. We're going to the Underground. Right *now.*"

"Ride with Jeff. I'll meet you guys there." He turned back to me with a sheepish smile. "I don't suppose you want to go to the Underground."

"I'd rather poke a sharp stick in my eye." The Underground was an eighteen-and-over club that catered mostly to the college crowd. I'd love to go, someday, but not with the Maleficent Six.

"What about next week? Come to my baseball game, and we'll go somewhere after."

"Sports give me hives."

"Then don't come to the game, and we'll go somewhere after."

I was playing with my cross and made myself stop, tucking my hair behind my ear instead, trading one fidget for another. "Look, Brian . . ."

"What are you doing, Kirkpatrick?" Brandon stood at the bottom of the steps, but still managed to loom somehow. "We're ready to go."

"I told Jess to go on ahead."

The alpha dog raked his eyes over me, then addressed his pack mate. "Jess will be real disappointed if you don't come with us."

"She'll live."

"Yeah, but I'll have to listen to her whine. So stop wasting time and let's go."

I looked Brian in the eye. "Go on with your friends. I'll see you around." I walked away, and he didn't stop me. I didn't really expect him to.

"Geez, Kirkpatrick." Biff didn't bother to lower his voice as Brian went down the steps to join him. "What are you doing? Some kind of science experiment?"

When I reached Lisa she glanced at me without sympathy. But she didn't say "I told you so," either. I guess that's why she's my friend. She just wrapped an arm around my shoulders. "Ready to go, kiddo?"

"Yeah." I figured my mom would have killed me by Monday anyway.

We said good-bye to Emily, congratulations to Suzie, and headed for the parking lot.

"What's with Dozer stalking Suzie Miller?" I asked Lisa. With black-clad Stanley hovering around after the show, I recognized her as the girl I'd seen him with backstage.

"Even dweebs can have crushes," she said.

I didn't see a need to mention how quickly his affections had shifted after he'd asked me to the prom. "I wonder if she'll give him the time of day now that she's a superstar."

Lisa snorted. "Suzie is a real-life ingenue. If she liked him before, she won't cut him off. And I say 'if' because . . . well, Stanley Dozer."

The butt numbing boredom of the play and the silliness

of Thespica's drama afterward had lulled me into complacency, but my Spidey Sense clawed the chalkboard of my nerves the moment we reached Lisa's compact Honda. Directly across from it, sharing the same island of halogen, were the Jocks and Jessicas. Biff opened the door of his Blazer for Jessica Prime, but rather than climb in she stopped to watch me with eyes full of venom.

Plenty of Evil there, but that wasn't what had fired the warning shot. Next to the Blazer was Jeff Espinoza's vintage Mustang, parked on the edge of the lamplight, not quite pristine, but lavishly loved.

There was a shadow within the shadow of the car. It squatted, waiting with an inanimate patience until I looked at it, and then it stirred, like smoke in darkness.

"Ow!" Lisa yelped. I'd grabbed her arm hard enough to bruise. "What's your problem?"

Brandon and all three Jessicas were climbing into his SUV. Jeff and Brian stood by the Mustang, discussing whether to stop and get something to eat before going to the club. I didn't realize I had changed direction until I heard my own voice.

"Brian!"

His head came up. Beneath the car, the darkness curled in on itself as if gathering to strike. My stride faltered as I felt its attention on me. Just like in my dream, I knew it *saw* me, even though it had no eyes. I couldn't make myself go any nearer, and stopped in the middle of the driveway.

Brian started toward me, his expression curious, but pleased. "What's up?"

"Don't . . ." My throat closed on the warning, choked by

self-preservation. I couldn't explain my knowledge, my Sight. If I warned him, everyone would know I was a freak.

Lisa called my name from beside her own car. "Maggie! What is *wrong* with you?"

"Don't get in the car," I whispered, reaching for his arm as if I could hold him back from danger.

"What?" He leaned closer. "I didn't hear you."

"Don't ride in the Mustang. Ride with Brandon."

Nails raked my wrist as someone snatched my hand from Brian's sleeve. I swallowed my heart when I realized it was only Jess Minor. Her face twisted with jealous fury, but it was nothing compared to what agglomerated in the dark.

"Don't you ever give up?" Her voice was reedy and thin, bamboo under the fingernails, and her complexion was flushed and blotchy in the streetlamp. "On what planet would one of *us* want anything to do with someone like *you*?"

Brian had stared at me with blank confusion. Now his gaze turned to Jess as if she were a space creature. Before he could say anything, though, Lisa was in Minor's face.

"Don't talk to her like that."

"Back off, egghead. Take your tramp friend and get out of here."

"Tramp!" I squawked in outrage.

Lisa pushed Jess's pointing finger aside. "Put that away before I break it, Michaels."

"Calm down, Jess—" Brian went unheeded as Brandon came up, Jeff lumbering behind.

"Hey! A catfight!"

"It's not a fight." I grabbed Lisa's arm and dragged her

away. I was shaking too much for the two of us to be any match for the six of them—five, if Brian abstained. "We've got better places to be."

"Good," Minor shouted after us. "Go poach someone else's boyfriends."

"Not hardly," Lisa threw over her shoulder. "We're going to Wal-Mart to see if we can find that outfit."

I should have just let Lisa handle her. They were both bigger than me. But when Minor launched herself at my friend's back, I acted without thinking, stepping between them and taking her weight full on. I stumbled backward, the hellcat's fists tearing at my hair, and banged hard into the fender of Lisa's Honda. Jess crashed into me and smacked my head against the trunk.

I swear to God, the thing under the Mustang laughed.

Brandon and Jeff hooted as Jessica Prime cheered and Thespica clapped and honked. With her friends egging her on, Minor put a knee in my gut and tried to twist my head off. She might not be the alpha bitch, but she was scrappy and mean the way the bottom of the pack had to be.

But I'm not the scion of Irish pub brawlers for nothing. I kicked her standing leg out from under her and followed her down, pinning her to the asphalt and dodging sideways when her French-tipped nails went for my face. She caught me in the neck and I felt the sting of drawn blood.

The shadow roiled, like a pot on the boil. The smell of rotting eggs and putrid meat grew stronger.

Off-balance, I couldn't stop her from flipping me like a tortoise, slamming me down with more force than I'd ever imagined a piece of fluff like her could manage. Her nails flashed at my face again. I flung up my arm to shield my eyes; when she scratched me again, the acrid stink surged into my throat, stealing my breath.

Or maybe that was her hands on my throat. "Meddling tramp!" She rattled my head against the pavement. "Stay out of my business."

I made a fist and punched. I felt the shock all the way to my shoulder. Jess reeled slightly, breaking her grip, then someone was pulling her away, lifting her bodily. Lisa's worried face filled my vision. I couldn't speak past the gagging, but I grabbed her hand, held her so she wouldn't go after Minor in retaliation. I could feel the shadow's hungry miasma of excitement, and knew the fight had to stop.

"Witch!" Minor shrieked at me as Brian held her, both arms wrapped around her waist. "You ought to be burned at the stake!"

"Jesus, Jess!" He struggled to restrain her, despite his size and strength. Even the Jessicas looked shocked, and Brandon and Jeff had stopped laughing.

"Freak of nature!" She screeched. The phantom stench was rolling off of her. Why couldn't they smell it?

I tried to crawl away, vomit rising in my throat. My hand touched the torn strap of my purse and, still gagging, tears running down my face, I pulled it to me and slid my hand inside.

"Calm down, Jess," I heard Prime say. "Jesus, what is wrong with you?"

"She's gone nuts. I told you not to play hard to get, Brian."

"Shut up, Jeff, and help me."

My lungs were on fire. I thought about what Professor Blackthorne had said about sulfur dioxide, about volcanoes, about brimstone. I was burning up, from the alveoli out.

"Just let her go. What's one less dweeb in the world?"

"Shut up, Brandon." Lisa crouched over me protectively, snarling up at Biff.

"Make me, Lisa."

I'd gotten my hand in the baggie of salt. On a whim, a hunch, a prayer, I gathered a handful and flung it out, covering the parking lot under Jess and Brian's feet with a smattering of white crystals.

The effect was immediate. Jess went limp in Brian's grasp and the shadow recoiled into the tailpipe of the Mustang.

And I took a deep, unfettered breath.

"Here." Brian said, as he shoved the flaccid Jess into Brandon's arms. "Take her."

I heard him crouch beside me, and his hand shook as it settled on my shoulder. "Get away from her," said Lisa, slapping him away.

"I'm just trying to help."

"Take your friends and get the hell out of here." Her slim arms wrapped around me, and helped me sit up.

I wiped my streaming eyes and looked at Brian, seeing the forces tearing at him. In that moment, I don't think he had any loyalty to the pack, but he didn't want to make things worse by breaking with them now. For the first time, he was right not to rock the boat. "Go." I sounded as hoarse as Thespica. "But not in the Mustang."

Still uncertain, he followed Brandon and helped lift Jess into the backseat of the truck, then climbed in himself. Thespica jumped in after, but Jessica Prime paused to cast a glance back at me, unreadable as an animal.

With the assistance of the fender of the Honda, I managed to stand up. Sort of. Lisa was helping me into the car when I heard Jeff arguing with Brian about riding in the Blazer.

"No way am I leaving the 'stang in the parking lot. What if those crazy bitches come back and do something to it."

"In case you haven't noticed, Jeff, we seem to have a lock on crazy bitches tonight."

"Screw it. I'm taking my car."

I tried to rise from my seat to stop him. But I didn't know how. Maybe I could puke on him. That seemed to be all I was good for just then. Lisa forced me to sit back down. "Leave them."

"But . . ."

"It's not your problem."

"You don't understand!"

"There is nothing you can do! I don't know what's got into you, but . . ."

The Mustang peeled out of the parking lot, ending the argument.

15

I expected it to be like that fifties song: The cryin' tires, the bustin' glass. But . . . Nothing. The Blazer pulled around so that Brandon could flip us off, then followed the sports car onto the street. The basso rumble of the truck's engine quickly caught up with the gravel-throated Mustang, and both faded quickly into the distance.

Lisa grabbed an empty soda can from her floorboard and flung it after the taillights. It bounced on the asphalt with an anticlimactic "tink."

"I hate those sons of bitches. Every last one of them. I hope they burn in a fiery conflagration that is only a prelude to the inferno of their everlasting exile in Hell."

Boy, Lisa could curse. I wished I could appreciate it, instead of flinching at shadows. "Please don't. You don't know what might hear you."

She covered her face with her hands, and when they dropped, she was in control again. We didn't have time to waste. I could see curious students, parents, and teachers approaching quickly. If Halloran was among them, he'd suspend me in a heartbeat, even if I'd only been fighting to defend myself.

"I'm not even supposed to be out of the house." The words scraped my raw throat. "Can we get out of here?"

"You bet." She jumped in the car. Just as we'd backed out of the space, Emily from English reached us and Lisa rolled down the window to answer her concerned question. "Spread the word that Jess Michaels went ape-shit when I made a crack about her wearing the softer side of Sears. They took off, and everything's cool now."

Emily leaned in the window. "Geez, Maggie. Are you all right? Your poor throat. And your blouse!"

I hadn't realized my shirt was torn. "Darn it! First my jeans, now this."

"She's fine, except for sounding like a frog." Lisa glanced in the rearview mirror at the gathering crowd, then caught Emily's gaze. "Just cover for us, okay?"

"Sure."

We zipped away, driving in silence until the school was out of sight. Then Lisa asked, "You want to tell me what's going on with you, Mags?"

"No," I croaked. "You wouldn't believe me."

"I don't know what to believe right now. What the hell

was that with Brian? When did you become so chummy? And the thing with the car? What do you think is going to happen?"

"I don't know why Brian suddenly finds me irresistible. I haven't exactly encouraged him. And I don't know how I know something's wrong with the car. Sometimes I just know things." I didn't mention the shadow creature. I didn't even know what to call it; how could I possibly explain?

She drove in silence for a moment. "What do you mean, you know things. Like the future?"

"No. Only the present. But sometimes that gives me clues that something might happen. Like if I know a teacher is planning a pop quiz, it's not the same thing as foreseeing a test. She could still change her mind."

We were cruising the main strip, the most direct way to my house. "Why didn't you ever tell me?"

"It hasn't happened in awhile."

"But now?"

I leaned my head against the window. I had a lump coming up, and it hurt to rest back against the seat. "Something is going on, but I don't know what."

She tightened her jaw, but didn't say anything else. My throat hurt, so I didn't encourage more conversation. Not until I put up my hand, and said, "Stop!"

"What?" Her foot tapped the brake. The speed limit wasn't very high along this curving stretch of Beltline, but everybody sped down it, in a hurry to get where they were going. "Another premonition?"

"No. There are flashing lights ahead. Oh God."

We slowed, along with the rest of the traffic, which was

being directed to the other side of the street by a uniformed cop. I glimpsed bright red, and my heart squeezed in my chest. Jeff's pristine Mustang was a misshapen heap of torn metal, wrapped like a fortune cookie around the front end of an SUV the size of a tank.

I rolled down my window, and I could hear the police officer talking to Jeff through the driver's door, telling him to stay still until the ambulance arrived. He was alive, at least for now. But the passenger side had taken the impact. Anyone riding with him would never have survived.

✳ ✳ ✳

The front porch was dark when Lisa dropped me off, which usually meant the parents had retreated into their room for the evening. I slid my key into the lock and turned it as quietly as I could. Slipping in the door, I closed it softly, then took off my shoes and crept to the stairs.

I'd left a note on my bed when I left. It's a strange dysfunction: Disobeying the parents was one thing, but it didn't seem right to worry them out of their minds. I wasn't surprised to turn my note over and read: "You'd better have a very good explanation for this. There will be consequences. —Dad."

Well, I expected that. I'm a novice rule breaker, but I suppose it was the price of being a crusader for justice.

I set my ruined bag on the dresser and pulled out my phone. I'd turned the sound off during the play, and now I saw that I had one text message from Justin (Call when you get home) and five missed calls from Gran (no message). Nice to know *her* Spidey Sense was operational. I went to the computer and left her an "I'm all right" e-mail.

Next, I phoned Justin, as ordered. I was quickly running out of steam, but I didn't want him to worry, either. He picked up the phone on the third ring, and for a moment all I could hear was music and laughter. "Hello?"

"Maggie! Are you all right?"

"Yeah. Are you at a bar?" Not that it would be my business if he was, of course.

"Hang on, let me go outside." More noise, then the slam of a door and silence. "My roommate. This is probably his last semester, so he's having a last hurrah."

"He's graduating?"

"He's flunking out."

"Boy, you attract the hard-luck cases." I pressed gingerly at the bump on the back of my head.

"So what happened? Anything?"

I was so tired, and the bed stretched out in front of me like a big, unmade ocean of temptation. "Yes. I'll tell you about it tomorrow."

"Why not now?"

"I'm too sleepy now."

"I have to study for finals tomorrow, or I'll be joining my roommate working at McWendy's."

Somehow I doubted that. Justin had an unshakable aura of studious industry. If he'd lived in the Middle Ages, he would live in an abbey and do nothing but transcribe ancient texts and preserve knowledge for the future.

"Okay. Short version? When I tried to stop the Jocks from driving their ghost-infected car, Jess Minor kicked my ass, and then Jeff wrapped the cursed Mustang around the front of a Hummer."

"Jessica *Minor* beat you up?" I had given him a rundown of the major players in this drama. Suffice to say, my opinion of Minor was rather dismissive, hence his stinging incredulity.

"Yeah, thanks for reminding me of my humiliation. It wasn't even the alpha bitch, just the wannabe."

"And what's this with the car? Is the guy all right?"

I shuddered at the memory of Jeff's blood-covered, pain-contorted face—the only part I could see, thank God. "They were taking him to the hospital. He was pretty messed up. No one else was hurt."

As Lisa had driven by—she had refused to stop—I'd seen the others clustered around the Blazer, and Jess Minor had been on her feet and clinging to Brian, so I guessed she'd had little lasting affect from her brush with the shadow.

"Look, if you want more than that, it's gotta wait for tomorrow. I'm gorked out." My sore head rested on my nice fluffy pillow, and it was getting hard to keep my eyes open.

"Okay." He paused, and I pictured his serious face pinched with worry. "But you're all right? You sound awful."

"I'm just tired."

"Did you escape detection?"

"Of course not." I yawned, and didn't bother to cover my mouth. "I can deal with my dad. He can ground me till kingdom come once this thing is . . . whatever."

"Vanquished?"

I rolled on my side and curled into a ball. "Or done."

"Done what?"

"With whatever it's trying to do." My eyelids had lead sinkers on them. Even the phone seemed to weigh a ton.

"How do you know it's trying to do something?"

"I dunno. I just do."

A pause. Or maybe I dozed off for a moment. Then I heard, "Hang up and go to sleep, Maggie."

"Okay." My thumb found the right button, even with my eyes closed. "'Night, Justin. Thanks for helping me tonight."

"You're welcome."

Almost immediately, I dreamed.

Sand and wind scoured the ground, and the sun blistered the sky. Before my squinting eyes, dunes stretched to the horizon, a molten sea of white gold.

I turned in a slow circle, getting my bearings. I stood on a rocky outcropping that jutted between the desert sands and a large oasis where I saw palm trees and some kind of cultivated garden, as well as small adobe huts and large tents. As I watched, a young girl shepherded a herd of goats toward a well, where a woman was drawing water. Dream or not, I was suddenly parched, the hot, dry air torturous on my raw throat.

Stumbling down the slanted rock, I hurried toward the oasis. The sand slid into my shoes, scorching my feet, and the sun, which hadn't bothered me at first, drove me like a living force. By the time I reached the blessed shade, I could barely put one foot in front of the other.

I could smell the water, like a perfume. The woman at the well looked at me with no surprise, as if modern-dressed girls stumbled into their oasis on a daily basis. Up close, I could see the detail of her clothes, from the loose and gauzy texture of her head covering, to the crosshatched weave of her robe. A leather girdle circled her waist; her skin was dark and her eyes kind.

The detail was stunning, from the color of her clothes to the smell of the goats. I didn't know what to call any of these things, but they couldn't be any more real if I had gone back in time. *Dad would be so jealous*.

I unstuck my tongue from the roof of my mouth. "May I have some water?" As politely as I could, I gestured to the full water skin she had drawn, because even in my dream, the only foreign language I knew was bad Spanish.

The woman took a dipper, filled it, and offered it to me with a smile. I drank thirstily, and then gave it back to her, bowing my thanks. I was trying to think of a way to ask where I was supposed to be, when I heard a shout from the edge of the oasis, joined by more voices, raising an alarm.

The woman ran toward the sound and I followed. A group of men clustered together, two of them carrying the torn body of a lanky young man between them. The woman from the well gave a heart-rending cry and threw herself forward, touching his wounds with her hands, as if she couldn't trust her eyes. One of the men tried to comfort her; she shoved him away and fell to her knees, her scream of angry denial becoming a wail of anguish as she tore at her hair with bloody fists.

I was afraid to go closer, terrified to look at the dead man's face. Was I seeing an event from the past, or a metaphorical picture of the present? Would it be Jeff staring up at the bleached sky, dead from wounds inflicted in the car crash?

The grieving woman fell over the body, and saved me from having to look. I listened to the men, not understanding their language, but interpreting the gestures of the guys who had brought the man back to his wife. They'd found him outside of the oasis.

I went the way they'd indicated, covering ground in a quick fold of dreamtime, and found myself in a spot where human feet and animal claws had disturbed the sand in a ten-foot circle, the fetid air thick over the scraps of cloth and hair. The odor of rot had become an indelible association, the way hospitals smell like disinfectant, and locker rooms smell like mildew. If the man had been attacked by carnivores, why the hellish smell? Was the pack more than it seemed?

A wind came up, blowing my hair around my face and obscuring my vision. I turned into it, brushing the strands from my eyes, and in the seamless way that dreams have, it was now full night, and the desert air was cold on my skin. The moon painted the sand silver, except for a circle of flickering blue firelight.

"This again?" I huffed in frustration.

The first time I dreamed, there had only been impressions of fire and smoke and danger. The second time, I'd seen the brazier and the blue flames. Now I had a setting, though it didn't make much sense to my present problem. Another metaphor? Or was I seeing the origins of something I still didn't completely understand?

The same brazier rested in the sand; no stand, just a beaten metal basin about the size of a large dinner plate, with designs of some kind engraved around the rim. The smell of the fire burning in the shallow bronze container brought to mind fireworks and made my throat ache. Underneath it, though, was the same rotten odor.

I gathered detail with some excitement, studying the symbols. Maybe I was getting better at this vision stuff. A rolled-up piece of parchment lay on the raised edge of the brazier, and the fire crawled slowly up the scroll.

With a courage I might not have possessed in real life, I snatched the small cylinder from the flames. It was a new element in the dream, and might be important.

I blew on it like a match, but the fire wouldn't go out. With the same odd lack of fear, I handled the parchment by the safe side, and unrolled it. The letters were ornate and completely foreign to me, but they made a list of some kind. I thought of my first dream, and the roll call of names. A hex maybe? A curse? That would make sense, except for the feeling of sentience that I got from the black shadow.

The blue flames traveled more quickly across the parchment. I wondered if that was the origin of the acrid smell. Wasn't parchment once made out of sheepskin?

The fire singed my skin, and I dropped the list to the sand. The flames, however, stayed dancing on my fingertips. I held my hand before my face, horrified as the flesh began to blacken and blister. The choking, burning odor was coming from my hand.

Terror shook me in its teeth. I tried to scream, but couldn't force any sound past my throat. I could only watch the flames lick down my wrist, as the skin of my hand began to crack and peel from my bones.

What had Justin said? That I was vulnerable in my

dreams. Could I die? Could I go mad? That seemed a very real possibility, as pain and fear chased each other around in my brain, making it impossible to think, filling my head with the shriek of blind, unreasoning panic.

My unblemished left hand went to my neck, grasped the cross that still hung there, even in my dream. Wake up. I ordered myself. Wake up, now. Wake up wake up wake . . .

* * *

"*Up!*" I screamed, propelled out of the dream and straight up in bed.

My chest heaved like I'd run a marathon, and my clothes and hair were clammy with sweat. My left hand still clutched Gran's necklace—*my* necklace—and the tangle of bedsheets hid my right. It didn't hurt, but I'd heard that third-degree burns didn't, because all the nerve endings were dead.

Trembling, I made myself let go of the cross, then reached over to flip aside the sheet. My breath whooshed out when I saw my pale skin, unblemished by anything but a smattering of freckles.

"Maggie?" Mom's worried voice called from below. "Are you all right?"

"Yes," I croaked, but the word didn't carry. I heard her footsteps on the stairs.

I was still wearing my clothes from the play. Even if Dad had told Mom I'd been out, I didn't want to wave the red flag of my disobedience in her face. Scrambling under the covers, I pulled them up to my chin just as she reached the landing. "I'm all right, Mom."

Her sleep-tousled head appeared around the bifold door to the bedroom. "I thought I heard you shout."

I pushed myself up onto my elbows. "I had a nightmare."

"Are you feeling all right? You sound hoarse." Concerned, she came into the room, then hurried to the bed when she saw me. "Oh, Maggie! You're drenched." She laid the back of her hand against my forehead—do all mothers have a thermometer there? "And you're burning up. Are you sure you're not sick?"

"No," I rasped, lying back and tugging up the sheet. "Just a nightmare. A bad one."

"Oh." She sat on the edge of the bed, her thoughts marching visibly across her face. I wondered if she was recalling, like I was, the last time we'd done this, the night her parents died. She must have been, because she seemed to waver in her curiosity, wanting to ask, not wanting to know.

"Was it a . . . What did you used to call them? A gut dream?" She didn't look at me, but at her knotted fingers.

I hesitated, my instinct still to avoid this ground with Mom. "Kind of. Yes."

"Oh." Her fingers unlaced, shifted, and knit again. "Do you want to tell me about it?"

"No." It came out harsher than I intended. I didn't mean to reject her, exactly. My mom fell into the very reasonable, rational part of my life, and I liked it that way. Whenever I needed to think of something logically, it was my mother's voice in my head saying, "Oh, don't be ridiculous."

I tempered that rejection a little. "Nothing I want you to worry about, Mom. Just school stuff."

"Is the stress getting to you, sweetheart?" Her hand brushed my cheek, cool against my flushed skin.

"Not exactly." Mom loved to hear what was going on in my life. It was a shame that her only child was so boring, and sadder still that once my life got interesting, I couldn't tell her about it. Whether she believed me or not, she would, as Dad put it, freak out, and take action to inhibit my girl detective responsibilities.

"There are these girls," I said, choosing my truths carefully. "Cheerleaders. You know the type. Beautiful. Popular. Wearing their air of entitlement like designer perfume."

"Oh yes." That agreement carried a world of understanding.

"Well, they're making me miserable." At least that was honest. "I'm trying to just stay above it all, but that's harder than it should be." Especially with a ghostly shadow forcing my involvement.

"I know." Mom patted my knee. "But you just have to ignore them. Remember those girls are just jealous."

The conviction in that cliché made me laugh. Motherless Nancy Drew might have more freedom in her investigations, but I'd trade a lot of fretting for moments like this. "I love you, Mom."

"I love you, too, Magpie." She leaned over and kissed my forehead, as though I were eight instead of (almost) eighteen. With one last frown, she tucked the covers closer around me. "But maybe you should take it easy the rest of the weekend. You don't want to get sick this close to the prom."

"Oh, Mom," I groaned. She suffered from the delusion that I might yet decide to go to the dance, and kept asking if we should go shopping for a dress, "Just in case."

"Oh, Maggie," she echoed. "I don't want you to have any regrets. It wouldn't kill you to behave like a normal teenager once in a while."

Wouldn't it? Look what happened the first time I ever snuck out of the house.

"I'll think about it."

It took so little to make her happy. She patted my knee as she rose, "That's all I ask. Sleep tight, Magpie."

" 'Night, Mom."

I waited until she'd had time to get to her bedroom, then threw back the covers. My clothes were strangling me. I stripped them off, pulled on my pjs, then went over to the desk. I was not eager to go back to sleep, even though, by the usual rules, I would be done dreaming for the night.

Picking up a pencil, I began to sketch as much as I could remember of the symbols on the brazier. I found that, just like my extra sense, I couldn't *make* it happen, but if I let my mind and hand drift, I could see the engravings and trace them on the page. Soon I was yawning, but I had six symbols I was reasonably sure of. They looked both familiar and strange, kind of a cross between Hebrew letters and the graffiti ciphers I saw spray-painted on buildings.

I dropped my pencil in defeat. Great. I had probably been influenced by the *Prince of Egypt* portion of the dream, and the last time I drove downtown. I hated not knowing what I knew.

At least the nightmare's power had faded with the detective work. I belatedly brushed my teeth, then switched off all but one small lamp in the corner.

I don't know what made me pause at the window. Maybe

I just wanted to see that the line of salt was still there, or comfort myself with those cheery red rowan berries. Brushing back the curtain, my eye immediately went to the moonlit street, and the amalgamation of shadows gathering under the neighbor's big pecan tree.

The inky darkness of the Shadow stood defined against the lesser gloom. It now had a distinct form, man-shaped, but not quite. There was a central mass, like a torso, and limblike outgrowths, and something head-shaped at the top. A breeze stirred the leaves of the pecan, and the Shadow's form shifted like a phantom, but with a core of material solidity.

It stepped out of the shelter of the tree, palpably obscure in the moonlight, a substance that cast no shadow of its own. The wind blew eddies of dirt and grass clippings around its half-formed feet.

How did I know it was trying to do something, Justin had asked me. The parchment, the list of names—maybe it was a curse, or maybe it was a means to an end. But I knew in that moment where this was headed.

Like some kind of nightmare Velveteen Rabbit, the specter was becoming *real*.

16

I woke feeling like I'd gone ten rounds with Mike Tyson instead of a skinny WASP Princess. It didn't help that I had slept on the ancient loveseat, as far away from the front windows as I could get. I hadn't planned to sleep at all, but as the small hours of the night crept larger and nothing happened, unconsciousness won out over fear.

I Frankenstein-walked to the bathroom, shedding clothes as I went. A hot shower eased my muscles but stung the scratches on my neck and arm. The joints in my right hand were stiff and I ached up to the elbow, but when I saw the bruises on my knuckles I realized this wasn't some weird transference from the dream. I'd gotten at least one good punch on Jessica Minor.

That happy thought gave me courage to consider my shadowy friend. The good news was the protections seemed to work at least a little, since the thing was on the street and not at the window. The question was, why was it here at all? Because I'd poked my nose into its business? From the acid words that Jess spewed while under the influence, the Shadow seemed to have a serious mad-on for me.

Which pretty much evaporated any improvement in my mood.

I pulled on jeans and a T-shirt and let my hair do its own thing. I was just thinking I should call Karen and see how she was doing, when my cell phone rang.

"Hi, Karen."

"Wow. Are you psychic or something?"

"Caller ID." I took the phone into the bathroom and reconsidered putting some powder on the bruise on my cheek. "How are you feeling? When do you go home from the hospital?"

"Maybe this afternoon. It depends." Something evasive lay under that, but she continued before I could ask. "Was that Jeff Espinoza's Mustang on the news this morning? They said that the driver was taken to the hospital."

"Yeah."

"Wow." She paused. "Is this anything like my accident?"

I'd given up on the mirror and gone back to the study, finding myself looking at the symbols I'd sketched during the night. I worried my lip, wondering how much to tell her. "Maybe."

"Huh. Well, okay." I stopped her before she could hang up.

"Karen, are you all right? Did you really call just to ask about the accident?"

There was another pause, a long, heavy one. "No. I don't know. Something weird is going on."

I sat down. "What is it?"

She made several attempts to start, as if getting up her courage. "I was trying to get caught up on my homework yesterday, and when I started my calculus the equations just . . . didn't make any sense. It was like trying to read Chinese."

"You've forgotten how to do calculus?"

"I can't make sense of any numbers at all." Her voice caught, a tiny, heartbreaking sound. "They think I may have swelling in a very localized part of the brain."

"Oh, Karen, that's so . . ." *Weird*. ". . . awful. I know how much you love math."

"I do, it's my best subject."

"I'm so sorry. But maybe if the swelling goes down . . . ?" I trailed off hopefully.

"If it does, the doctor hopes the ability will come back." She gave a laugh, half brave and half ironic. "You know, ever since I blew the answer in the State Mathlete Finals, I've had this fear that one day I would just lose it."

"You're not losing it," I reassured her. "It'll come back when the swelling goes down."

"I hope so. I didn't mean to whine about that. I mostly called because of the news. The whole school knows how much Jeff loves that car."

"Yeah." Something about that was important, but my brain needed time to work on it.

"Jessica Prentice was on the news. She looked haggard." Karen sounded only a little pleased with this report on Prime's appearance. "Is she sick?"

"Only in the head."

"Gotta go. Doctor's here."

Our time was up. I wished her good luck and closed the phone slowly, my mind spinning.

Karen loved math. Henchman Jeff loved his Mustang. Thespica loved the limelight. They had to be the first few turns of a pattern. Not enough to see what the completed shape would be, but definitely interlinked.

I went downstairs, still wearing a distracted frown.

"Everything all right, Maggie?" Mom and Dad had a Saturday-morning routine: sofa, bathrobes and slippers, newspaper, coffee, box of doughnuts. I grabbed one of the latter.

"Yeah. Karen's been out of school for a few days, so I was catching her up on the gossip."

Mom held up the local section of the *Avalon Sentinel.* "Is this boy one of your classmates?" Mouth full of doughnut, I nodded, and she tsked. "That section of Beltline is awful. They need more traffic lights."

The doorbell rang. "I'll get it." I snagged another dough-nut on the way to the door.

Brian Kirkpatrick stood on our front stoop, looking like he hadn't slept all night. He skipped right past the pleasantries and demanded, "How did you know about the crash?"

It was dumb luck I didn't choke to death on my doughnut.

"Who is it?" Dad called from the living room.

"Jehovah's Witness!" I yelled back as I stepped out and shut the door behind me. "What are you doing here? How did you find out where I live?"

"There aren't that many Quinns in the phone book. How did you know what was going to happen?"

I shushed him, as if my parents could somehow still eavesdrop. "I didn't. You haven't told anyone what I said, have you?"

"No. The others didn't hear you. Jess just thinks you were coming on to me."

Lovely. "Is she okay?"

"Yeah. And what the hell was *that* all about?"

"I couldn't tell you," I said in perfect honesty. "What about Jeff?"

"Compound open fracture of his leg is the worst of it."

"That's pretty bad."

Brian shook his head, looking grim. "He's lucky. And so am I. If I'd been in the passenger seat, I would have been crushed like a bug on the grill of that Hummer."

I glanced away, knowing it was true and unable to look at him with the mangled sports car superimposed on my memory. "Would you believe I just had a bad feeling about it?"

He stared at me for a long moment, evaluating my sincere expression, and the impossibility of any other explanation. Then he shoved his fingers through his short mop of blond hair. "Okay. I'll buy that."

I slanted a nervous glance up at him. "You won't tell anyone, will you?"

He seemed surprised at the idea. "No."

"Good. Because the last thing I need right now is the head cheerleader screaming, 'I saw Goody Quinn dancing with the devil in the moonlight.'"

A slow, reluctant smile turned up the corners of his mouth. "Yeah. Those girls in *The Crucible*. They were totally Jessicas."

We were laughing over that when Justin pulled up behind my Jeep in the driveway. Naturally. He climbed out of the car, pausing uncertainly when he saw me entertaining a gentleman caller on the front stoop.

I waved him over, trying to sober toward dignity. "Hi! I thought you had to study."

"I do, eventually." He started up the walk. "I tried to call you, but your phone kept sending me to voice mail."

"I must have been talking to Karen."

Justin glanced curiously at Brian. Brian slanted a look at Justin. And then they both looked at me.

Awkward.

"Justin, this is Brian Kirkpatrick, from school. Brian, this is Justin MacCallum, my, um, friend."

Brian offered a handshake instead of his usual "Hey." His forearm flexed handsomely during that hearty clasp, and Justin's knuckles went slightly white. Their expressions, however, were genially inscrutable.

See, this was when psychic mojo would come in handy. But my inner eye gave me no clue. My inner nose, on the other hand, detected the strong odor of testosterone.

The door behind me opened. "Phone for you, Mags. It's—" Dad stopped, looking at the two guys on our front walk. It was probably a sign of the apocalypse. "What is this? Grand Central Station?"

Brian took it as a cue to leave. "I'd better run. See you on Monday, Maggie?"

"Sure," I answered blithely, then remembered that he had asked me on a *date* for Monday. What had I just agreed to? From Brian's ear-to-ear grin, more than I'd intended. Consciously, anyway.

He nodded courteously to my dad, then to Justin, and took off toward the sporty car parked beside mine in the driveway. Dad glanced at me, one brow raised. "School stuff," I said evasively. "Can Justin come in?"

"Sure."

Justin followed us into the house, and I went straight to the phone extension in the living room. "Hello? This is Maggie Quinn."

"Hello, Miss Quinn. This is Dr. Smyth at the university's Chemistry Department. I hope you don't mind. I looked up your father's number in the faculty directory."

"Not at all! Thank you for calling."

"I've finished the gas chromotography on the sample that Silas Blackthorne gave me, and have the results for you."

Silas Blackthorne? Why was he teaching high school chemistry instead of penning lurid gothic novels?

"That's great news, Dr. Smyth. I've been anxious to hear from you."

"I imagine you have. You say you *sat* in something?"

Justin and Dad watched me curiously. "Uh, yeah. It's a little complicated to explain. Can you give me the information over the phone?"

"I could, but the results are as complex as your

explanation would undoubtedly be. I'll be in the lab for the rest of the morning. Are you busy?"

"No. I'd be happy to meet you." She gave me the building and room number. Justin peered shamelessly over my shoulder. "I'll be there in half an hour or so."

"No hurry."

I hung up and faced my audience. "I need to go to the Masterson Building. What street is that on?"

"I know where it is," said Justin, eager curiosity lighting his face.

"Let me put on some shoes."

Dad blocked my way to the stairs. He gave me a laser beam look, virtually identical to the ones I got from Gran. "Magdalena Quinn. What are you up to? I don't buy that you had to take pictures for the yearbook last night." He transferred a little of the intensity of that glare to Justin. "And I still have questions about what you two were doing on the roof."

"I explained that, Dad."

"You gave me a load of codswallop."

Codswallop? I knew it wasn't going to help my case to laugh so I forced my face into a concerned frown.

"Does this have to do with the nightmare you had last night?" he asked.

I didn't have to fake a scowl. "Dad."

"Your mother is worried about you. And your grandmother says to just let you be, which makes *me* worried." We could have stayed at an impasse all day, because I definitely get my stubbornness from his side of the family. "Just tell me this," he asked, "are you in danger?"

I paused to consider a lot of evasions. But meeting his

eye, I took the chance that he was as much like Gran as I was like him. "I don't think so, but others are. This is something I have to do, Dad."

This much I knew: I was in a race to learn as much as I could about the phantom before it grew any stronger.

He studied me for another long moment, then shook his head in defeat and stepped back. "All right. Go see Dr. Smyth. We'll talk more later."

"Thanks, Dad." As I ran upstairs, I heard him ask Justin, "Don't you have an anthropology paper that's due next week?"

"I'm on top of it, sir." Dad said something else, something that I couldn't hear despite straining my ears. Justin answered him, "I'll do my best."

He could have been talking about class work, but something told me not.

✳   ✳   ✳

Justin and I argued briefly over who should drive; I liked being in the driver's seat—big surprise—but in the end it came down to efficiency. His car was parked behind mine.

"What were you and Dad talking about while I went upstairs?" I didn't waste time once we were on the road. "You weren't making some macho, keep-the-little-woman-safe pact, were you?"

He flicked me a glance but otherwise kept his eyes on the road, Mr. Conscientious behind the wheel. "I can't imagine that any man who knows you would make that mistake."

A dogleg of an answer if ever I heard one. I spiked a volley in another direction. "You're not going to flunk out or anything because I dragged you into this mess, are you? I'm not sure I can afford the karma hit if you do."

His mouth turned up in a crooked smile. "I'm not going to flunk out. And you didn't hold me at gunpoint." I acknowledged that was true. "Anyway, I wouldn't be able to concentrate wondering what you'd left out of last night's drama."

"Did I leave anything out?" Sleep had been dragging me down when I'd talked to him on the phone. "I can't remember."

"Just start from the beginning. The long version."

I didn't have time for the long version; Avalon isn't that big of a town. I had just gotten to Jess Minor going postal, and the Shadow's malicious delight, when we pulled into one of the university's big parking lots, virtually empty on Saturday morning. Justin turned in his seat to face me, his square jaw set, one hand still grasping the steering wheel tightly.

"I wondered about the scratches." He reached out as if to touch my face, then redirected the movement, pointing to his own cheek instead. "You've got a bruise, too."

"Yeah." I held up my hand, knuckles out. "But look! I got in a punch, at least."

"Good for you." I couldn't interpret his tension, but I thought it might be that he was trying hard to restrain old-fashioned protectiveness. He confirmed my hunch when he asked, as if he couldn't help himself, "But you're all right? Your voice still sounds awful. I can't believe you didn't mention the almost dying part last night."

"I didn't almost die." I refused to believe anything different. "Do you think she was really possessed? I mean, her head didn't spin around or anything, but it was freaky."

"Possession is a term with a lot of baggage. Let's say, 'Overshadowed.'"

I shivered. I'd started thinking about the whatever-it-was as the Shadow, with a capital S. The word fit. "I'm cool with less implied *Exorcist* in my life."

Justin tapped his fingers thoughtfully on the steering wheel. "I wonder why the Minor one and not the leader? Or one of the boys, who might have easily done real damage to you?"

I shrugged and reached for the door handle. "Weak-minded but mean. She was the perfect hostess."

17

the Earth Science Building was limestone and granite, surrounded by a green lawn, spreading oaks, and tall pines. Bedivere University nestled just north of the center of town, an old, relatively small private school. A strong emphasis on arts and humanities doubtless accounted for the low enrollment. A shiny new science building was in the planning stages, but I would miss the cozy anachronism of the present one.

The chemistry lab lay on the second floor, up the stone steps and through a rabbit warren of plaster and paneled hallways. We found the room and peered in. It wasn't much different from the high school—rows of slate-topped lab benches, each with a sink and a gas spigot. (I'll bet the college kids were allowed to use theirs, though.) It was bigger, and had more equipment along one wall, as well as a computer workstation where a woman typed diligently.

"Dr. Smyth?"

She looked up. "Miss Quinn?"

"Maggie," I confirmed. "This is my friend, Justin MacCallum."

The professor was about my mom's age, with some of the same no-nonsense demeanor. Dr. Smyth had flaming red hair and a wildly curving figure not really hidden by her lab coat. She picked up a piece of paper and gestured us over, her expression serious. "Before we begin, I have to ask. Did Professor Blackthorne put you up to this?"

I blinked in surprise. "No ma'am. I asked him for help."

Dr. Smyth subjected me to an exaggerated scrutiny, then clicked her tongue and nodded. "All right then." She laid the paper on a meticulously neat lab bench. "What you have here, Miss Quinn, is a rather fragrant potpourri of organic compounds, amino acids, and a few minerals."

I scanned the list, as indecipherable as the foreign symbols in my dream. A couple of the suffixes rang a bell, though. "Ethanethiol and methanethiol? Those wouldn't be, ah, putrescine and cadaverine, would they?"

"No. Those are from the sulfhydryl group." Dr. Smyth sounded a little pissed, so I tried to prove I wasn't an idiot wasting her time.

"Dr. Blackthorne mentioned the thiols. Rotten egg smell."

"Yes. And swamp gas and cabbage. Skunk odor, too. Down here—" She pointed to two lines on the printout I wasn't even going to try to read, let alone pronounce. "Those are the two smelly little buggers that cost me a steak dinner."

"You bet a steak dinner on putrescine and cadaverine?"

"What would you have bet?" she asked curiously.

"That I might never eat meat again."

Justin had been reading over my shoulder. "I'm guessing those names are fairly descriptive?"

"Oh yes." Dr. Smyth explained with relish. "Both are released by the breakdown of amino acids during the putrefaction of animal tissue. In small amounts, they are present in living flesh as well, but we only notice them when things die and start to rot."

"Nice," I said, ready to move along. "Sulfur, sulfuric acid . . ."

Justin took the sheet from my hands. "That's green vitriol. It was a standard ingredient in alchemy formulas."

"Exactly," said the professor. "You see why I thought Silas might be pulling my leg. Especially with this one." She pointed to the list. "*Artemisia arborescens L.* Tree wormwood."

"Wormwood?" I asked. "Where have I heard of that before?"

"You may have heard of absinthe."

"There's a biblical reference, too," Justin added. "And C. S. Lewis used it as a name for a junior demon in *The Screwtape Letters*."

That all sounded familiar. "Isn't it a poison?"

Dr. Smyth shook her head. "Not this variety. It comes from the Middle East, and was brewed into a medicinal tea."

Justin spoke thoughtfully. "In Russian folklore, the literal translation for the plant is 'bitter truth' and it's associated with a spell to open the eyes of deluded people."

Dr. Smyth gave him an odd look and I explained, "His thesis." She nodded like this clarified everything. Maybe to another academic, it did.

I took the list back. "What's *Cinchona officinalis*?"

"That's where your fluorescence comes from. Quinine."

"Quinine?" Boy, which one of these was not like the others. "Like, for preventing malaria?"

"Yes. It's another organic compound. It binds to the blood cells so tightly that the malarial parasite cannot."

My mind was spinning, drawing a strange sort of picture. I flipped over the printout and sketched a flat, vaguely bowl-like shape. "Let's say I'm an alchemist."

"Okay," said Dr. Smyth, in a humoring-the-nutcase sort of voice. "Why are we saying that?"

What could I say that wouldn't get us tossed out of her lab so fast we bounced? She already suspected that Professor Blackthorne had set her up. I glanced at Justin, but he was no help. My next accomplice was going to be a much better liar.

"I'm working on a project." Dr. Smyth continued to gaze at me, bemused. "A creative writing project," I said with sudden inspiration.

The corner of her mouth lifted. I still got the feeling she was humoring me, but she said, "Okay, I'll bite." She leaned her elbows on the lab bench and looked at my drawing. "Is that your cauldron, then?"

"It's more of a brazier. For a fire, you know?"

"What is it made out of?"

"Does it matter?"

"Certain metals may be reactive with your potion." She seemed intrigued now. My dad was the same way, a sucker for an intellectual discussion, no matter how off the wall. "I assume that's where this exercise is headed."

I took up the gauntlet. "Say I start a fire, then add sulfur, which burns blue, right?"

"Yes." Dr. Smyth gave me a quizzical look. "But what purpose does it serve? It can't be just for aesthetics."

I considered the question. Professor Blackthorne is my favorite teacher, but chemistry is not my strongest subject. "Fire supplies the energy for the chemical reaction, right? What if the sulfur—or brimstone, since we're thinking like alchemists—is meant to evoke the energy of the earth?"

"Or of Hell," Justin added. I frowned at him, but he didn't back down.

Dr. Smyth nodded. "Right." She wrote "Fire and Brimstone" on the sketch and then, "Energy source." "If we allow for supernatural in your plot, then we allow for Hell."

"Can't we leave that out of the equation for the moment?" I could rationalize alchemy. It was, in its way, a science. "'Hell' sounds so melodramatic."

"Let's say the power of the underworld for now," said Dr. Smyth, writing it in parenthesis. "That covers the physical and spiritual possibilities. Now, what are we trying to accomplish with our spell?"

Their eyes went to me expectantly. I had been chewing on the idea for a while, but it was a struggle to voice. Talk about melodrama. "A curse. We're trying to curse someone."

Justin held my gaze for a silent moment. It was the first time I had acknowledged out loud that this wasn't a random spirit or undirected supernatural event. The thought that someone could have meant to kill or injure Karen or Jeff was an uncomfortable one.

"Excellent!" The professor continued with a brisk enthusiasm that drew me back to humor. We bent over the table to watch her scribble notes. "Wormwood—the bitter truth. We want to teach the cursee a lesson. The quinine . . ."

"It binds to the blood," I said. "Binds the curse to the victim." A thought distracted me: Or binds the servant spirit to the summoner.

Dr. Smyth continued. "Right. Putrescine and cadaverine. Well, those are harder."

"Not really," said Justin. "Eye of newt, toe of frog. Or whatever else is handy."

Dr. Smyth looked at him. "But why? Literary tradition? If the character goes to the trouble of putting this formula together, everything must have a purpose."

"A burnt offering," he suggested.

"Toe of frog?" she scoffed. "Not much of a sacrifice."

I straightened. "Decay is a kind of breaking down. Maybe we're trying to break down our victim, reduce him."

Dr. Smyth tapped the pen. "Seems a bit of a stretch metaphorically."

"So is 'bitter truth,'" I protested.

"That has a folklore precedent. But then, so does eye of newt and toe of frog." She jotted down "newt & frog." "But of course, it's your story, so you can write it any way you want."

Didn't I wish.

She and Justin squabbled amiably over what icky rotting things could be added, for what metaphorical or alchemical purpose. To Dr. Smyth it was an academic exercise, an amusement, and for a little while, listening to them, I let myself think of it that way, too.

But I realized what she didn't. The organic compounds, the nasty ones, didn't have to be part of the formula. They could be intrinsic to the thing that the spell had called.

✳ ✳ ✳

I thanked Dr. Smyth again as we left. "I appreciate all your help." We stood at the door of her office and I had the printout, with all our notes on it, folded in my hand.

"Not at all," she said. "I enjoy an esoteric puzzle, now and again. Good luck with the project." It took me a blank moment to realize she meant my very fictional fiction assignment. She pushed her hands into the pockets of her lab coat and continued. "The main thing to remember is that the supernatural has rules, just like the natural world. You simply have to figure out what they are."

"Right. Well. Thanks again."

We turned to go, but her voice called me back before we'd gone more than a few steps. "Maggie?"

"Yes, Professor?"

"I'm still curious. This substance that seems to have inspired your story. You never said where you came across it."

"The school gym," I said, because I was out of lies.

"Hmm." Her expression was doubtful, but she let it go. "Well, that would definitely convince me to wear flip-flops in the shower."

18

"**Y**ou're quiet," Justin said once we were in the car.

"I'm trying to banish the mental image of Drs. Smyth and Blackthorne playing McGonagal and Snape in their off-duty hours."

He chuckled. "I'd like to meet Professor Blackthorne someday."

"He's a trip. I wish he taught English."

"It probably wouldn't be the same."

"It would have to be better than what I've got. Ms. Vincent has no sense of humor."

"I'll bet that's hard on you."

"What's that supposed to mean?"

"Only that you sort of live and die by the wisecrack."

I wondered if that was a good or bad thing in his eyes, and how much it mattered to me. "I like to keep my tongue honed to a sharp edge. I never know when I'll need it in a fight."

He navigated the left turn onto Beltline before he spoke again. "Want to get some lunch?"

"Don't you have to study?"

"I have to eat, too." Taking my silence for assent, he pulled into one of the restaurants on the strip. The Cadillac Grill had been a diner in the fifties. Back when *Grease* and *American Graffiti* were hot, someone had refurbished the building to all its *Rock Around the Clock* glory. Kitschy, but the food was good. We got one of the last tables without a wait.

I ordered a Coke, a cheeseburger, and fries without looking at the menu. Justin had iced tea and the chicken finger basket.

"Did they have chicken fingers back in the fifties?" I asked. "And what kind of name is that for food? Chickens don't have fingers and if they did, I wouldn't want to eat them."

His brows screwed up in the center. "I'm not really supposed to answer when you do that, am I?"

"No. I'm just showing you how clever I am."

"By mocking my food? Not very."

The waitress brought our drinks; I took a deep gulp of mine, and settled back in the vinyl seat. "So. What's your deal? You know practically everything about me, and I know almost nothing about you."

He clearly couldn't decide whether to be amused or not. "What do you want to know?"

I started with, "How long have you been at Bedivere?"

After a sip of his iced tea, he answered, "I transferred here last fall. I'm finishing my bachelor's and taking some grad-level courses."

"Are you in a big hurry to tackle that ivory tower?"

He smiled sheepishly. "There's a graduate internship I want to do this summer, and I had to have some preliminary courses to apply."

"Why Anthropology of the Bizarre? I mean, that wasn't something they really talked up at *our* Career Day."

An odd reserve entered his expression. "It's a long story."

I leaned forward, elbows on the table. "I hear the service here is slow."

He seemed to be considering things on some deep level, and I realized this was not something I could tease him about. But before he could tell me—or not—I heard my name.

"Maggie?" Instinctively, I turned.

"Oh hi, Jennifer." Great. The town crier, here at my table. "What are you doing here?" Besides spying on people.

"Eating, same as you." She addressed me, but her avidly curious gaze was on my tablemate. "Having a nice time?"

"Yes." I gave in to the inevitable. "Jennifer, this is Justin. Jennifer and I work on the school paper together."

"Nice to meet you." He smiled amiably.

"Same here." She beamed back, her shining brown curls falling over her shoulder as she turned her head. I couldn't decide if she had assumed he was my date, or assumed he wasn't, or which notion annoyed me more.

I shoved an unruly chunk of my own hair behind my ear. "So what's up?" I intended only distraction. I didn't expect her to pull up a chair and make herself comfortable, but that's what she did.

"I had to come tell you what I just heard, since we were talking about her the other day."

"Who?" A lot had happened in the last twenty-four hours.

"Jess Michaels. She was arrested for shoplifting a D&B bag."

Justin glanced at me curiously, and I mouthed "Minor" to clarify. I couldn't help him out with "D and B" though. I assumed it was a designer, and expensive. "But I thought she had money."

"*Everyone* thought so. As it turns out, her mother has the moolah, and she buys Jess stuff on her custody visits. But her dad can't afford the newest Prada, I guess, so she took a five-finger discount."

My mind circled back to the day I'd played tabloid reporter in the bathroom. "With Jessica Prime telling everyone her clothes were fakes, maybe she felt she had to have something new to save face."

"I know. But here's the thing." Jennifer leaned in close, as if revealing a secret. "I saw her wearing that blue Ralph Lauren sweater in September, and I swear it was the real label. But when I saw her yesterday, it was such an obvious copy I couldn't believe I'd ever been fooled."

"How strange." I spoke noncommittally, disinterested.

"Maybe Jess had to sell her good clothes," she mused, "and bought cheap replacements so no one would know."

"That's one explanation." A perfectly *un*natural alternative occurred to me, but why would a phantom care about fashion? "But that's just speculation, Jennifer," I cautioned. "I wouldn't spread it around."

She pantomimed locking her lips, but I didn't feel reassured. "I'll get back to my friends. Just had to say hi! Nice to meet you, Justin."

She fluttered off while the server put our lunch on the table. I sagged back in the booth, smacking the lump on my head on the wall behind me. "Ow. What just happened?"

"You were hypothesizing." Justin kept his voice neutral. "In unwise company."

"Just say it." I sat up and began to take the lettuce, tomato, and onion off my burger. "I was gossiping."

"I didn't know you were interested in fashion." He tested a poultry digit and found it too hot to handle.

"I'm not." I picked at my burger a moment longer. "It occurred to me this morning that all these people are losing what's most important to them. Image is extremely important to Jess Minor. She's always trying to keep up with the others. Losing status is the worst thing that could happen to her. Maybe there's some kind of illusion on her stuff."

He chewed a french fry thoughtfully. "That's why you suggested the chemistry experiment might be a curse."

I nodded. "I think that's why the Shadow leaves behind that stuff. If the—recipe, spell, whatever—creates it . . ."

"Or summons it," he said, ignoring his food now.

I didn't much like where that thought was headed, but a good journalist stays open-minded. "Or summons it," I allowed.

"So the question remains, what *is* the Shadow."

"Some kind of agent," I hypothesized, "fulfilling the curse. Like a messenger spirit."

Justin caught my gaze. "Like a demon, you mean."

"Well, I was trying to avoid that word." Especially in a crowded restaurant.

"Why can you say 'ghost' or 'spirit' without flinching, but not 'demon'?"

Good question. I tucked my hair behind my ears. "I don't know. Too many of those melodramatic connotations. Horns and pitchforks and things."

Leaning his elbows on the table, he gave me a long look. "That's a relatively modern, Western caricature, and not what I'm talking about at all."

"I know." I shook my head. "But I have to wrap my brain around this in stages."

The one thing I knew was this: If I was right, and someone had summoned some *thing* to bring down the Jocks and Jessicas, then regardless of the source, of the justness of the targets, the intent was Evil. With a capital E.

Justin looked like he might press the issue, but after a moment he let out his breath and reached for a chicken finger. "All right. Let's get back to Jessica Minor's shoplifting arrest. Do you think she might still be overshadowed?"

"No. I think that, robbed of what she valued, she'd do anything to try and recapture it." I picked up my burger. "Besides, I broke the connection, remember."

"You didn't finish telling me. How'd you do that?" he asked the instant my mouth was crammed with food. I tried to chew with undignified haste, then just picked up the saltshaker and mimed throwing it on him. He fell back against the bench, staring at me in surprised joy. "You mean it actually worked?"

My eyes bugged out of my head. I swallowed the much-too-big mouthful of burger and choked out, "What do you mean 'it actually worked'? You didn't *know* it was going to work?"

"Well, on paper, sure. But . . ." My outrage popped his bubble of satisfaction. "What? Everything I'd read said it should work as well as anything I could have given you."

"Everything you've *read*?" The sorority girls at the next table turned to see what I was squawking about. I lowered my voice, leaning against the table. "You mean you've never actually dealt with anything like this before?"

"Not personally, no."

"I trusted you!" My throat squeezed out the words, trying to be quiet. "I thought you knew what you were doing."

He threw the chicken finger into the basket. "It isn't as if I made this stuff up. It may be secondhand knowledge, but at least I'm not basing it on Bill Murray movies."

"That was just a starting place!" Indignant, I forgot about whispering. "I have been as logical and methodical as I can, under some pretty extraordinary circumstances."

He waved a hand in frustration. "You're trying to force this thing to fit in a real-world box, but you won't even fully admit it exists."

The truth that didn't make it any easier to swallow. "At least I admit I don't know what I'm dealing with."

His eyes hardened to chips of stone. "At least I'm willing to commit to my hypothesis without closing my mind to the more unpleasant possibilities."

That stung. "Closed" and "minded" were fighting words for me, and I struck back below the belt. "Yeah, but you tested your hypothesis on me. Some paladin you are."

The angry color ran out of his face. I felt a prick of guilt for smacking him right in the self-image, for knowing how to hurt him and using it. But I was still too mad to take it back, even if I knew how. So I dropped my gaze and climbed out of the booth, digging into my pocket to pay for my burger. "I told you when we met, I didn't want to be your research project."

"Maggie, sit down."

"No. I'm too angry to eat."

"Then put your money away." He leaned on one hip to pull out his wallet. The waitress appeared as if conjured, like a pert blond genie from the lamp.

"Is there a problem?"

"We're going to need some to-go boxes." He handed her a twenty and she vanished before I could give her the wadded up bills for my half of the meal. Furious at being treated like an invisible child, I shoved them in Justin's direction. "Here. This should cover me."

"Stop being such a brat, and sit down."

That was the final straw. My face flamed with hurt anger, and rather than prove him right by bursting into a tantrum, or tears, or both, I turned and left.

"Have a nice day!" said the poodle-skirted hostess as I made a beeline for the door. I knew they made her say that, so I didn't tell her *exactly* what kind of day I was having.

Justin caught up with me in the parking lot. He didn't have the to-go boxes. "Don't even think about walking home."

How had I ever thought he was Mr. Nice Guy? "It's not that far."

"With everything that's happened around you? Across the street is too far."

"That's not your problem." I waved him off. "I absolve you of responsibility."

He clenched his jaw and ground out between his teeth, "I'll see you back safely." End of discussion. I ached to tell him he wasn't the boss of me, but didn't want to be called a brat again.

I stomped to the car instead, fumed while he unlocked the door, then huffed into the bucket seat. Justin went to his side, but paused for several calming breaths before he climbed behind the wheel.

He drove with tense deliberation while I sulked. The urge to scream or explode had evaporated; that only left the threat of tears. "Why don't you just say it?"

He kept his eyes on the road. "Say what?"

"Whatever is making that muscle in your jaw twitch."

"Because I'm focusing my anger on getting to your house in one piece so I can dump your ungrateful"—He struggled a moment, then settled on—"backside, and be done."

I folded my arms. "Oh, just say 'ass.' The world won't end if you're rude. My universe would have imploded a long time ago if rudeness were fatal."

He turned off of Beltline and onto a smaller, safer street. "Really? I thought you were making an exception for me."

I twisted to face him. "I thought you had experience with this stuff. I trusted you."

"I never said that, Maggie. Sure I have a broader base of knowledge than you—though that's not saying much. I've done research and interviews and studies. But it's not like there's some kind of paranormal lab practical."

Unreasonably I clung to the idea that it *was* his fault for projecting such confidence that, desperate to believe someone was equipped to deal with the supernatural, I'd given him more credit than he claimed.

He turned onto the residential road that led to my house. "Why are we even arguing about this? It worked, didn't it?"

"It might not have." Now I was just being stubborn.

"But it did!" Finally he was raising his voice.

"But you should have *told* me it might not work."

Another turn, onto my street. "Half of the power of a talisman is the belief that it will work."

"Like Dumbo and his stupid magic feather?"

"Yeah." He pulled into the driveway and stopped so abruptly that my seatbelt jerked me backward. "Exactly like Dumbo."

He unbuckled and got out of the car. I scrambled out after him. What kind of guy walks a girl to the door even in the middle of an argument? "What does *that* mean?"

"That for a smart girl you're acting pretty dumb, fighting over technicalities." He faced me, arms folded across his chest. "You need me. Who else is going to believe you, let alone help you?"

My posture mirrored his. "Apparently I can simply read a book."

"Great idea. Because a book will definitely give a damn

what happens to you when you get in over your head. *Further* over your head."

He seemed to be waiting for me to say something else, but reeling from the fact that (a) he'd cursed and (b) he gave a damn what happened to me, I hesitated too long.

"Fine." He dropped his arms and turned away. "You know where to find me."

I needed to respond. I wanted to say *something*. But I didn't know what would fix the mess I'd made of things. Except "I'm sorry" and even that wouldn't come out past the stubborn stranglehold of emotions in my throat.

So I just let him leave.

19

the real world marched along, for the moment at least. Regardless of what went on in the supernatural realm, I had an English paper due in a couple of days. As I plugged away at it without enthusiasm, my dad came halfway up the stairs and peered through the banister rail. "Mom and I are thinking about Chinese food for dinner. Are you in?"

"Yeah." My stomach growled at the thought. Those three bites of cheeseburger hadn't gone far. "I want egg foo young and an order of spring rolls."

But instead of going back down the stairs, he came up to the study. "Did you and Justin have a fight?"

"What makes you say that?"

"The shouting on the lawn was a clue."

I groaned and slithered down until my butt was nearly hanging off the chair. "I was such a brat."

"Probably."

"You're not supposed to agree with me."

"Why is that?"

"Because you're my father."

He bent over and kissed the top of my head. "That only guarantees that I'll love you when you're a brat, not that I'll never think you are one."

I sighed, deeply. "That's fair, I guess."

His curious glance fell on my desk. "What's this?"

I spun the chair with my foot. "My theory that the microcosm of the American high school is represented in the lands that Gulliver encounters in his travels."

"Interesting theory, but I was talking about this." He held up the sketch I'd made that morning, of the symbols engraved on the brazier.

"Oh." How much to tell him? If I spilled it all, he might believe me. And then he'd lock me in my room and call for a priest. That would put an end to my Nancy Drew–ing.

So I parceled out a little of the truth. "I dreamed about an oasis, with tents, and a woman at the well. There was a campfire, and those symbols were carved in the brazier that held the coals."

Dad raised his brows. "Interesting. They look Assyrian, or maybe Babylonian. That's not really my area."

"I thought they looked Hebrew."

He considered them again. "Perhaps the same family. I

can ask Dr. Dozer if you like. She's done a lot of work in the Middle and Near East. Went on some expeditions there, before the first Gulf War."

I stopped listening after the name "Dozer." Stanley. How could I not have seen it before?

Dad had stopped talking, expecting an answer. I backtracked to his question. Thank God for mental TiVo. "No, thanks. Let me do a little more research, okay? It could be just nonsense."

He laid the paper back on the desk. "Okay. You know I'll help you however I can."

I smiled up at him. "I know."

He headed for the stairs. "Egg foo young and spring rolls," he confirmed before he left.

I rooted through piles of paper and books until I found the flash drive where I'd stored those pictures from the week before. I plugged it in and clicked on the folder marked "in_case_of_death."

The first photo popped open, showing Stanley's face frozen in terror, his long legs hooked over the brick wall of the elevated walkway, while Brandon and Jeff, laughing like maniacs, held him suspended over the two-story drop. Brian stood back, looking torn and miserable, and the Three Original Jessicas pointed and twittered like the birdbrains they were.

Of the seven people in the snapshot, four had something strange happen to them. Only Karen wasn't in the picture. Did she not fit the pattern, or was I not seeing the whole thing?

I clicked "print" and picked up the phone to call Justin.

Then I stopped. I wasn't angry with him anymore, but my pride still stung. We'd both thrown a lot of darts, and maybe his were more just than mine. It was all very complicated, even more so because I was unsure if this was a friends and colleagues argument, or a guy/girl thing.

I had guy/girl thoughts about Justin, but I had no idea if he thought about me that way. When he met Brian today, his careful neutrality could have meant anything from "Me, Tarzan. You in my tree," to "Maggie's like a sister to me."

Brian, on the other hand, hadn't quite thumped his chest, but when I accidentally agreed to Monday's date, he was pretty clearly thinking "guy wins girl." If only I didn't have this picture of him, standing by and doing nothing while his friends terrified Stanley.

I stared at the photo, studying the faces, frozen in that pivotal moment. Stanley Dozer. "You'll all be sorry," he'd said. Had he found some otherworldly alternative to a black trench coat and an AK-47?

✳ ✳ ✳

I tossed restlessly in bed. Time had dilated somehow, and my paper was due tomorrow. Besides the Swift theme, I needed to write an article about Jeff Espinoza's accident, finish two chemistry lab reports, and compose a one-page essay for civics. No wonder my brain felt feverish and overheated.

I didn't remember getting up, but abruptly found myself at my computer, facing a blank document on the screen, my paper not even begun. I wondered briefly how I could have forgotten to start the darned thing; some deep, muted voice in my head said that wasn't right. Something was off about

184

this whole scenario. But the immediate panic of the looming deadline drowned out all logic. I had to get cracking.

Let's see. Jonathan Swift. Irishman. Satirist and misanthrope.

I typed the title: *Satire for Social Change*. So far so good. Too bad I'd waited until the morning it was due, not to mention the seven chemistry reports and a six-page essay on the judicial branch of government.

Thesis sentence: *Jonathan Swift was a real good writer. When he rote stuff for the Irish noospaper, it pissed off the government and they said, we can tacks you all we want, because we're English, and we have a big army and a cool flag.*

Class started in fifteen minutes, and at this rate, I wasn't even going to be able to start those ten lab reports. I scrolled up and looked at what I'd done so far.

What the Hell?

Who wrote this crap? An illiterate twelve-year-old?

I deleted and tried again: *Jonithen Swift rote about stuff that was bad and made fun of it, and it was real funny, and made people think . . .*

I shoved back from the computer, rejecting the words there. They were moronic. Infantile.

"How did you get in this class?" asked Ms. Vincent, appearing at my desk. I wanted to ask what she was doing in my room, but I saw we were actually in her classroom, complete with the cartoon pencils and erasers dancing over the chalkboard.

"You should never have been allowed in AP English," said Vincent. "You'll have to finish the year in that class, over there." I turned to where she pointed; a door led to another classroom—this one filled with three football players (in uniform), a couple of Drill Team Barbies (doing their nails), a few stoners (stoned), and a pimple-faced, greasy-haired boy wearing a Wal-Mart smock, who pointed to a desk beside him and said, "You can sit by me, Maggie."

I turned to Ms. Vincent to protest, but all that came out of my mouth was gibberish. She looked at me pityingly and I ran from the room, into B Hall.

Halloran was there and I tried to tell him there was a terrible mistake with my schedule, but only nonsense words spilled from my lips. "Very funny," he said. "That's what you get for pretending you're so much smarter than everyone else."

This wasn't true, and I told him so, but still I could only speak Martian.

"Stop horsing around, Quinn," he barked, "or I'll put you in detention until the end of the year."

I ran the B Hall gauntlet of mocking laughter, sick heat spreading through me at the jeers and taunts. I found Karen, stitches on her head, and I tried to tell her what was happening. She looked at me in sweet-natured confusion. "I don't understand, Maggie. Is this a joke?"

"It's the thing I value most . . ." But of course my words made no sense to either of us.

At the end of the hall, Stanley and Lisa stood side by side. "You did this," I yelled at Stanley. "It's not funny!"

"Sorry, Maggie," Stanley sneered from his towering height. "I can't understand you. I don't speak loser."

I grabbed him by the plaid western shirt and pulled him down to my level. I wanted to hit him, to hurt him. To punish somebody for the panicked terror seizing my mind. "Take this curse off me!"

"You're dreaming, Maggie." Lisa's sensible voice. Just as it had while I was wigging out about the locker room photo, her droll practicality cut through my rioting emotions to the rational person inside. "Wake up now. Everything will be fine."

I turned my head to look at her, a bubble of hope rising in my chest. "Bewop?" I said.

"Yeah, really."

And with an abruptness that was almost anticlimactic, I woke up.

* * *

The room was dark, except for the nightlight casting shadows on the wall. I snaked a hand out from the covers, irrationally afraid something waited to grab it. The bedside lamp was more effective, and I sat up to cast my eyes suspiciously around the room. I didn't see or smell anything, but I could feel the sweat of panic drenching my nightshirt, and the dampness of tears on my face.

So, what had I learned from the dream? That I prized my communication skills above all else. And I was probably more proud of my brains than I ought to be. Sobering thought. Perhaps it wasn't so much a question of what they—okay, what *we*—valued most, but where our vanity lay.

I forced myself out of bed and to the computer; a jiggle of the mouse brought it to life. I let out a breath as I saw my nearly completed English paper on the screen. Then I sat down, opened a new document, and poised my hands over the keyboard.

I typed: "To be, or not to be. That is the question. Whether 'tis nobler in the mind to suffer the slings and arrows of outrageous fortune, or by opposing, end them."

I got up. Paced the room. Sat down. Read the words on the screen. They looked exactly as they should.

Then I entered: "The core dilemma for Hamlet is the question we all face: Do we endure the crap that life dishes out, or do we fight against it, even if it would be easier to just lie down and let fortune have its way?"

Not the most eloquent, but when I looked back at what I'd written, it didn't say: "Trouble, bad. Sleep, good."

I got up from the desk and rubbed my hands over my tired face. *To sleep, perchance to dream.* Screw that.

Walking to the window, I paused a moment, then brushed back the edge of the curtain. I saw no shadows other than those cast by the pecan tree, rustling lightly in the breeze.

I'd always thought *Hamlet* was a dumb play about a guy who can't make up his mind. I mean, I face the same drama in the lunch line. But at that moment I understood: When it comes to the big stuff, it *is* hard to decide whether to let things just happen, especially when its to other people, or to take a stand and cause yourself a world of trouble.

The dream could have just been the egg foo young, or the pot of my fears stirred by the events of the day. But no. I hadn't seen fire or smoke in the dream, but I'd felt the threat. I'd been warned, told to let slings and arrows have their way.

Like that was going to happen. Old Smokey had no idea who he was messing with.

20

Monday morning I took up arms against a sea of troubles. I marched into the school office, asked to see the nurse, and learned we only have one on Tuesdays and Thursdays.

"What if someone gets sick on a Monday, Wednesday, or Friday?"

The secretary looked at me without humor. "Then you get to go home."

"I'm just learning this now? All those civics classes I suffered through, for nothing."

She sighed. "What do you want, Maggie? You know we're super busy before school."

I chewed my lip, deciding how to proceed. "What if I'm worried about the health of a student? Who would I talk to?"

The secretary tilted her ash-blond head. I could see her flick through the mental card catalog of possibilities—drugs, pregnancy, depression. "You could talk to one of the assistant principals."

"Is Mrs. Cardenas available?"

"No. Just Mr. Halloran. Would you like me to see if he has time to see you?" Her drolly bland expression said she knew the answer to that question.

"Uh, maybe later. First I have to make an appointment for that root canal I've been putting off."

"Right. See you, Maggie."

"See you, Ms. Jones."

I grumped out of the office, irritated to be sidelined so quickly. Bad enough I had to rescue Jessica Prime at all. I wanted to get it over with.

"Maggie!" Brian found me in the busy courtyard, a smile on his handsome face. He made a token effort to sober up. "I heard you and your friend had a fight at Cadillac Grill. I'm sorry."

"No, you're not."

"If he's just your friend, then I am. If he's more than that, maybe not." He flashed an unrepentant grin and I had to give him points for honesty. He handed me a ticket. "That will get you into the game this afternoon. When it's over, I thought we could get something to eat."

I had a lot to do that afternoon. Besides homework, newspaper, and yearbook, there was saving the world as well. Where was I going to fit in a date?

But none of these excuses actually made it to my lips and

Brian took my silence as assent. He dashed off before I could tell him to be extra careful.

I turned to go to my own class, but stopped when I saw Jessica Prime staring at me from near the picnic tables. There was malice in her eyes, but that didn't shock me. It was the sunken hollows in her cheeks and the collarbones jutting out like knives. She looked like a walking toothpick with a pair of grapes stuck on the front. Her fake boobs were the only things with any life. The rest of her was deflated down to the bones.

How had this happened so quickly? Was the change so fast, or was I looking with new eyes? Either way, it was clear I wasn't going to be able to wait for the nurse to return tomorrow. I had to take action immediately.

✳ ✳ ✳

I arrived in the locker room early, which should have given Coach Milner's marathon-conditioned heart an attack. She glanced up from her desk as I tapped on her office door. "Got a minute, Coach?"

"Certainly, Quinn. Have a seat. If you're worried about your grade for the swimming portion of the six weeks—"

She broke off with a raised eyebrow as I closed the door and sat down purposefully. "It's not my grade. Though I will point out that lots of people have phobias about the water. But this is about Jessica Prime—I mean, Prentice."

"Prentice? What about her?"

"Last Friday, when I went back to get my goggles, I heard her throwing up. In secret."

The coach's eyes narrowed. "You shouldn't jump to con-clusions, Quinn. Maybe lunch wasn't agreeing with her."

"I don't think *any* food is agreeing with her."

"Look, Quinn. Not everyone with a trim figure is anorexic or bulimic. As a cheerleader, Prentice must be rigid about diet and exercise. You shouldn't let jealousy color your perceptions."

I sat back in the molded plastic chair. "Jealousy?"

"Yes. You struggle in every physical activity, when you bother to try at all. For your height, you could stand to lose at least five pounds. I've been teaching P.E. for a long time, and I can tell you, a healthy body comes with hard work."

"Yeah, well, I don't think that includes sticking a finger down my throat." Furious, I surged to my feet. "I thought you'd be an advocate for a healthy person, not just a thin body. My five extra pounds means an extra book read, or another banana split I shared with my dad. I'm happy like I am, and I am certainly not jealous of Jessica Cheers-for-Brains Prentice."

"That's detention, Quinn." Milner's face went red beneath her sun-bronzed tan. She shoved a D Hall slip at me. "Take it and go."

"Fine." I grabbed the pass from her. "But open your eyes and take a look at her *today*, not how you remember her looking last week. Just help her. Please."

I stormed out, leaving the door open behind me. I ran into a crowd of girls in various stages of dress, their changing interrupted as they gathered to stare in confusion at Jessica Prentice. It was impossible to call her "Prime" while she gazed at herself in the mirror and wept in unfeigned anguish.

"How did this happen?" she wailed, unable to tear her

eyes from her reflection. "I haven't eaten anything. I've exercised two, three hours every day."

I could sense the funeral pyre stench at the back of my throat. I was attuned to the smell by this time; it seemed faint. Days old.

Thespica stood to one side of the mirror, her face twisted with anxiety. "You don't look fat, Jessica." She wrung her fingers into a fearful knot. "Maybe, if you're worried, you should see a doctor."

The crowd parted for Coach Milner. If the scene weren't so pathetic, I would have relished her shocked expression.

"What's going on, Prentice?" Milner asked when she had recovered herself. She pitched her tone somewhere near its usual go-get-'em bluster.

"Look at me, Coach." Jessica could not tear her gaze from the mirror. "I'm so . . . fat."

"You're not fat, Prentice." She moved slowly, reaching to take the girl's arm. "You're going to be fine. Why don't we go in my office and talk?"

"No!" She pulled away. "I know you think I must be eating like a pig, but I'm not. I'm not eating at all." Tears slipped down her gaunt cheeks.

"I know you're not. Let's just go in my office. . . ."

Milner turned her gently away from her reflection. Jessica saw me, and started to shriek. That was always such a pleasure.

"It's her, isn't it? Did she tell you I'm crazy? She hates me, you know."

"Let's leave Quinn out of this."

"She's just jealous!" The girl began to sob. "Or she *was*. Now look at me! I'm disgusting."

I looked. Not at her, but in the mirror. When Jessica opened her eyes and gazed at her image, I saw her toothpick-and-grape figure burble and warp. In its place was a girl I had never seen before. It wasn't merely that she was fat. She was certainly overweight—rolls of flesh strained against her too-small clothes—but a wardrobe change would do wonders.

No, this girl in the mirror, wearing Jessica Prime's clothes, her hair, her boobs, was ugly. She had piggish eyes and a bulbous nose and as I watched, her face erupted in a minefield of gaping black pores and pus-filled pimples.

Jessica screamed. The sound echoed off the metal lockers and the tile floors. Some of the girls put their hands over their ears. Some were too appalled to move. They couldn't see what Jessica saw in her reflection. To their eyes, her perfection was marred only by her emaciation and slipping sanity.

She reached her hands to her face and began to claw at it, to tear the skin. I jumped forward to stop her, dizzy from the dual vision of the girl, nearly perfect and utterly grotesque. As she raked her nails over her cheeks, in the mirror the pimples popped and ran, and I gagged on the putrid smell. It was as if, in the vision-Jessica, all the rot inside her oozed out of her face.

I squeezed my eyes shut and dragged her hands down as Coach Milner came to help. Jessica fought us like a wild thing, flailing and kicking, shrieking at the top of her lungs. Milner got her in a restraining hold, wrapping whipcord arms around her from behind, and gently but inexorably lowering the struggling girl to the floor.

"Call nine-one-one," she said as Jessica went limp. In her weakened state, she was no match for the coach. She subsided, sobbing, a wretched heap of sticks on the cold tile floor.

21

I met Lisa after school at Froth and Java, desperate for a caffeine boost and some debriefing. "On the other hand," I told her at the end of my tale, "I did avoid landing in detention for the second day in a row."

Battlefield humor. We sat outside and the balmy afternoon with its endless blue sky stood in glaring contrast to my gnawing worry.

Lisa leaned back in her chair, arms folded. "How do you keep ending up in the thick of these things?"

I sipped my vanilla latte. "Believe me, it's not by choice."

"What do you care if Queen Jessica wastes away to

nothing? She took that humiliating picture so she and her friends could cackle at you."

"Thanks for reminding me."

Lisa plopped her elbows on the table. "I'm serious. If you were a different kind of girl, you might have slit your wrists."

"But I didn't. I never even thought of it." In fact, I was shocked at the idea.

"That's because you're reasonably together, and you have me for a friend. But you *were* hiding in the toilet."

My cheeks heated up. "That was temporary."

"And yet you know how it felt." She stabbed her finger on the glass table, nailing home her point. "How many girls commit suicide because of witches like Jessica? If not all at once, then slowly, by starving or eating themselves to death. Or by sleeping around to try and find some self-esteem."

"So that makes it right that Jessica Prime got hauled away to the funny farm?" Her screams still echoed in my head.

Lisa scowled and traced a figure in the condensation that dripped from her soda. "It seems fitting, if a little extreme. But you can't expect a Jessica to do anything without going over the top." She took a drink and set the cup back down.

I could see her point. The bane of so many girls' lives, flipping out in the locker room and having to be taken away in restraints? There *was* a kind of cosmic justice to it. But the cosmos, or Fate, or deity of your choice hadn't set this in motion. Someone earthly had meted a malicious and disturbing vengeance.

Lisa changed the subject and I was happy to let her. "Who is this guy you were arguing with at Cadillac Grill?"

"Justin. A friend of mine."

"Uh-huh. So why don't I know this 'friend'?" she asked.

I twisted the insulating sleeve on my cardboard cup. "Because he's . . . new."

"I heard he was cute."

"Very."

She gave me a squinty, what-is-your-damage sort of look. "Then why in heaven's name are you going out with Brian Kirkpatrick tonight?"

"I sort of agreed to it by accident." And since he was one of the six in the picture, I figured it might be a good idea to stick around him.

As if reading my mind—and I wouldn't quite put it past her—Lisa said, "I don't know what I think about your having this ESP, or whatever it is, if it's going to keep you hanging around the Jocks and Jessicas."

"Well, they're dwindling fast, aren't they? There aren't any Jessicas left."

"Oh, Minor will be back." Lisa paused with a devilish smile. "When she makes bail."

Now *that* I could laugh at.

✳   ✳   ✳

Avalon High's home games were held on the university's baseball diamond. I arrived during the third inning; I could see the scoreboard from the parking lot. This was my compromise, to avoid seeming too eager for this to be a *date*.

It was a perfect baseball evening, with the kind of temperate weather that makes me love spring in Avalon. Under a very slight breeze, the sun bowed out gradually, lending a warm light but not too much glare: the magic hour, in photography terms.

I brought my camera with me and took pictures of the spectators with the light of the setting sun on their faces, bags of popcorn in their hands. Of the left-field guy, hands on knees in an anticipatory crouch, dirt-streaked uniform against the vibrant green grass. Idyllic, boys-of-summer stuff.

Eventually I found a seat behind the home-team's dugout. Brian got on base the first time I saw him go to bat. He was tagged out at second on what the guy beside me called "a really nice squeeze play." He was of a parental age, and wore a blue-and-gold Avalon T-shirt. This was either very cute or very sad.

When Brian jogged back to the dugout, he seemed unsteady on his feet. He waved his coach's concern away. Mine was less easily put aside.

"You all right?" I asked when he came over to say hi.

He pulled off his hat and rested his elbows on the fence. Even hat hair looked good on him. "I'm fine. Just a little hot. Are you having a good time?" he asked.

"Sure. Too bad about that squeeze play." I hope that impressed him, because it was the only baseball I spoke.

He shrugged. "That's how the game is played."

If you say so. What did I know?

The coach called out to him, "Hey, Kirkpatrick. Stop flirting and get on the field."

"See you on the next side out," I said.

Brian laughed and put his hat back on. "Funny. See you

next inning. Bye, Dad!" He waved at Mr. Squeeze Play, and then grabbed his glove from the bench and ran onto the field.

I reevaluated the parental unit. "You're Brian's dad?"

"You must be Maggie." He grinned and offered his hand. Yep. They were definitely related. "Glad to meet you."

"Likewise." Heck. How did an accidental date turn into a meeting with a parent? "Enjoying the game?"

"I'd enjoy it more if we were ahead. But it's only the fifth inning."

"Right." I returned to my seat. "I don't know much about baseball, I'm afraid."

"I'll explain it if you want, but I know my wife finds it equally satisfying to just enjoy the weather and cheer when I do."

"Sounds about my speed."

The opposing team's batter came up to the plate, and went back to the dugout. The next player hit two foul balls, then another one that managed to stay in the lines. He was out at first base, though, thanks to Brian. I cheered for that, too.

"Brian's a pretty good player, isn't he?" I watched as he took off his hat again, and wiped his face with his arm.

"Well, I think so. But the scouts from the University of Texas must agree. They offered him a full scholarship."

"That's great!" I tried to smile naturally while a chill spread through me. Anyone who has ever seen a movie— ever—knows that nothing dooms a character quicker than a bright future: pregnant wife, farm in Montana, baseball scholarship. . . . All the same to cinematic irony.

My eyes searched the grounds for Old Smokey. Though

the shadows around the field were lengthening, they weren't deep or dark enough to hold the phantom as I'd last seen it, and I didn't smell anything but peanuts and popcorn.

Out on first base, though, Brian swayed on his feet. He put his hands on his knees, but it wasn't the usual wait-for-the-pitch stance. Even from the stands he looked green.

"He doesn't look well," I said, stating the obvious.

Grimly, his dad shook his head. "He's been feeling bad all weekend. At first we thought it was because of his friend. You know, Jeff."

The coach called for a time out. He walked to first base and talked to Brian, as if telling him not to be a macho idiot. Or maybe that was what I would tell him, if I were out there. Finally, the coach signaled another player in from the dugout.

Halfway off the diamond, Brian's legs folded up under him. Mr. Kirkpatrick yelled in alarm and ran to the fence. "This way," I said, and led him to the gate behind the home-team's bench. We ran out onto the field, ignoring umpires, players, and the confused and concerned murmur from the stands.

Mr. Kirkpatrick dropped beside his son, putting a hand to his face, then placing his fingers against the pulse in his neck. I crouched by them. "Is he all right?"

Brian opened his eyes, blinking at the worried circle of faces that gazed down at him. "What happened?"

"You fainted," I said. Pained embarrassment crossed his face, and I remembered that his teammates were clustered around us. "I mean, passed out. Uh . . . took a header." What was the macho term for "swooned like a girl"?

"Did you lose consciousness?" his father asked, looking

into his eyes. I wondered if he was actually a doctor, or had just watched a lot of *ER*. "How many fingers am I holding up?"

"Three." It was the wrong answer.

"Can you squeeze my hand?" Apparently the answer to that wasn't good, either. "Raise your head? Move your legs?" He could, but with trembling effort, as if someone had tied sandbags to his limbs.

"Do we need to call an ambulance?" the coach asked.

Brian protested. "No, Dad. Let the guys help me up."

Dr. Kirkpatrick—I felt pretty sure about the profession—sat back on his heels, and his son's frightened gaze followed him. "You need to get checked out. Now. And I'm not taking any excuses."

"I promise. We can go straight to the emergency room, if you want. Just let the guys help me off the field."

Men.

I stood back as his teammates hoisted him up, his arms over their shoulders, and half-carried him off the field while the spectators clapped their encouragement.

Dr. Kirkpatrick went to move his car closer. On the field, play resumed, as Brian sat on the bench to wait, leaning wearily back against the surrounding fence. His hand caught mine and weakly pulled downward. I obliged the silent request and sat beside him.

"What's going on, Maggie?"

"Your dad is taking you to the emergency room, I think." The school should get a discount rate.

"No." He shook his head, then swayed woozily, grasping my hand to steady himself. "I mean, first Jeff, then Jessica, and the other Jessica. What's going on?"

His voice was so weak, I didn't think his teammates

could hear. Still, I leaned closer, clasping his hand between my own. "I don't know, Brian. Something bad."

"You have to figure it out, Maggie." He met my worried gaze, his eyes vivid blue in his pale face. "It's all of us from that day, isn't it? From the day with Stanley."

He'd figured it out more quickly than I had. "Yeah. Except Karen."

"Why didn't you give the pictures to Halloran?"

It took me a moment to realize what that meant. "*You* told Halloran about the pictures? Why?"

"Crisis of conscience, I guess. Too afraid to stand up to them alone, but didn't want them—us—to get away scot-free." He rubbed his hand over his eyes. "I guess we're not."

"Don't give up." I squeezed his hand. "I'm working on it."

He smiled. "I feel better already." His expression seemed almost shy. Or maybe that was his weakness. "Can I call you to ask how it's going?"

"Sure."

When his dad reappeared, Brian had regained enough strength in his legs that it only took one teammate to help him to the car. I followed behind, distant enough to ask Dr. Kirkpatrick if he had any idea what was wrong.

He shook his head, not quite in denial, but in disbelief. "I know what it *looks* like, but it's impossible for it to progress this fast."

Impossible had become a relative thing in my life. "What does it look like, then?"

"Well, it *looks* like MS. But he's never had any symptoms before. This is like a year of deterioration in a matter of days."

Multiple sclerosis? Didn't people with MS end up in wheelchairs?

I watched them drive off, then stood in the parking lot, unsure what to do next. I had failed to save anybody. Events had been escalating from mildly amusing to life-altering. As a ghost hunter, I was a total failure. I wasn't much of a detective, either, since I still didn't know exactly what the Shadow was or how to stop it. I'd even managed to lose my best ally. So far it was Powers of Darkness six, Maggie Quinn zero.

Time to face facts. I sucked at being a superhero.

22

by the time I'd finished two cups of tea and a piece of chocolate cake, I'd also caught Gran up on my extraordinary lack of success.

"I thought Karen was going to be okay. And the first two Jessicas, what happened to them was kind of funny. But then there was the car accident and Karen might have brain damage, Jessica Prime might be on psychtropic drugs for the rest of her life, and poor Brian may end up in a wheelchair."

"That's not certain, dear." Gran refilled my cup and pushed the sugar bowl my way. She had just come home from her retiree's dinner group at church, and was dressed in a fashionable skirt and top, her short red hair styled with a casual flair, much too mod to be pouring tea.

"I've screwed everything up. I haven't made any progress, and things are getting worse instead of better."

"Things always get worse before they get better. And I think you've made a great deal of progress. I think it was very clever of you to have that . . . what did you call that ghost goo?"

"Ectoplasm?" I sighed. "I watch too much TV."

"And I would never have thought of a curse potion."

"It's just a theory." I sulked into my tea. "And to top it off, I argued with Justin, so I've lost my best ally."

Gran set her cup in her saucer with a clatter. "Now that *is* stupid."

"Thanks for your support."

"What did you argue about?"

"Something that seemed important at the time."

"Well, it can hardly be more important than your overall mission." She gestured to the phone on the kitchen counter. "Call him up."

"Oh, Gran." I slumped back in my chair. "He said he doesn't want to help me anymore."

She rose and got the handset herself. "Of course he said that. Men have to save face. What's his number? Never mind. It's on the caller ID." She beep-beep-beeped through the recent calls while I made weak protests. Truthfully, I wanted to talk to him, but if he hung up, or told me to get lost, it would hurt. A lot.

"Hello? Is this Justin MacCallum?" Gran's accent always deepened on the phone. "I hear that you've had a bit of a row with my idiot granddaughter."

"Gran!"

She waved me silent. "Right. No, I wouldn't expect you to tell me what it was about. But she'd like to apologize." I held out my hand for the receiver. Gran ignored me. "Where would you like her to meet you? Well, where are you studying? At the library? She'll be there in twenty minutes."

Gran put the handset back into the cradle and turned to me expectantly. "Maybe you should freshen up a bit before you go."

"I could have just talked to him on the phone." Rejection would be a lot easier with AT&T as a buffer.

"Making up after an argument is better done face to face." She hauled me out of my chair. "Go powder your nose and comb your hair."

I bowed to fate. Easier to simply suffer the slings and arrows of my outrageous grandmother.

✳　✳　✳

The sun had gone down, but streetlights kept the campus well lit. So close to finals, there were a lot of people coming and going from the library, and probably would be for hours yet.

The west half of the building was built early in the last century; the other part dated back only to the eighties. Justin waited for me in the east lobby, on the far side of the theft prevention gates. The fluorescent lighting made his unsmiling face look forbidding, sculpted the lines of his cheeks and jaw too harshly.

A trick of the light. I hoped. I lifted a hand in tentative greeting. "Hi."

He cut right to the chase. "I don't want you to apologize just because your grandmother made you."

My eyes narrowed. "I don't do anything just because someone tells me to."

He raised his eyebrows. "True enough." Unfolding his arms, he jerked his head toward the stacks. "Let's get out of the lobby."

I followed him up some steps and through the rabbit warren of the humanities section. The tables and carrels were filled with students, heads diligently bent over their work. I'd used this library for school research, but I hadn't been to the enclosed meeting rooms before. Justin had one to himself; he'd spread his books out over the football field of a table, clearly not inviting company.

"Did you get your paper finished?" I warmed up with some banal small talk.

"Almost." He didn't invite chitchat, either.

"I won't take up too much time then." My nerves were balled up in my stomach, like a wad of Christmas tree lights when you get them out of the box in November. His resolutely blank demeanor gave me no clues how I'd be received. I took a deep breath and plunged into the frigid waters of apology.

"I'm sorry we argued," I said sincerely. "I don't know why I blew things so out of proportion, but once I got going I didn't know how to back up."

His shoulders relaxed; the air in the room seemed to palpably warm. He paused long enough to acknowledge the dodge in my phrasing. "I'm sorry we argued, too."

I took a relieved step forward, my heart lightening. "Thank goodness. I do need you, Justin. Your help, I mean."

A corner of his mouth turned up. That was progress. "I know what you mean."

"I shouldn't blame you because I wanted so desperately to think that someone knew what was going on." I laughed a little too loudly. "I know it's not me."

He shoved his hands in the pockets of his jeans and shook his head. "Your instincts are good, when you listen to them. You knew to throw the salt on the Jessica-shadow."

Sighing, I sank into one of the heavy wooden chairs. "Half of my brain still rejects this as impossible. You were right about that, too."

"No wonder you got so angry." I slanted a suspicious look up at his too-bland tone. He smiled crookedly and sat beside me. "To defeat this thing, you are going to have to commit your left brain, too, Maggie."

I rubbed my hands over my face. "I'm failing, Justin. Two more of the Jocks and Jessicas have fallen."

His hand brushed my shoulder, briefly comforting but not coddling. "Tell me."

"You need to work on your paper."

"It'll wait. Tell me what's happened."

I told him about the picture I took, about Stanley's humiliation, and the clique of six. I described Jessica Prime's breakdown, and Brian's collapse.

"Brian, the guy I met at your house?"

"Yeah." I couldn't help fishing a little. "Why?"

"No reason."

I also told him my theory, which I didn't get to explain on Saturday, that the spirit became more developed, more *real*, with every victim. I saw the telltale tightening of his jaw when I described the thing lurking in my yard.

He rubbed an irritated hand through his hair. "Why do you wait so long to tell me these things?"

209

That was a complicated question, and probably rhetorical anyway, so I went on. "Do you think it could become solid?"

"I don't know. Maybe it's just a sign of its growing power." He shifted through the papers on the table. "I was doing some work yesterday, and I found something. Does this look familiar?"

He set a Xeroxed photo in front of me. Color pictures never copy well, but I could still make out the wide, flat bowl with etchings along the rim. "That's the thingy from my dream! Where did you find it?"

"In the catalog of the university's archives. The brazier was found on an expedition to Mesopotamia back in the sixties."

I picked up the paper to study the symbols more closely. I had to squint. "Where is Mesopotamia, exactly?"

"It *was* between the Tigris and Euphrates rivers."

Those were names I'd heard on the news. "Where Iraq is now?"

He nodded. "My adviser, Dr. Dozer, did some expeditions there, before the last regime made that impossible."

"So on the edges here— Is that writing between the hatch mark things?"

"Yes, but the hatch mark things are letters, too. Cuneiform, one of the most ancient forms of writing. The squiggly looking bits are the language that replaced it. Kind of a proto-Hebrew."

I scrunched my brows in memory. "In the dream where I saw this, there was a big, biblical-looking village in an oasis. Some wild animal had killed a young man." I traced the picture with my finger. "But maybe he was the victim of the same curse. Someone cast it then, like someone is casting it now."

"Well, quinine hadn't been discovered yet. But everything else had." He pulled forward another book, flipped to a page he'd marked. "Most cultures have some notion of an evil spirit, something to blame for the random tragedies of life. The ancient Babylonians had a demon for everything—bad crops, bad weather, bad health."

He showed me a picture of a very ancient worn statue or fetish. "Is that one of them?" Just barely man-shaped, the thing reminded me of the quasi-human form the Shadow had taken.

"Possibly. This statue represents a personal god. They were supposed to serve an individual's interests, so I guess benevolence and malevolence could be relative." He reached over and tapped the photocopy. "What if this artifact actually invokes someone's demigod or demon?"

I rubbed my hands over my arms, my T-shirt completely inadequate for the air-conditioning. "Can you read the letters? Or do you know someone who can?"

"Not from that photo."

"What about from the actual artifact?"

Justin gave an ominous sigh. "I got permission to go to the archives, but the brazier wasn't there. Just a 'removed for cleaning' card."

My fingers fiddled with the copied page. "I wrote down what I remembered from my dream. Not the cuneiform—I thought that was just decorative. But I think I got the others right."

"I can find someone to translate them," he said with more excitement than I felt.

"Not Dr. Dozer."

Justin sat back in his chair. "You can't honestly think she might be cursing her son's classmates."

"No." I framed my suspicion obliquely. "But I know how much I pick up from my dad, just living in the same house."

"You didn't even know where Mesopotamia was."

"I knew it was in the Middle East somewhere, smarty-pants." I pushed out of the chair and started pacing. "It's too much of a coincidence that Stanley is connected to all the victims *and* the brazier."

"Well, you can't just march up to him and accuse him of cursing his classmates."

I paused to imagine the scenario and admitted, "Okay, I guess I can't. Not with only circumstantial evidence, anyway." How could I find out if he'd bought wormwood or quinine? You could get just about anything off the Internet, but unless I had either his computer or a Dozer-family credit card number, I was at an investigative dead end.

Justin watched me, reading the thoughts on my face; I'm not exactly Ms. Impassive. "Maggie." His eyes were sober, his tone cautious. "If it *is* Stanley, you should be careful not to let him know you suspect him. It would be easy for him to set the demon on you."

My hand crept up to clasp my necklace. "I'm not in the picture. I'm not part of the pattern."

"But you are. You're behind the camera." I blinked in shock. I hadn't thought of that. Were we back to Karen taking my place on the diving board?

He seemed to regret pointing out the connection I was too close to see. "I'm sorry. But I want you to be careful."

I tucked my hair behind my ear in a determined motion.

"I'm not trying to antagonize it. But it's hard to try and *stop* a thing without making it, you know, a little pissed."

"I realize that." He rose and took my fidgeting hand. "I'm not trying to be overprotective. But it's hard to know you're in danger and not be able to do something about it."

How strange, that a little thing like a hand could be the center of so much feeling. The nerves on the back of it where his fingertips brushed, in the palm securely wrapped in his, fired like sparklers. The sensation rushed up my arm and alighted, fizzling, in the middle of my chest.

"You put all those charms on my room," I said. "You put that salt in my purse. I'm not sure I'd be here if you hadn't. The fumes . . ." I broke off. I didn't like to think about that.

He shook his head. "But I'm just shooting in the dark. That's why I got so angry on Saturday. I wish I knew exactly what would protect you. But I can only make my best guess."

I glanced at the books and papers taking up eighteen square feet of table. "I think your best guess is better than a lot of people's certainties."

His smile warmed me from the inside out—crooked, rueful, and unwittingly charming. "Yeah, but it's not the same thing as riding in on a white charger."

I laughed, precisely because I could picture him doing just that. Justin was a throwback to another age. A scholar knight.

"I'm not much of a damsel in distress, though. Too mouthy."

"Too stubborn," he nodded.

He didn't have to agree quite so quickly. Not that I wanted to be a damsel in distress, of course. "So what do we do now?"

He looked at the books on the table and sighed. "I have to finish my paper tonight. Send me the letters you wrote down. Your dad can give it to me in class tomorrow. Meanwhile, note down everything in your dreams. And watch out for Stanley. And keep an eye on the last guy. What's his name?"

"Brandon." I frowned. "I wonder why nothing has happened to him yet."

"If I were a guy who'd been beaten up and humiliated by someone for years, I'd definitely save the big kahuna for last."

"Good point." Justin seemed to have accepted my theory of Stanley-as-puppetmaster.

He wrote "Still in use" on a piece of notebook paper and stuck it on top of his pile of books. "I'll walk you out to your car."

"You don't have to do that. You need to get back to work."

"Look, I know you don't need a white knight, but at least let me be a gentleman."

I gave a sheepish grimace, and agreed.

We left the library, winding back through the maze, past the dedicated students with their laptops clicking and pens scratching. On the short walk to the parking lot, Justin and I talked about college, and the pleasant night, and anything other than demons and curses and gangly, vengeful nerds. We reached the Jeep too quickly, and he saw me buckled in and on my way before returning to his work. It was just a few minutes of peace in the turmoil of the week before, and it would have been perfect, if only he'd taken my hand again.

✳ ✳ ✳

I went to bed with both determination and dread, certain I'd meet Old Smokey in my dreams. I woke the next morning to the brain-melting beep of the alarm clock, tired and grumpy, but without any recollection of a vision or nightmare. Grumbling all the way, I schlepped into a hot shower, and stood under the spray until the cobwebs began to clear from my head and the bathroom was thick with steam.

Turning off the water, I reached for my towel, wrapping it around myself while I grabbed another one to wipe away the fog from the mirror.

The sweep of the cloth revealed nothing but roiling black mist and a pair of sulfurous yellow eyes, blazing out at me from the glass.

23

i screamed. Shrieked like the most girly, helpless damsel on the planet. I fell against the bathroom door, fumbling with the knob, whimpering and struggling like a rabbit in a snare. Steam hung in the air, stroked my skin. The demon didn't have to touch me; I was going to give *myself* a heart attack. My heart beat against my ribs like a caged bird—just like I beat against the bathroom door.

Footsteps thundered up the stairs, then the door flew open. I tumbled out, catching my towel close around me, staggering to stay on my feet.

"Close the door! Close the door!" I yelled.

Dad slammed the door closed. "What the Hell?"

"Yes. Exactly. Oh my God, it was in the mirror." I jab-
bered like a madwoman. "It has eyes now, and it was in the
mirror."

"What are you talking about, Maggie? What has eyes?"

"The thing! The smoke thing from my dream!" My pulse
still pounded. I could feel it in my brain, in my vital organs.
"Get away from the door!"

He moved away, but only to get the afghan from my bed.
Until he wrapped it around my shoulders, I hadn't known
how icy cold my skin was. "It sounds like you were still
dreaming," he said worriedly.

"I didn't dream last night." I could not drag my eyes
away from the painted wood panels of the bathroom door.

"Mike?" Mom's worried voice floated up the stairs.
"What's going on? Is she all right?"

Dad gave me a look and called back in answer. "She's
okay. She says a mouse ran across her foot."

"That's absurd. We don't have mice."

"So I'm telling her."

Indignation helped chase away panic. "I'm not afraid
of mice."

"Do you want me to tell your mother you think you saw a
smoke monster in the bathroom?"

I pictured that scene and answered, "No, I guess not."

He rubbed a reassuring hand over my back. "Maybe you
did dream, and got in the shower still half asleep."

"Yeah." That actually made some sense. More sense than
Old Smokey getting past all my defenses and into the bathroom. I wrapped the afghan more tightly and shuddered,

but the blind, flailing terror had abated. "Now I feel a little silly. It must have been just a dream. Sorry, Dad."

"Don't worry about it, Magpie." He hugged me in tight reassurance. "Do you want me to open the door before I go?"

If we saw nothing, I would feel even more foolish. If something was there, I didn't want it to see my dad. "No. I'm good."

"Actually," he looked a little sheepish, "it will make *me* feel better."

He smiled, but I saw him surreptitiously wipe sweaty palms on his trousers.

"Okay. But wait a second." I grabbed the canister of salt that still sat on the nightstand. Pouring a handful into my palm, I indicated with a jerk of my head that he should open the door while I stood ready to fire at whatever lurked inside.

Dad and I had seen the same action movies, so he got into place, all very *Lethal Weapon*. I mouthed, "One, two, three!" and he yanked open the door so hard it banged into the wall, showering plaster onto the carpet. The crash startled me, and I flung my barrage of salt into the bathroom with a stifled squeak.

Nothing waited inside. Only the humid blanket of air left over from my shower. The last of the condensation cleared from the mirror with the rush of air. There was no black smoke, no burning eyes. Not even a whiff of brimstone, just the clean, herbal scent of my shampoo. Well, plus the mess of salt on the floor.

"I'm getting too old for this shit," said Dad, making me laugh, mostly with relief. He examined the big hole the doorknob had made in the wall. "Your mom is going to kill us."

"I'll move the bookshelf over until we can fix it."

He didn't say anything about the empty bathroom. "I'll have the coffee ready when you get down." He went downstairs, and I heard Mom at the bottom ask him, "What in heaven's name are you two doing up there?" and Dad answer placidly, "Looking for the mouse."

For the record, I was never afraid of mice. I was, however, worried I'd slipped a mental gear.

* * *

When I got to English, Lisa ambushed me, dragging me back out into the hall where the noise of students hurrying to their first-period classes covered our voices.

"What is going on with you?" Hands on her hips, she glared down at me. She wore a black-and-red blouse I hadn't seen since her Goth days, and though she'd paired it with faded blue jeans, the severe color still made her look very pale. "I tried to call you until eleven, and you didn't answer."

"I was in the college library. The reception is bad there." I shifted my heavy backpack. She hadn't even let me put my stuff down. "Why didn't you leave voice mail?"

A sophomore glanced at us curiously as she got her books out of her locker. Lisa grabbed me by the arm and pulled me a few doors down. "I heard about Brian. Why are you always around when these things happen? You have got to . . . I don't know." She pressed her fingers over her eyes. "You can't do that anymore."

"There *aren't* any more," I said. "Only Brandon. He's the last one."

She dropped her hands and stared at me. "The last what?"

"The last— Man, this sounds so crazy when I say it out loud." I whispered back, keeping our heads close together. "Remember I told you yesterday, I thought all these freaky things were connected? Well, Brandon is the last link in the chain."

Lisa shook her head in denial. "You have lost it. They may call me D and D Lisa, but at least I know the difference between fantasy and reality."

Ouch. I didn't quite flinch. "I know it sounds wild."

"It sounds certifiably insane!" She didn't bother to lower her voice now. "Paranoid and delusional."

I snapped back. "Maybe you could use the intercom. I don't think the whole school heard." She clamped her jaw in annoyance, but at least she stopped yelling.

"Look," I said as reasonably as I could, "it sounds crazy because you don't know the whole story. I haven't told you what's been going on, because, well, I know it's unbelievable."

She fell back against the lockers, folding her arms across her slim body. "You couldn't have left me happily in the dark?"

"Not with you getting up in my grill the second I walked in the door!" The hall was clearing; I didn't have much time to cajole her onto my team. "I'm telling you now. The fact is, I could really use your devious brain."

She stared at me for a hard moment. Then the bell rang, and she was forced into a decision. "After school?"

"Yeah. My house."

"There'd better be snacks."

I had to go out to the Jeep at lunchtime and find my chemistry lab book. Used to be, if you came to Professor Blackthorne's class unprepared, you had to wear the Molecule Hat, an absurd thing made out of Nerf balls and Tinkertoys. But a parent had complained that this was damaging to the students' self-esteem, so rather than be liable for a lot of expensive psychiatric therapy, the administration nixed the hat. Now unprepared students had to copy out the periodic table.

I didn't have the patience for charting elements, which is why I was in a mostly empty parking lot when Brandon cornered me between my Wrangler and an Explorer the size of Nebraska.

"Heya, Quinn." He filled the gap between the cars. To my rear, someone had parked their Mazda across two spaces, blocking any graceful exit. Bravado it was, then.

"Hi, Biff. No backup today?"

"Like I would need backup to talk to you." He leaned his mammoth shoulders against the SUV. "But now that you mention it, I *have* noticed that my friends aren't doing too well, lately."

"Oh really?" I decided to play dumb, which was an ironic reversal for any conversation with Brandon. "What could that possibly have to do with me?"

"You tell me." He walked forward, tall and muscular, a lot bigger than me. But even more unnerving was his confidence, his certainty that he could get away with things that ordinary people couldn't.

"You interviewed Jessica for the paper," he said, "and then

she lost her voice right before the play. You fought with Jess on Friday, and Saturday she got caught shoplifting. You were around before Jeff crashed the Mustang and you were there when Jessica got taken to the nuthouse. And now Brian."

"That's a fascinating recap, Brandon." The book retrieved, I swung my heavy backpack onto my shoulder with a whump. "You could write for *Paranoia Digest*, if there was such a thing and it wouldn't require some literacy." I stepped toward the exit, willing him to get out of my way. "There's no way I could be responsible for those things happening to your friends."

"Well, I was thinking about what Jess said that night of the play." He didn't budge, just folded his arms, making his broad chest look even more impassable. "Maybe you *are* a witch."

Laughing was probably not my smartest move. It really pissed him off. Go figure.

He moved fast, pushing me up against the SUV, his arms trapping me on either side, blocking escape.

I stopped laughing, and got pissed, too. "Get off me, asshole."

"Make me, Quinn."

"If I am a witch, what's to stop me from shriveling your testicles into raisins with my evil eye?"

His beefy forearms braced against my shoulders. I could smell his deodorant, see the flecks in his irises as he leaned down to look me in the eye. A dominance ploy. If I squirmed, he would win.

"I don't believe any of that magical bullshit," he said.

"But there's nut jobs that'll buy any rumor that goes around. It doesn't have to be true to royally screw up your life."

My stomach knotted. Witch hunts scared me. Not for the obvious reasons, but because they were so irrational that there was no defense against them. But I couldn't actually be hanged for a witch. Could I? I wouldn't put anything past the Republicans.

"What do you want, Brandon?" I bit the words out.

"I want those pictures to disappear. The ones you took of me and Dozer."

"Is that all?" A smart guy would have demanded to know what was happening to his friends, or worried he might be next. But you don't have to be smart to be a bully. "Sure. Whatever."

"And if they show up in anyone's e-mail—"

"It's a stalemate. I get it." He still had me cornered against the Explorer, and didn't look ready to move. "Are we done?"

His eyes narrowed, summing me up, and I realized we weren't done, because what he really wanted wasn't for those pictures to vanish, but for me to be scared of him.

"Well," he began, leaning in closer, "I'd like to know why Brian has been panting after you all of a sudden." Elbows against the car, he pinned me with his weight. "You got some hidden talent, Quinn?"

I dropped my fifty-pound backpack on his foot. When he bent over, cursing, I slammed my knee up into his gut. He was lucky, because I was aiming for the place where he kept his brain.

"You bitch!" he wheezed, the wind knocked out of him.

"Oh, *I'm* the dog?" I yelled, because I *was* scared of him, and I was furious with him for making me feel that way. "I thought you were just a bully, Brandon, not an oversexed sociopath."

"What's going on here?" That ringing voice could only mean Halloran. Oh, yeah. The screwing continues.

"Nothing, Mr. Halloran," said Brandon, trying to stand up straight.

"Nothing except sexual harassment," I said, still livid. "Maybe even assault."

"Now, Margaret. I'm sure there's just been a misunderstanding." The assistant principal made a placating gesture. "These mix-ups can happen between young men and women."

I stood trapped between him and Biff, and I didn't like the symbolism any more than the fact. "I don't think so, Mr. Halloran."

"And now you've gone and overreacted." He oozed soothing condescension. Brandon didn't even bother to fake innocence; he just smirked. Sure, I'd hit him, but not before he'd seen my fear.

"I'm going to overreact all the way to the school board if you don't get out of my way."

"There's no need for that," said Halloran, still trying to convince me we were all good friends.

I slung my bag over my shoulder and marched forward. He moved aside, proving he was at least a fraction of a point smarter than Brandon.

24

I pulled a steaming bag of popcorn out of the microwave just as Lisa called to say she couldn't come over. She had an appointment she couldn't change. "Just don't do anything stupid until we talk," she said, with traffic noise in the background. "Other people have noticed that you're always around when stuff happens. So stay away from Brandon, and don't talk crazy to anyone."

"Yes, my liege. Right now I'd rather take a chum bath in a shark tank than go near Brandon Rogers."

"I have to shut up and drive now. See you tomorrow."

Mom came in as I hung up. "Company coming?" she

asked, probably because I'd put the popcorn in a bowl instead of eating it out of the bag.

"Lisa was supposed to, but something came up."

"That's too bad." She took it as permission to raid from the snack bowl.

"Do you want a Coke?" I asked.

"A diet. Thanks." Mom sat on one of the barstools. She eats popcorn one piece at a time, but I prefer it by the handful. "Lisa is an interesting girl," she said.

"That's one way to describe her."

"Well, I didn't know what to think when you started hanging around with her back in junior high, when she wore nothing but black and had all that spiky jewelry."

I popped the top on my soda. "She grew out of that phase."

"Well, not completely. She was still wearing striped socks the last time I saw her."

"Yes, but they weren't *black*. And neither is her hair."

Mom waved that aside. "Anyway. I just mean that I think it's neat that she's going to be valedictorian. And has a full scholarship to Georgetown. That must make her dad so proud. He worked hard to raise her on his own."

My hand froze over the popcorn bowl. By mentioning the scholarship, had Mom just jinxed Lisa, too? She wasn't in the bully picture, but she had AP calculus with Stanley and Karen. In my last dream, they'd been standing next to each other. Did that mean anything?

That user's manual would come in real handy right now.

"Is Lisa going to the prom?"

I shelved my worries for the moment. "I don't know,

Mom. We don't talk about the You-Know-What. We made a pact."

"You could go together, if you didn't want to mess with dates and things."

"I don't want to mess with the prom at all, Mom."

She ignored me, placidly eating popcorn, piece by piece. "Some girls in my high school class did that and had a wonderful time. They weren't lesbians or anything. Not that it would matter if they were."

"That's nice, Mom. I'm glad you're so open-minded." I grabbed my Coke can and the popcorn bowl and headed for the stairs, because I could go my whole life without ever hearing my mother talk about lesbians again.

"Maybe you could take Justin to the prom," she called after me, laughter in her voice. "He is such a hottie."

Shoot me now.

✳   ✳   ✳

I was doing the last edit of my English paper when I heard footsteps on the stairs. "Come on up." Saving the document, I turned to greet Justin. "I didn't hear the doorbell."

He climbed the last steps, looking exhausted. I wondered if he'd stayed up all night working. "Your mom was heading out. She said I could come in."

"Did you get your paper done?"

"Yeah." He fell onto the battered sofa. A burgundy slipcover hid a multitude of sins, including burnt-orange-and-brown-striped upholstery that was older than me. "Done, turned in. Now I'm free until finals."

"Cool."

He opened his own backpack and pulled out a folded

sheet of paper. "I e-mailed a friend and asked him to translate the letters you drew."

I scooted the desk chair closer to look. "That was fast."

"He's got a degree in biblical history, so he knew right where to look in the library."

"Not the public library, I assume."

"No, Henry's in seminary, studying to be a priest."

My eyebrows climbed. "Really?"

"Yeah. We went to high school together."

"Catholic school?"

"Yes," he said. My bemusement must have shown, because he asked, "Why is that surprising?"

"It isn't. Your love of khaki trousers and oxford shirts should have been my first clue."

He gestured to the paper, where he'd jotted down normal letters under the strange ones I'd sketched. "You want to see what I found out?"

I did, but I wasn't done with this line of inquiry just yet. "Do you still go to Mass?"

"Sometimes." He answered matter-of-factly, then pointed to my crucifix. "What about you?"

"Not in a long time." I chewed my lip, uncertainly. "Do you think it matters? I believe in God. I'm just not sure about the outward trappings, you know?"

"I do know." He contemplated my question. "I think that faith—in something bigger that yourself, no matter what form it takes—gives you a certain spiritual or psychic protection. If, say, the room caught on fire, it might not keep you from burning . . ."

"It did for Shadrach, Meshach, and the other guy."

"I said it *might* not. Can I make my point here?"

"Sure."

He seemed to reorganize his thoughts. "Bible stories aside, faith can't keep you from burning, but it might give you calm to, say, think of a way to put the fire out or escape. If you were under spiritual attack, however . . ."

"Like if a demon made me think I was on fire?"

That earned me a suspicious look, justified, since that was one of those things I'd neglected to mention. "Exactly like that. You might be able to see through the illusion, and overcome it. So I guess it depends. Is your evil a spiritual or physical construct? Personally, I do believe in miracles. But physics is physics so I always wear my seat belt."

I touched the small, gold cross that had become a talisman to me. Not of a religion, but of my strengthening conviction that if there was Evil with a capital E then there must be Good with a capital G, and I wanted to be on its side.

"Can we get back to work?" Justin asked.

"Sure." I took the paper from him and frowned at the letters. M A E L A Z. "I think it made more sense in Mesopotamian."

Justin pulled out the copied catalog page. "The problem is, the symbols go in a circle, and you can't tell exactly where to start reading."

"Let's see what happens when we Google it." I rolled over to the desk and opened the browser. On the search engine's main page I typed in: "maelaz." Google helpfully asked if I meant "Maalox."

"I guess that's a no." Next I typed: "Aelazm." The Internet netted nothing.

Justin leaned on the back of my chair, peering over my

shoulder. I was distracted for a moment by the warmth of his arm brushing mine. "Keep the first three letters together," he suggested. "Move them all to the back."

I typed in: "Azmael." The search engine churned for a moment and finally displayed a page of links to archaeology and anthropology sites. "Look!" I said, because I'm a dork when detective work pays off. "A site about ancient Babylon. That's in Mesopotamia."

"Yeah." He didn't look nearly as happy.

"How did you know to put the 'ael' at the end?"

"El was the top dog god to a lot of people in the region. The 'ael' would mean 'of El.'"

I clicked on the link. The hard drive spun and clicked as the page tried to load. "It must have a lot of graphics. My computer hates bells and whistles."

The whirring intensified, but the browser window remained dark. I felt Justin tense behind me. "Close the window, Maggie."

I clicked the mouse, but nothing happened. "It's locked up."

"Force quit the program."

The Internet had taken my computer hostage. "It's not quitting." I smelled ozone and burning plastic and my voice cracked in panic. "It's not doing *anything*."

Smoke poured out of the CD slot on the front of the tower and I jerked back, thinking phantom. But no. Just plain old burn-your-house-down fire.

"Get down." Justin pulled me out of the chair as the monitor exploded in a shower of glass. He reached under the desk and yanked the surge protector from the wall, then scrambled back as the CPU began to melt, flames licking out of the case.

The smoke detector went off, piercing my ears. I half-crawled into the bathroom and grabbed the little fire extinguisher from under the counter. I'd never used it before, so I struggled to read the instructions with the fire alarm turning my brain to Jell-O. Justin grabbed the extinguisher from me. He turned something, pointed the nozzle, pressed something else; frosty mist and foam shot out at the flames.

He emptied the entire canister, continuing to spray even after the last flicker disappeared. Finally I climbed onto the chair and turned off the screaming alarm.

My ears rang in the sudden silence. I jumped off the chair and joined him, staring at the melted hulk of the CPU. "I guess that's what you call a physical construct."

"Yeah."

"At least we got the word figured out." He turned to look at me, and I wondered if my expression mirrored his dazed look. I felt numb. "My mom is going to blow a gasket."

He slid a comforting arm around my shoulder. "It could have been worse."

I nodded, and rested my head against him. The desk was scorched, but otherwise the fire hadn't gone farther than the computer. Of course, the peripherals were all shot: the printer, the scanner, and . . . A bone-deep chill seized me, followed by a rush of liquid-hot fury through my veins.

"My English paper was on that computer! Ten thousand words, up in flames! That bastard!"

"Didn't you back it up?"

I blistered my fingers pulling a misshapen lump of plastic from the USB port. I held up the ex–flash drive and Justin's dark brown eyes softened with exquisite sympathy as he echoed, "That bastard."

25

I woke facedown on the kitchen table, with Dad's hand gently shaking my shoulder. "Hey, kiddo. Did you get your paper done?"

My thoughts struggled upstream against the current of exhaustion. Rewrites. Dad's laptop. Parental freak-out over the fire. My paper going up in smoke. Oh yeah. I remembered that.

"Yeah." I creaked upright and tried to straighten my neck. "Just need to print it out."

"What time did you fall asleep?"

"More like passed out, I think." I rubbed a desert's worth of grit from my eyes. "Maybe four?"

"Go take a shower. I'll print your paper and you can do another proofread before school."

I dragged myself up the stairs and turned on the shower, then went to get clean clothes while the water heated up. When I came back, I was so sleepy, it took me a moment to be surprised by my name written in the fog on the mirror.

Hello, Magdalena was what it said.

I've got to remember to turn on the vent fan was the first thing that came to my mind.

And then my brain caught up, and dread crawled over my skin. The thing knew my name. That couldn't be good.

Maybe I was dreaming, still lying facedown in a puddle of my own drool, having a nightmare. I closed my eyes, but it was much worse *not* seeing what I knew was there.

The rivulets of condensation that dripped from the letters reminded me of too many horror movies. Steeling myself, I wiped away the fog. Acid yellow eyes stared at me, and I flinched back, but didn't scream.

The black smoke drifted in the mirror like a negative reflection of the steam in the bathroom. I cast no reflection, but the sulfur-colored orbs floated where my head would be. Fear skittered over my nerve endings, but I was also pissed at the whole Peeping Tom routine, not to mention the destruction of my Senior Theme.

"How do you know my name, you smoky bastard?" I growled at it without expecting an answer, like you growl at the car when it won't start. So my heart lurched against my ribs when a reply appeared in the quickly refogging mirror: *Summoner knows.*

The summoner knew my name. Super.

"Then what the"—I edited myself under the circumstances—"heck are you doing here? What do you want?"

See you.

"Great. Just what I always wanted. A stalker." A semiliterate one at that.

You see me. The words appeared above the first ones. I saw the demon, so Old Smokey wanted to see me. I got it. It was scary how I got it.

"Well, I don't want to see you, so bug off."

In a new patch of fog appeared: *Soon you'll fear.*

"Why not now?" Stupid question. I was pretty darned scared, at the moment.

Not allowed.

Everything has rules, Dr. Smyth had said. You just have to know what they are.

Soon, it wrote. *Magdalena.*

There was a huge power in a name. I wasn't simply scared that it knew mine. I was sickened. I wanted to curl into a ball and just give up. Soon, it said. The taunting and toying would end, and I would be dead or wish I was.

Soon, but not yet. The mirror was like the dream, I realized. A spiritual construct. I took a deep breath of the steamy air and let the panic run out of me, leaving space for rational thought.

What came instead was an irrational idea. I put my own finger to the fog and wrote: "Azmael." The eyes recoiled. "Get out of my bathroom, you stinky son of a bitch."

The blackness in the mirror twisted and contorted in fury, and then turned in on itself and disappeared, leaving the word *Soon* superimposed on my pallid reflection.

✳　✳　✳

I called Justin from the car on the way to school, waking him up. "It's the name."

"What?" he asked groggily.

"It's the thing's name. I think I may have banished it." I explained what had happened with the mirror. By the time I was finished, he sounded completely awake.

"I don't think you banished it completely," he said. "But you found a way to control its spiritual presence."

"What do you think it means that it can't get at me now, but soon it will?"

"I think it's what you said. The demon is getting stronger with each victim. The last one might not only make him solid, but also free him from constraint."

"Yikes," I said.

"That would be bad," he agreed.

"How do we know the magic number?"

"We don't know. When he finishes the list maybe. Or perhaps there's a numerology thing. I'll read up on it."

"I'm having Lisa over to my house this afternoon since she couldn't come yesterday. Can you be there?"

"Sure. No point in studying for finals on Monday when the town might be invaded by a demon before then."

"I like your sense of perspective." I pulled into the parking lot. "See you then." I grabbed my backpack and made it inside with little time to spare. It was amazing how bandying words with the Hell-spawn could eat into your morning.

✳ ✳ ✳

I told Ms. Vincent about the fire, and asked her if I could have until the afternoon to proofread the paper one more time. She replied coldly, "You shouldn't have waited to the last minute, then."

A thousand arguments sprang to my tongue, but I'd already dealt with one demon today, so I simply laid the paper on her desk and took my seat.

Lisa watched me drop into the seat beside her. "You look like crap."

"Thanks. Battling the forces of darkness will do that to you."

"If you mean Vincent, I agree."

We settled in. I wondered if Vincent was going to actually teach for once. I could use a nap.

"Hey, Lisa," I said. "Are you going to the prom?"

"Yeah. Tessa and Katie and I are going stag. We didn't ask you to join us, because we knew you'd rather die."

"I wonder if Stanley ever got a date."

"He's going with Suzie Miller. You know from the play?"

"Really?" I was stunned. Suzie was so cute, and riding her five minutes of fame. She was going to the prom with *Stanley*?

When the bell rang, Vincent rose and came to the front of the room, straightening her cardigan—apple red with school buses for the pockets. No lie. "Today," she said, "we start your last novel of the year. Fittingly, as you end one segment of your life and begin a new one, we will read *Brave New World*."

She paused, as if for applause. At the smattering of murmurs and groans, she set her mouth in a thin line and went to the shelves to hand out books.

"Have you read *Brave New World*?" Lisa asked me.

"Doesn't the future world kind of . . . suck?"

"I think that sums it up pretty well."

✳ ✳ ✳

At lunch, I had a table to myself, which was not that unusual, but everyone kept staring at me, which . . . well, was becoming more common.

Halfway through my doughy burrito, a girl I'd never met plopped into the seat across from me. I actually did a double-take, because this—the jet-black hair with pale roots, the black nail polish—was Lisa's old look before she'd given up monochrome as a lifestyle choice.

This girl had a pentagram hanging from a leather strap around her neck. She set her elbows on the table and asked avidly, "Is it true you're a witch?"

"*Excuse* me?"

"They're saying you cursed the Jocks and Jessicas. Is it true?" I stared at her stupidly. "If it is, you can tell me. I won't hold it against you. I mean, those stuck-up posers . . ."

"You should be careful." Another girl stood beside me. Unlike her dark counterpart, she was dressed in a flowing pastel blouse over jeans and flip-flops. She looked like a hippie and smelled of incense. "You know the Wicca Rede."

"The what now?" My fork full of burrito hung midair. From my hand, I mean. Not levitating. Considering the company, maybe I should make that clear.

"The first rule of the White Path: 'An' it harm none . . .'"

"What's that in English?"

"Do what you want, as long as it harms no one." Flowers-and-Light Girl sat down beside me, but not before shooting Pentagram Poser a glare. "Whenever you cast a spell to do harm to someone, it will come back on you, three times as bad."

"Yeah, well." I dropped my fork onto my tray. "That sucks for someone, but not for me. I didn't do anything to anyone."

Wicca girl put her hand on my arm. "I sense a terrible darkness around you."

That shook me slightly, but then I realized . . . duh. "Yeah, they call it high school."

Her mouth detoured into a sulking frown before she rerouted it into a smile. "When you are ready to admit your wrongdoing, my friends and I can help you. We can cleanse your aura and help you remove the negative energy . . ."

"Well," said Goth girl across the table, "if you're ready to rock and roll, *my* friends and I are down with that."

"Thank you both." I climbed over the bench and grabbed my tray. "I'll look for you where the freaks come out at night."

"Blessed be!" Hippie chick called after me.

I started to say something rude but then figured, what the heck. I needed all the blessings I could get.

Heading out of the cafeteria and into the courtyard, I ran into Stanley. Only as I stumbled back and muttered automatic apologies, it took me a moment to recognize him.

I'd been thinking a lot about Stanley over the last few days but I hadn't actually *seen* him since Friday. I stared, trying to figure out what he'd changed. And then I realized, nothing much. He'd gotten some clothes that fit—that was the biggest difference. Other than that: skinny, pale, insanely tall, drab, colorless hair. Check. No briefcase, but otherwise, that was Dozer.

But looking at him was like watching a DVD when you've been used to VHS. He looked sharper, more alive. I couldn't explain it better than that. His shoulders were back, his head was up. And he was *smirking* at me.

"Meet some new friends, Maggie?"

"Don't even go there. I had to rewrite my entire English paper last night because of you."

He looked genuinely surprised. "Because of me?"

"Yeah." I forgot I wasn't supposed to antagonize him. "You look good, Stanley. Walking around with five less bullies on your case must agree with you."

His eyes narrowed. "It would agree with anyone. Maybe I should thank you for casting that magic spell everyone is talking about."

"That's bunk and you know it."

"Do I?" He smiled. It was an expression I'd never seen on Stanley's face. He looked like a cat with a mouthful of canary feathers and whiskers coated in cream. "Unless you mean that the idea of magic is bunk, and then I agree. I mean, you'd have a real hard time proving something like that."

"You have no idea what you're dealing with, Dozer."

"Right now, I'm dealing with a runtish busybody and, according to some people, a jealous witch." He waggled his fingers and took off. "Buh-bye, Maggie."

At least I didn't have to wonder anymore. He did it. The power had given him a burst of confidence equal to any magic spell. The old Stanley could never have gotten the last word with me.

I hoped he enjoyed it while it lasted. Because I had a feeling that when the demon got loose, it wasn't going to be too happy with the guy holding the leash.

26

"It was the eyes that got me." Lisa and Justin and I sat in my study. I'd lit some candles—I was trying to clear the smell, not my aura—and the aroma of fresh baked cookies reminded me of Gran's house, and feeling safe. It made it easier, slightly, to talk about things like demons and curses.

Lisa's body language made it more difficult, though. She sat on the sofa with both her arms and her legs crossed, a scowl of rejection on her face. "The smell of brimstone, Mags? Doesn't that seem a little cliché?"

"Clichés have to come from somewhere, don't they?"

"But a demon." She glanced at Justin, and then back at

me. "You two realize we live in the squarest town on the planet, right? And you think this thing is a *demon*?"

Justin, sitting in my desk chair, read from the e-mail he'd received from his friend. He'd brought his laptop since my computer had undergone a meltdown.

"According to Henry, Azmael was a minor Babylonian demon. He mentions that the concept of 'demon' wasn't necessarily bad. It basically meant it was a spirit. Like those personal gods we talked about, Maggie."

Lisa stopped jiggling her crossed legs and relaxed her tightly folded arms. "So this thing might not even be evil. It might just be doling out justice."

"Karen Foley wasn't doing anybody any harm," I said.

"Maybe she was just an accident?"

"It's connected. But I'm not sure how." I picked up the sheet with the symbols. "There are six letters in its name. There were six in the clique, three Jocks, three Jessicas. I thought maybe when it reached six, it would be real, or free, or whatever. But judging by this morning, no."

"Maybe it's one plus," Justin suggested.

"Or two plus, or three." Lisa returned to foot jiggling. "Maybe it's like . . . roulette, or something."

Justin met my eye and shrugged. "It could be that as easily as anything else."

I rubbed my forehead, as if I could massage out the answer. "Maybe it's not just the number of victims, but how much juice it gets off each one."

Lisa rose from the couch and paced restlessly. "This just keeps getting grosser and grosser."

I half regretted bringing her in. She was the smartest

person I knew, but she was having a lot more trouble accepting this than I expected from someone called D&D Lisa.

Justin turned my thoughts back to business. "What do you mean, juice?"

"Why tailor everyone's tragedy to bring the most fear and loss? There must be a purpose to all that angst. Maybe that's what the thing is feeding on, what's making it stronger."

"Pretty sophisticated for an ancient Babylonian evil spirit." Justin cast an eye toward the sheet-covered mirror in the bathroom.

"It's pretty sophisticated for Stanley," I said. "I wouldn't think him capable of crafting something like Jessica Prime's breakdown. But if the demon knows what the summoner knows, maybe it picked up enough to make its own choices."

Justin leaned forward, elbows on his knees. "So, when will it be? What does your gut tell you?"

"That it is very close. That one more victim will hit the jackpot."

"I see . . ." Lisa put a hand over her eyes and held the other out straight-armed, with stage magician drama. ". . . a trip to Las Vegas in our future."

"Very funny." The doorbell rang, and I jumped like a cat.

Justin smiled crookedly. "If the demon is solid enough to ring the doorbell, we're in real trouble."

I gave him a that's-not-funny look, and rose to answer the door. Neither of my parents were home yet.

Brian stood on the doorstep, on his own two feet. I exclaimed in delight and gave him an impulsive hug. "You're standing up! I was so worried."

He kept me close longer than I had intended, but not so long that I minded. Only when I stepped back did I notice the cane he carried. "It's not all bad, but it's not all good," he told me. "I need help as the day goes on. But the good news is, it may remit."

My relief faded a little. "What may remit?"

"My medically impossible MS." He said it with a lot more humor than I would have.

"Come in." I backed out of the doorway. "Lisa and Justin are here. We were just talking about what's going on."

"Have you figured it out yet?" He followed me down the hall, toward the living room. I used the travel time to hedge my answer, not knowing quite how much to tell him.

"It's strange and bizarre. Twilight Zone stuff."

"I guessed that much." He stopped beside me, met my eye. "Brandon is next, isn't he?"

"Looks that way." I held his gaze steadily, gauging his fortitude, letting him see mine. "We're going to stop it, somehow. Not because of Brandon, but because of what might be set free if it builds up enough freedom points."

Brian stared at me, not really understanding, but getting the gist. He squared his shoulders, an unconsciously heroic gesture. "Right. We're the good guys. We stop the bad thing, so it doesn't take over the world. Simple enough."

"Man, I wish Lisa were so easy to convince." I gestured to a chair. "Sit. I'll call them down."

He caught my arm before I moved away. "Wait a sec. I want to ask you something."

I paused, curious at the break in his usual confidence.

He'd taken the news about big bad evil with ease. What had him looking so shook up?

"This is embarrassing, because it makes it sound like you're my second choice." He smiled at me, a little sheepish, a little roguish. "And you're not. But I was stuck going with Jess Michaels to the prom, and now she's dumped me, thank God, so I can ask you."

My jaw didn't quite drop, just dipped a little. "You're asking me to the prom? A Jock—"

"Ex-jock," he said, waggling his cane. "Jess didn't want to go with someone who'd had to drop off the baseball team."

"I don't know, Brian. I hadn't planned to go." I wondered if he knew this, or if he'd just assumed I wouldn't have a date.

"Why not?" His surprise answered my question and made me answer *his* more sharply than I meant to.

"It's just so overwrought. All the angst beforehand, about the date and about the dress. All the expectations: How much money will he spend? Will she put out?" I shrugged. "So much wasted emotion on—"

I broke off as a thought struck me, like an Acme Anvil of Inspiration. I stood there, mouth hanging, while the logic rabbits chased each other through my brain. *So much wasted emotion.*

"Maggie?" Brian sounded worried. I held up a wait-a-minute finger and ran to the staircase.

"Hey, guys! Come down, quick!" I shouted up, ignoring for the moment Brian's baffled stare. "Come on!"

Justin and Lisa rushed down the stairs, both of them

stumbling to a halt when they saw Brian. They exchanged awkward "Heys" all around, but I overrode them.

"I know when it's going to happen."

"When what's going to happen?" Brian, confused.

"How can you know that?" Lisa, disbelieving.

"When?" Justin, succinct and to the point.

"The thing feeds on emotion, right? On grief and terror and angst and woe. Where can it find all that in one place?"

They stared at me, varying degrees of comprehension in their faces. "So," began Justin tentatively, "your plan is . . . ?"

"God help me, I'm going to the prom."

27

by suppertime we'd worked out a plan. It maybe wasn't the best plan, but it was the best we could do, considering that by "we" I mostly meant Justin and his theoretical knowledge and me and my freaky intuition. Possibly this meant we were doomed, but that was certainly true if we did nothing, so this was better odds.

Or so I told myself.

Lame as it sounds, my first step in the plan? Buy a dress. As the saying goes, I had nothing to wear.

Lisa came with me to the department store; she had an uncanny gift in the clearance racks. I'd seen her reach into a bargain bin full of polyester seventies-revival rejects and come up with a beautiful silk chemise that everyone had overlooked because it wasn't the current fashion. Which of course didn't matter to Lisa, as long as it looked good on her.

I was counting on this talent as we hit the mall, because this late in the prom season, everything was on sale, and usually for good reason. She sent me to the dressing room with orders to strip, while she went through the racks like Attila the Hun. By the time I was out of my clothes, she had amassed two armloads of gowns for me to try on.

"What's with that?" she asked. I'd draped my clothes over the cubicle's mirror, unsure I'd ever be comfortable in front of a looking glass again. I wondered if Alice spent the rest of her life leery of the Red Queen's reappearance.

"I have issues," I explained succinctly, and took the dress on the top of the pile. "White? I'll look like the bride of Dracula if I wear this."

"Then don't try it on." She whisked the gown out of my hands and replaced it with a purple one. "Maybe you should have come up with an ingenious scheme that didn't involve formal wear."

Lisa did not suffer a witch to whine. I stopped complaining and obediently slithered into the slinky purple monstrosity.

"You don't have to help, you know."

She zipped up the dress before she answered. Just as quickly, she made a face and unzipped it. "It's a crazy plan. But if you're going through with it, I'd better be around to pull your fat out of the fire."

"Please don't say 'fat' while I'm standing here in my underwear."

Ignoring that, she turned to rifle through the sartorial candidates. "Say you're right and this . . . thing is really waiting for the prom to attack Brandon. He's not exactly going to stand still to be the bait."

"He's not bait, exactly." Except he sort of was. "He's just the only known element in a lot of speculation."

"See, that's what I mean. Speculation." She handed over a deep blue dress, ferreted from the bottom of the pile. "Are you sure the salt is effective against it?"

"Yes. I'm certain about that." I'm not sure my muffled voice sounded very convincing as I struggled to extract my head from the smothering folds of satin. I knew I could fight the demon. Whether I could kill it was another thing.

"But salt. That seems so simple."

"There's a folklore precedent." I wrestled the dress into submission. "Justin could explain it."

"That's another thing," she said, tugging the strapless bodice into place with more force than necessary. "If I had a smart, cute guy like Justin at my beck and call, I sure wouldn't be dangling after Brian the Jock."

I turned on her, indignant. "Okay, back up. Dangling after? And what do you mean, my beck and call?"

She put her hands on my shoulders and spun me back around, going to work on the zipper. "Suck it in. I liked this, but they didn't have it in your exact size."

I sucked. "Explain 'beck and call.'"

"I mean that every time you pick up the phone, he comes running."

"He's helping me with this problem. It's an academic exercise—Ow!" She'd pinched my skin in the zipper.

"Sorry. But the thing is, Mags, guys don't do that for an academic exercise. They don't come running when something goes 'bump.' They don't climb on your roof and check for boogeymen. They don't stay up all night researching ancient Mesopotamia, just so they can impress you."

She finished zipping; I couldn't breathe, but I was more concerned about her point. Justin had, in a very short time, made himself invaluable to me. Not just for his intellect, but for his friendship. If he walked out of my life tomorrow, I'd be the worse for it. But I hadn't let myself think—well, not seriously—that he might view me as more than a friend.

"But I'm *not* dangling after Brian."

Lisa rolled her eyes. "All I'm saying is, don't blow the opportunity you have with Justin just because a hot guy totally out of your league suddenly pays attention to you."

"Give me a little credit, Lisa. Brian's backbone is still in the embryonic stages. But he's not like the others."

Her jaw tightened stubbornly, and I knew there was no point in continuing. "They are all made of the same stuff. He's just figured out the way to work you is to let you develop his conscience." She collected the rejected dresses and flung them over the partition. "He's probably got a bet with Brandon that he can get into your pants."

Embarrassment scorched my face. "Trust me. He'd have a better chance getting into the space program than my pants."

She went on as if I hadn't spoken. "Especially now that he's got that cane. He's got to prove something to regain his place in the pack."

The blind edge to her jock-hate distressed me. Not to mention her lack of faith in *my* common sense.

"You think I'm that easy to manipulate?" Hurt and anger threaded through my voice.

"No. But I don't trust any of that crowd not to just take what he wants."

Something in her tone made me look at her, hard and questioning, but I found her gaze turned inward. Though she spoke with an odd conviction, I couldn't include Brian in that. Not that my judgment was so infallible. I just couldn't picture Mr. Don't-Make-Waves taking unwanted liberties, as Gran would say.

But there wasn't any point in arguing with Lisa when she made up her mind about something. As I learned when she announced that the blue satin dress was the one.

"But it's too tight and too long."

"Yes, but it makes your boobs look great and I'll get one of my minions to hem it up tomorrow."

"I can't pay very much."

"If the world doesn't end this weekend, give her one of your Gran's cookie recipes."

✳　✳　✳

School flew by on Friday. Half the senior class was absent, mostly the female contingent. Apparently, the prom takes hours of preparation—hair, makeup, nails, etc. What did I know? When I'd asked my mother to explain the use of cuticle cream to me, I thought she would cry in joy. If I'd realized it would take so little to make her so happy—just one day of shared girly-ness and the opportunity to buy me shoes and proper undergarments—I would have mugged some guy and made him take me on a date a long time ago.

Too bad I was doing it now solely in the cause of fighting Evil. But Mom didn't have to know that.

When I arrived at school Brian was in the crowded courtyard, sitting at one of the tables. He stood when he saw me. "Hey!" I said. "You're not using your cane."

"I don't really need it first thing in the morning." His smile grew forced and I was sorry I'd mentioned it. "Are you all set for tonight?"

"Yeah. I think so." As ready as I could be to face one of my worst nightmares. Not to mention an ancient Babylonian demon.

"I didn't know what color your dress is, so I just got white flowers. Is that all right?"

I stared at him blankly. "Is there some secret code for flowers?"

"No. But Jess— I was told it was important that they match your dress."

"Oh. My dress is blue, so that would be a trick." I ducked automatically to avoid a football, lobbed across the court-yard. "But you didn't have to get me—"

And then I saw his face. Yeah, he *did* have to get me flow-ers, because secret mission or not, he thought I was going as his date. Call me clueless—Lisa would—but I'd been think-ing of my allies as individually wrapped Ding-Dongs, and he'd been thinking two-packs of Twinkies.

Boy, for a smart girl, I could be an idiot sometimes.

"I love flowers," I assured him as the football flew by us in the other direction. I saw the big body hurtling after it, right before Brandon bumped heavily into Brian, knocking him over. I wrapped my arms around him, sort of propping us both up and doing nothing to dispel the Twinkie notion.

Brandon ran by us with a grin. "Sorry, crip. Maybe you should use your cane."

It was getting harder and harder not to just give that guy up for demon chow.

✳ ✳ ✳

Upstairs in my room that evening, I risked a peek in the mirror to see if I was remotely prom-worthy, and was pleasantly surprised to find I'd turned out passably well. I rather liked the dress. Hemmed to lower-calf, the indigo satin stood out in a full, Dior-esque bell. The tighter-than-it-ought-to-be bodice cinched my waist and gave me actual cleavage. Mom had found a deep rose shrug and a crocheted bag that matched. My shoes were pointy and uncomfortable, but looked great with the dress. Even my hair was cooperating. It lay in a smooth, seal-brown bob, and I'd pinned two blue sparkly clips on one side. Besides the matching earrings, my only other jewelry was Gran's cross. Better safe, as they say.

My camera would explain my presence at the dance, since I'd been vocal about not going. If Old Smokey sensed a trap and stayed away, I didn't know if we'd ever be able to anticipate it this well again. Assuming I was correct, which, as Lisa pointed out, wasn't exactly a certainty.

It also gave me an excuse to carry my camera bag, which was packed with canisters of salt. I'd be well armed and prepared, but nothing really stopped the nervous churning in my stomach.

The doorbell rang. No more time to fret about my appearance, or the possibility of my imminent demise.

Justin stood in the living room, chatting with my mom

and dad. I froze on the stairs, a funny sort of stab in the middle of my gut. He looked amazing in black trousers and a white dinner jacket, with his hair brushed tidily back from the rugged lines of his face. He reminded me of Indiana Jones at the beginning of the (vastly inferior) second movie. Not so much in looks, but in the easy way he wore the formal clothes, and his crooked smile when he saw me.

Oof. Stabbity stab.

"Magpie, you look beautiful." My father beamed. So did my mother. I blushed awkwardly, especially when Justin's grin widened; he knew me well enough to read my discomfort.

Mom hugged me when I reached the bottom of the stairs. "I'm glad you decided to go. You see? I doesn't kill you to act like a normal girl once in a while."

Boy, I really hoped those weren't famous last words.

"Take a picture, Michael," she told my dad.

"Oh," I rushed to correct any misunderstandings while Dad went to get his camera. "Justin isn't . . . I mean, we're not . . . I'm going . . ." I'd gone incoherent. I blamed the dinner jacket.

"Maggie is trying to say that we're sort of a foursome." Justin came to my verbal rescue. "We're not really a couple."

"So you can't take a picture?" asked Mom. "You two look great together."

Dad came back with the camera. "Put your arm around her, Justin." He obliged, his hand warm against my waist. Let's just pretend my sudden breathing trouble was due to the corset-like constriction of my dress, and leave it at that.

The shutter clicked, preserving my flustered expression for posterity.

The doorbell rang again. Did I imagine that Justin was slow to drop his arm? The cool spot his touch left behind was real enough. I avoided his eye, quipping poorly, "That'll be the next member of the Scooby Gang."

It turned out to be both of them. Brian looked spectacular in his tux, the tailored jacket smoothed across his broad shoulders, the formal black emphasizing his blue eyes and his wavy blond hair. Next to him stood Lisa, echoing her Goth heritage in a dark-green-and-black silk dress with a corset-type bodice and flowing sleeves. Her coppery brown hair was twisted up in a knot of trigonomic complexity and she looked beautiful, except for the icicles forming around her at having to share air with Brian.

It was a good thing we would have demon hunting to distract us, because otherwise it was going to be a very awkward night.

28

$f$ortunately, I hadn't gone to the prom to have a good time, because I definitely wasn't. Nerves stretched tight as violin strings, I watched for Brandon, jumped at every shadow, and sniffed the air so often that Brian finally asked if his deodorant had stopped working.

"No," groused Lisa, her elbows on the table. "Maggie's brain has."

The hotel staff had cleared away our plates of rubbery chicken, leaving the vaguely coral-and-seaweed-shaped centerpieces and a littering of fish-shaped foil confetti on the table. The theme of the evening? *Under the Sea*. One of the many items on which I'd declined to exercise my voting rights. We'd entered the Marriott's ballroom through a thick curtain of aqua crepe streamers, most of which were now on the floor. A painted paper mural covered the walls, full of sand, seaweed, cartoon fish, and even a diver getting eaten by a shark. Lovely.

"Where's Brandon?" I had lost sight of him for the fourth time since the DJ started blasting "Louie Louie" so loudly that the silverware bounced on the tables.

"On the dance floor." Brian nodded to the large parquet area laid out for our terpsichorean pleasure. Or, more accurately, for wiggling around like a trout on a line. At least that fit the evening's theme.

Brandon and his second-string friends had arrived so late that I'd become certain I'd misread the signs, and Biff lay in an alley somewhere while the freed Shadow went to town. But Stanley towered over the crowd, looking a lot like Lurch from the *Addams Family* in his tux. I was betting heavily that he would want the satisfaction of seeing the big dog taken down.

The Jocks and Jessicas, version 2.0, arrived staggering drunk. Jess Minor hadn't let any grass grow under her feet. With Jessica Prime exiled to the nut farm, she had latched onto the BMOC. Literally. His arm was probably the only thing keeping her upright.

"She looks like she thinks she's won the big prize." Brian wore a concerned knot of pity between his brows.

"The booby prize," Lisa added, as Brandon and his new entourage wove through the crowd.

"Nah." I watched Jess and Thespica giggling tipsily,

trying to stay upright on their high heels. "That's what they give to the first girl to fall out of her dress."

Justin choked back a laugh. Lisa had almost started to smile, too, then caught herself and went back to scowling.

Presently, we sat with our chairs turned toward the dance floor, wincing as the DJ turned on the mike with a squeal of feedback that made the whole room groan. "Amateur!" shouted someone over the last blast of music.

"Whooooooooooo!" shouted DJ Cliché. "Hello, senior class of Avalon High School! Are you ready to paaaaaaaaarrrrrrty?"

"Geez," I said. "Did this guy time warp out of *Animal House*? Why couldn't we have a band?"

"I think the class voted on it," said Brian, as Jessica Simpson started singing some song I hadn't liked back when it was actually popular. That would teach me to neglect my role in the democratic system.

I craned my neck, searching the dance floor. The flashing lights and brain numbing volume made it impossible to keep track of anyone. "Do you see Brandon?"

Beside me, Lisa pressed her fists to her eyes. "Jeez, Maggie. Would you just chill? If you're right, the . . . thing will show up. If you're not, there's nothing you can do about it."

I glanced from Brian to Justin, who admitted, "She's right."

"Of course I'm right." She dropped her hands to the table with a thud. "But this waiting is making me nuts. I need to take a break."

She pushed her chair back and strode off before I could

stop her, even if I wanted to. Justin turned to me, bemused. "I thought you said she was pretty much unflappable."

"She is. Normally." I stared at her retreating back as she headed toward the door. "Should I go after her, do you think?"

Brian shook his head. "Let her go. It's not like this is a normal situation, and trying to protect Brandon can't sit well with her."

I frowned. "She has a serious hate for all of you. Brandon especially. What's that about?"

"I have no idea." This was clearly a lie, but I didn't have a chance to challenge him, because he glanced over my shoulder and said, "I see him. I think he's headed to the john."

Justin rose to his feet, looking resigned. "You get the next pit stop. There's bound to be a few, from the way he's staggering."

When he was gone, I twisted in my chair to face Brian. "You don't think I'm crazy, do you?"

He returned my gaze soberly. "Last week I had two base-ball scholarships to chose from. Now I'm walking with a cane because I have advanced MS."

My fingers covered his on the table. "I'm so sorry, Brian."

He turned over his hand so that he could grasp mine. "Geez, Maggie. I'm not dead, crumpled like a tin can in Jeff's car. I owe you for that. So no, I don't think you're crazy."

Sighing, I looked at the corsage around my wrist, white roses. Very classy. "I'm sorry for ruining your prom. I know this isn't what you had in mind when you asked me."

"Life is full of surprises." He levered himself up with the

help of the table and then tugged on my hand. "Come on. Let's dance."

One bubblegum pop song finished and something else started, equally brainless and rhythmic. "You sure?" I conspicuously avoided looking at his cane.

"I can probably manage to stand in one place and swing my arms around." He led the way toward the booming music and flashing lights.

I wondered if he'd been a good dancer when he was steady on his feet, and didn't have to worry about his legs giving out under him. Because now . . . not so much. But when one of his baseball teammates noticed him out on the floor, and flashed a thumbs-up, Brian grinned gamely. Then the boys around him started a sort of synchronized head bob. Pretty soon there was a cluster of guys dancing like Brian: feet in one place, kind of bobbing to the beat while the girls gyrated around them. Mostly around Brian, actually.

Some people are popular because they're the stars of the team, and some people are popular because they're not afraid to dance like a complete dweeb.

Despite all the slinky girls around him, when the music ended he pulled unslinky me into a tight, laughing hug. It felt just as nice as you might imagine being squeezed against the chest of a butterfly-swimming, home run–hitting jock would be. Which is to say, very.

"Hey, Crip-patrick. Hard to keep you down, huh." Brandon's voice carried in the silence between songs. Brian loosened his grip on me, but not completely. I felt one arm heavy on my shoulders, and stayed pressed against his side so as he turned, he could lean on me.

"Hey, Brandon." The kids around us swung their heads back and forth like tennis spectators. Behind the looming footballer I could see Justin, lifting his hands in an apology, though I didn't see how he could have warned us.

"Jess told me you were here with the snitch. I couldn't believe it until I saw for myself." Biff's eyes lingered on my constriction enhanced cleavage and I resisted the urge to tug at my dress. "That must be some secret talent you've got, Quinn."

Like I needed a reminder of our last meeting. "Not everyone can get by on muscle alone, Brandon."

Jess Minor wrapped both arms around her date's meaty bicep. "It's not like you can get by on looks," she said, in a pointed sort of way. And I don't mean the obviously insufficient support of her clingy pink bodice.

I smiled sweetly. "Nice outfit, Jess. Find a good sale?"

Her claws dug into Brandon's black sleeve as she looked from me to Brian. "I'm not the one here with castoffs."

Brian's arm tightened around me. I had bruises from underestimating her once. Maybe I would have gotten more if one of the teacher chaperones hadn't appeared before I could voice my next smartass retort.

It was Professor Blackthorne, who took in the situation with a glance, and a Monty Python quote.

"What's all this then?" He cast an eye around the cluster of students.

"Nothing, Teach." Brandon turned on the smarm.

The chemistry teacher was unmoved. "Do I detect the characteristic aroma of ethanol on your breath, Mr. Rogers?"

"Uh . . ."

"The correct answer would be no and a prudent retreat," Blackthorne said, confirming my love for him.

"Er, no, Professor Blackthorne," said Brandon, smart for once. With a last glare at me, he went to another part of the dance floor, taking Jess with him.

"Thanks, Professor Blackthorne," I said.

"Think nothing of it, Miss Quinn. I take my duties of chaperonage very seriously." The gleam in his eye made me doubt the total truth of that. "And now I must be about them," he said as he left.

A girl from my gym class, Amber Somebody, slid up to us in the lull between songs. "Hey, Brian. I asked the DJ to play a slow dance next." She ran her hand down his lapel. "Dance with me?"

Brian hesitated. "Well, Amber, I'm here with someone."

"It's just a dance. Maggie won't mind." She barely glanced my way. "Do you, Maggie? D and D Lisa said you wouldn't."

"How helpful of her," I said. Brian was standing on his own feet again, if tentatively. "But she's right. I don't mind."

Amber leaned in and said more softly. "Come on, Brian. Show Jess you're no castoff."

"Well." He gave me another glance, then looked back at Amber and gave in with a sheepish sort of grin. "But only to show Jess what's what."

Call it a hunch, but I had a feeling Amber wasn't asking just to tweak Jess Minor. Likewise, except for his reluctance to leave me on my own, Brian didn't seem unhappy, either. It was nice to see something work out tonight.

Justin waited for me at the edge of the dance floor. "You lost your partner."

"S'okay." The mirror ball started up and the slow strains of a ballad flooded the ballroom. "I think he'll be all right."

Hands in his pockets, Justin nodded to the floor. "You wanna dance?" I didn't answer immediately, but cast a searching gaze over the room. He assured me, "I've got my eye on Brandon."

"I was worried about Lisa, actually."

"She's over there." A tilt of his head indicated a group of girls ensconced at a table far from the blasting speakers. When Lisa caught my gaze on her, she scowled, pointed to Justin and mimed us dancing. Or something. Looking quickly back to Justin, I smiled tentatively. "Dancing sounds good."

He smiled and reached for my hand. I stepped closer, my legs suddenly stiff and awkward, feeling my face heat, my heart flutter. Then he slid his arm around my waist, drawing me in, and we were swaying to Sarah McLachlan, and I thought maybe the DJ had redeemed himself. Justin turned my hand in his, tucking it close against his chest, like a prized item. I sighed a little, feeling the knot between my shoulder blades ease for the first time all night.

"We shouldn't let our guard down." I said it to myself more than to him.

"Lisa will watch."

Would she? I wasn't so sure. "I knew that Lisa hated Brandon and his friends, but I thought it was because they were basically assholes," I mused aloud as we danced.

I'd gotten used to doing that around Justin. "But something Brian said makes me think there may be more to it than that."

He sighed. His breath smelled very slightly of peppermint, and stirred the wisps of hair by my ear, tickling my neck. All thoughts raced out of my head, as quickly as that. One breath. "Maggie?"

"Yeah?"

"Before we talk about Lisa or Brian or anyone else, can I ask you a question?"

How could I answer, when all I could think about was the way the fabric of his jacket rubbed the bare skin of my arm. Ah, friction. Finally I knew what the big deal was about.

"Brian who?"

He made a sound that might have been a laugh or a sigh. His arm tightened imperceptibly on my waist, pulling me closer still. It was the most natural thing in the world to lay my head on his shoulder and let the too loud music drum out awareness of the world.

"Justin?"

"Hmmm?" His cheek rested against the top of my head. For the first time in my life, I was glad to be short.

"Were you going to ask me a question?"

"Hell if I know."

I smiled as we swayed in a slow circle. I saw Amber with her arms around Brian's neck. She raised her eyebrows at my partner, and gave me a covert thumbs-up.

I closed my eyes again, and when I opened them, we'd gone almost full circle. I saw the klatch of wallflowers, and Lisa's empty chair.

An icy chill crawled over my skin, leaving a clammy feeling of wrongness in its wake, the sudden certainty that something *bad* was happening.

I jerked up my head, hitting Justin in the jaw. "Lisa's gone." I clapped a hand to my skull and ignored the watering of my eyes.

He held his chin and squinted toward the table in the corner. "Maybe she went to the ladies room."

"No. Something's wrong." I searched the crowd.

"Where's Biff?"

"Who?"

"Brandon! Where's Brandon?" I saw Jess hanging drunkenly from the arms of a guy definitely not her date. "Where's Stanley?" He, at least, should be impossible to miss.

Justin scanned the crowd, summing up the futility of his search with a brief but eloquent word.

"Come on." I grabbed his hand and wove through the intertwined couples until we reached Brian and his partner. "Did you see where Brandon went?"

His head turned with aching slowness. "What?"

Amber looked down at me with annoyance. "What the Hell, Maggie?"

"Exactly." I pried Brian out of her grip. "Sorry, Amber. You can have him back later. I hope."

Hurriedly, I explained my worry as we left the dance floor, summing up with, "Brandon, Stanley, Lisa . . . they're all missing." Stopping at our table, I felt underneath it for my camera case. My fingers met only carpet and crumbs. I lifted the tablecloth to look, then straightened, feeling my stomach sink impossibly lower. "And so is my bag with our stuff in it."

This was definitely not how the plan was supposed to go. We'd lost track of our bait, our quarry—the human part, anyway—our ammunition, and our ally.

"Okay." Justin used a let's-not-panic voice. "Maybe Lisa saw Brandon leaving the ballroom and followed."

"By herself? She doesn't even really believe what we're dealing with."

"Exactly. She might think she can handle it on her own."

There was still something not right about that, but I couldn't think clearly with the alarm bells going off in my head. I snatched the saltshaker off the table and turned for the door. "We have to find them."

We exited the ballroom by the double doors and paused in the hallway to get our bearings. The lobby lay in one direction, the bathrooms in the other, and straight ahead were glass doors leading to the terrace.

"Check the restroom," Justin said, "just to be sure. I'll check the lobby." Brian's breath had grown labored just from the walk from the dance floor. "Stay here in case they come back."

I hiked up my skirts and dashed for the bathroom in a noisy rustle of satin. I don't know how those girls in the action movies do it. After I'd scouted, I had to slip off my heels and jog back in my stocking feet.

Justin returned as I did. "They didn't go that way."

"I know where they went." It wasn't entirely the process of elimination. Maybe I was getting the hang of this psychic stuff. I straight-armed the glass door leading to the terrace that circled the conference level of the Marriott, overlooking the golf course.

Brian followed us out, then had to stop and lean a trembling hand against the wall. His face looked ashen in the dim light. "You guys hurry. I'll catch up." When I hesitated in concern, he waved me on.

"He'll be all right." Justin grabbed my hand; heart pounding, ribs heaving against my too-tight dress, I ran behind him, down the moonlit path.

29

the plan had been simple. Stick to Brandon. Follow him if he left, especially if Stanley left, too. Use the salt to protect him from the Shadow, since it was the only thing we knew worked. See? Simple.

The stench hit me the moment we rounded the corner. Oh yeah, the demon was here, all right. My gorge rose in my throat and I fell against the terrace wall, losing my struggle to keep down my dinner.

"Jesus Christ, Quinn!" Brandon's voice rattled my skull. "You're here, too? What is this, the whole goddamn circus?"

I blinked stupidly, trying to fit the puzzle together.

Brandon stood in the center of the patio, his tux jacket thrown over a wrought-iron chair, a smoldering joint pinched in his fingers. Oddly enough, this was the only part that made sense. What I had to wrap my head around was Lisa with my camera case at her feet, empty now of easy-pour canisters of salt, and Stanley, wild-eyed and belligerent, clasping the now-familiar brazier in his arms.

Justin came to my side, looking green, so possibly he could smell the demon, too, though the other three seemed oblivious.

"Lisa?" She hadn't even glanced at me. "What's going on?"

"Yeah, Lisa," said Brandon. "I'm just out here getting some fresh air, and this one"—he pointed at Stanley—"shows up talking crazier than a shit-house rat. And this one"—meaning Lisa—"starts playing Betty-effing-Crocker."

I looked at the ground and saw a salt circle on the pavement, white in the moonlight. It looked as though most of the pattern had been put in place earlier and closed just now, where the line was cleaner. Raising my eyes to Lisa's grim face, I realized she'd been holding out on me, and protesting entirely too much, perhaps from the very beginning.

"Lisa?" I repeated her name.

"I'm fixing this, Maggie." She still didn't look at me. "Just let me handle it."

"Why are you interfering?" Stanley's drab hair stood up in wispy spikes as he confronted her. "You hate these assholes as much as I do."

"Shut up, Dozer," she snapped. "You don't even know what you're dealing with."

"Yes I do." He held the brazier in both hands. It looked smaller in real life, but somehow . . . more. As if the evil contained in it were distilled down, latent in the beaten brass. "I'm the one who found the key. I'm the one who realized what it could do. I'm the one who can control it."

"That thing doesn't control it, idiot."

"Lisa," I cautioned, seeing Stanley's face flush blood-dark. "Maybe you shouldn't piss him off too much." Just in case he could let the leash go early, better not antagonize the crazy guy.

Brian arrived then, leaning heavily on his cane. He stared in obvious confusion and Brandon, seeing him, made a disgusted sound. "You, too, Crip-patrick? This is a real loser convention. I'm out of here."

"Stop!" At least three of us shouted at him. Justin because he was about to step across the salt barrier, Stanley because he was in full raving lunatic swing, and me, because I could sense the demon waiting, its anticipation invading my brain the way its stink invaded my lungs.

The footballer paused at our outburst, and Justin stepped into his path. He raised his hands in a gesture both calming and emphatic. "You really don't want to head back right now."

"Look, dickhead. I don't even know who you are, but you'd better move before I kick your ass."

Justin's eyes narrowed and his face hardened. "You could try." He may have been bluffing, but he convinced me.

The tension seemed to thicken the air, growing dense

with every harsh word. I didn't know whether to warn them or not. If we drew the Shadow out of hiding, we could fight it, with Brandon safe in the protective circle. The uncooperative bait, however, was one wild card. The other pushed his way past Lisa to get in my face.

"Do you think you can stop me? No one can stop this now."

"Geez, Stanley. Did you get your dialogue from an old James Bond movie? Listen to yourself."

"No, you listen, Margaret Quinn."

Margaret?

He pushed my shoulder with the hand not holding the brass artifact. Brian stepped forward with a protective "Hey!" but Stanley ignored him. "You are an interfering little bitch and I don't know why you're not lying at the bottom of that swimming pool right now."

I remembered the list of names in my dream, offered to the demon in parchment and blue flame. "You put my name on the hit list?" I don't know where I found the room for indignation. "What did I ever do to you?"

"You *pitied* me," said Stanley, pushing at my shoulder again. "And you *meddle*. So I put you on the list. I don't know why it missed you, but . . ."

I shoved him back, remarkably restrained in confronting someone who'd tried to kill me. "Maybe because my name isn't Margaret, jerkwad."

Stanley stumbled backward; his heels scuffed the line of white crystals, but didn't break it.

"Maggie!" Justin shouted a warning and a remonstration. I saw immediately why. In the shadows by the terrace wall a nightmare coiled in on itself, writhed into being.

Lisa grabbed Dozer by the arm and yanked him away from the circle and away from me, trying to reestablish control of the situation. "Stop it. Now."

I looked at her, tried to sort out her involvement in all this. The demon knew my real name, but Stanley didn't. If Azmael knew what its summoner knew . . .

Still inside the circle, Brandon took one last hit off his joint and pinched it out, letting the smoke escape slowly on a lazy laugh. "Are you the loser queen, Lisa? These your court jesters?"

. . . then Stanley didn't actually summon the demon.

"Or maybe you got it bad for one of them." Brandon continued his languid taunt, while Lisa stared at him, loathing in her eyes. "Is it Quinn? Did I put you off guys for good?"

"Shut. Up." Her voice bit frozen chunks from the night air.

I stared at her. We all did. Nothing moved but darkness and shadow, growing in the corner of my vision.

Stanley didn't know my full name. But Lisa did.

"I was drunk." Bone-deep hatred twisted her words.

Brandon met it with indifference. "Duh. It was a college party. Everyone was drunk."

A vague memory flitted through my head: spring break, leaving for Colorado with Mom and Dad, and Lisa telling me that she and Katie and Tess were going to get a feel for campus life while I was gone.

Her fists clenched at her side, gathered more air and clenched again. "I was too drunk to say no."

Brandon's careless shrug was another assault. "Not my fault you changed your mind."

I took a furious step toward him, trembling with the temptation to do violence on him, to wipe that indifference off his face. "You unconscionable bastard." Justin put out a hand, kept me from crossing the line. I glared at him, then turned my anger on Brian next. "You knew about this?"

He avoided my gaze, swaying on his feet. "I drove her home that night. I offered to take her to the police, but she didn't want to."

"Why not?" I looked at Lisa. Her whole countenance, her entire being rejected sympathy. "Why didn't you tell me?"

"I didn't want anyone to know." Her gaze flicked to Brian, and I glimpsed part of her unreasonable hatred of him. He'd witnessed her weakness.

I grabbed for Lisa's hand, didn't let her push me away. "He did wrong, not you." Brandon snorted, and I ignored him.

Her chest heaved with the effort to control her emotion. "No, I was just stupid and naïve." Two fates worse than death in Lisa's book. She turned to Brandon. "All I wanted to do was punish you."

Two burning yellow sparks flickered in the solidifying darkness. "Lisa," I cautioned. "Don't do anything stupid."

"Something more stupid than summoning a demon, you mean?"

"No!" Stanley wrapped his arms around the brazier. "It was my idea. Mine. You just helped me, threw some ingredients in the pot." He stared, transfixed, at the agglomeration of shadow. "And now it's here, and you'll see who is in charge."

"You are *all* bat-shit crazy," said Brandon with almost as

much horror as contempt. The only time I would ever agree with him. "I'm done listening to this crap."

The darkness broke free from the corner and spread across the patio in a dank, hell-born fog. "Don't move," Justin ordered.

"You are not in charge here!" shrieked Stanley.

The Shadow chortled, less a sound of laughter and more the noise of bugs scuttling across rock.

"Christ on a crutch!" Brandon frantically searched the dark. "What was that?"

Lisa's face shone white in the moonlight. "I came up with the formula to evoke it. I can control it."

"I found the brazier." Stanley backed away from the fog, pressing his back to the wall. "I gave it the list of names."

"Shut up, Stanley."

Brian collapsed without warning. Justin turned instinctively to break his fall, and Brandon took his chance. He stepped out of the circle. As soon as his foot broke the line, it happened, more quickly than my mind could completely process.

The haze wound together, spinning into a noxious cyclone that amassed into a malformed approximation of legs and arms and trunk, sulfurous orbs where eyes should be.

Stanley dropped the brazier, three millennia of burnished brass hitting the concrete with a clang that echoed all the way back to its forging. Brandon's arm jerked suddenly up and back, like a police control hold, and kept going until I heard a crack and a wet pop and a tearing sound, then it fell to his side like a dead thing.

The pain reached his brain and he began to scream. His

other shoulder cracked, the joint splintering. Then the rib cage . . . Oh God, the sounds it made.

Do not pass out, Maggie. Think! I still clutched the shaker I'd taken from the table. My fingers lost precious time fumbling to unscrew the top. The metal cap bounced on the ground, and I poured the fine white crystals into my hand, until they ran through my fingers.

The screaming stopped.

Lisa fell to her knees, doubled over with horrified sobs. Stanley pressed himself to the wall as if he could crawl through it. Brian lay lax and still, but I could hear his breathing in the grisly silence.

Justin stood slowly. We watched as the Shadow dropped Brandon's broken body over the terrace wall, like so much rubbish, then turned to face us. It looked almost the same, a mostly human shape with a miasma of smoke clinging to it, trailing as it moved.

"Now we meet in the real world, Magdalena," said the demon Azmael. "At last face to face."

30

It knew my name because Lisa did. I hadn't quite wrapped my head around that, but I didn't take the time to analyze it now.

I flung the handful of salt. It hissed and fizzled against the creature's cloaking outer layer, and the acrid smell redoubled until I choked on the burning fumes, my eyes streaming until I couldn't see to defend myself. That was some deflector shield.

"Don't be rude," he —it?—chided. "I've waited so long to meet you."

"Sorry," I wheezed. "I left my book of demon etiquette

at home." I don't know how I found the courage to quip. But I figured collapsing in a gibbering puddle of terror wouldn't do anyone any good. Least of all me.

Justin's hand slid into his pocket. I knew he was armed, too, and I drew the demon's attention to me with another lame verbal sortie. "I gotta tell you, buddy"—Behind it, Justin silently opened his Ziploc bag—"now that you've got armpits, I suggest some deodorant. Because . . . damn."

"This century is full of wonders." A tendril of its smoky layer snaked toward me, winding as it came, twisting into a thin rope of shadow. I forced myself not to retreat. "The human capacity for false courage is just one of them."

The cord snapped around like a bullwhip, and I flinched as it struck Justin's hand, sending an arc of fine white crystals flying harmlessly across the paving stones. The tentacle lashed again and wrapped around Justin's throat.

His fingers tore at the blackness without effect. The demon didn't even look at him, but cocked its head at me. "Was that sporting, Magdalena? No. I think not." It lifted Justin higher, until he was hanging from the smoky extension, his back bowed as he tried to find purchase. He couldn't even draw enough breath to choke.

"Let him go!"

"Drop your weapon." I tossed my carton to the ground, next to Lisa whose fingers twitched, just barely. Justin made tiny, gasping half-coughs, and his grip on the demon noose began to slide away. "Now ask *nicely*."

Slowly, as if forcing my stubborn knees to bend, I took a supplicant's position. I couldn't read the creature's expression—I could only see its eyes through the concealing black miasma—but I sensed its surprised pleasure.

Arrogant son of a bitch. "Please," I said, my fingers creeping across the stone until they met cold brass. Lisa's hand inched to the carton of salt. "Let . . . him . . . Go!"

On my word, Lisa and I moved together. She snapped the canister up, throwing the contents across Justin and the demon-tentacle that held him. I lurched to my feet with the brazier, and slammed the metal with all my might and momentum into the monster's amorphous head.

Solid was a relative thing. The weapon clanged, I felt the impact up my arm. Acid yellow eyes dripped like the yokes of two rotten eggs, then congealed and rolled back up to where they belonged. Where the salt struck, its smoky extension sizzled and evaporated; Justin fell to the ground as the creature reeled back, making an animal squeal of pain.

"Close the circle," I shouted at Lisa. The demon had stumbled backward into the broken ring. "Close it!"

Lisa jumped forward and poured salt over the gaps. I felt a strange subliminal buzz as the line became complete again, a scant instant before the demon collected itself.

I hurried to Justin, who pushed himself up, wheezing painfully. Pulling loose his tie and opening his collar, I saw his skin was blistered and bruised, but his breathing eased quickly. "You all right?"

"Yeah. Help me up." He staggered to his feet, squaring his shoulders as we turned to face the trapped demon.

"Oh Lisa," it said, disappointment in its tone. "You had such potential. That one"—it gestured to the unconscious Stanley—"was just a clown. I had high hopes for you."

"That's enough, Azmael." I stepped forward, speaking the creature's name aloud for the first time, bringing it into the open and reducing its psychological power.

It hissed at me, eyes burning brighter for a moment. "Your bravado annoys me. You will be very afraid before I'm done with you, Magdalena."

The demon knew the power of a name, too. "You're trapped, Ass-my-el. And I'm going to punch your return ticket."

A tendril of its cloaking layer gestured carelessly to Lisa and Justin. "I will kill these two first, to give you great pain."

I raised the brazier like a shield. "It would give you a lot of pain, too. I know you're solid now."

"Not that solid." Its voice skittered with amusement, like dry, multilegged things in the dark.

The creature gave a heat-mirage shimmer. A layer of its swathing haze pulled away, like a wet peel of sunburned skin, and fell to the ground in a congealed lump. The blob twitched and writhed, as the demon shed another layer to plop beside the first. Clump after clump became semisolid until the imprisoning circle was filled with contorting masses of ectoplasm, heaving and struggling to be born into something vile.

I stepped instinctively back; beside me, Justin went taut with the same revulsion that held me transfixed. Stripped of his outer coating, Azmael looked as though someone with no real understanding of human form had tried to sculpt it out of dry and filthy earth. Eyes sat in sockets without lids and the nose recalled the vestige holes on a mummified corpse. And when the misshapen mouth moved to speak, my skin crawled at the *wrongness* of it.

"Do you not like my inner form, Maggie Quinn?" The demon taunted me. "Perhaps you liked me better as a shadow?"

"I certainly liked you better before you could talk."

The pseudo-face showed little more emotion than the veiling layers of smoky ectoplasm, but it managed anger pretty well. "And I prefer you quivering with fear."

The first Hell-blob leapt up. It wasn't done cooking, but it had too many legs, too many eyes, and its gaping maw seemed impossibly large, impossibly full of ragged, sharklike rows of teeth. The jaws snapped; I stumbled back, even as the thing hit an invisible barrier at the circle's limit.

"What are those things?" Lisa stood at one shoulder, Justin at the other.

"Trapped," I said, relieved, but not entirely. The beasts pawed the ground, a distorted hunting pack, growling with foul, sooty breath.

Azmael stood in the center of its minions. "It has been a pleasure doing business with you, Lisa." The beasts at its stubby feet snarled and sniffed the air. "I'm grateful to you for opening the door for me. The tasks you and the boy set before me allowed me to gain a liberty I haven't had for centuries."

"I never wanted—" Lisa began.

"I knew what you wanted better than you knew yourself." It made a tsking noise, almost droll. "Yet you give me no thanks."

I picked up one of the discarded cartons of salt. "I hope you enjoyed your leave, Smokey, because your pass is about to be revoked."

A derisive, dismissive snort. "I think not." The sulfurous eyes turned to me, anticipation making them swell. "You were right about this much, Maggie Quinn. I am hungry after so long without a solid form. And your kind is a wealth of rampant emotion."

With a certain drama, it crouched and brushed clear a section of the white line. Its hand smoked and blistered and stank, but remained intact. "Oh, that does sting."

The pack of demon-spawn slipped their invisible leash, poured out of the gap. They scrabbled on phantom claws past our horrified eyes, buffeting us as they rounded the corner and headed for the smorgasbord of teenagers dancing in short-lived blissful ignorance.

"Oops!" said Lisa. At least, the voice was hers, but the tone was Azmael's taunting humor. She turned, and I recoiled from the otherness in her eyes. "You'd better get going, Supergirl." She reached out and took the salt that I cupped, forgotten, in my hand, and let it run out of her fingers. "I think you know where to find us, if you survive."

Her body turned, walked away, stiff-jointed like a puppet. I took a step after her, but Justin caught my arm.

"Leave her."

"But Lisa . . ."

"Is one person." He pulled me insistently toward the front of the hotel. "We have to stop those things, or they'll kill everyone inside."

Stanley hadn't roused from his faint, and Brian was still unconscious. I didn't know if Brandon was even alive. But those demon-dogs were going to cut a swath through the senior class unless we stopped them.

I gave up arguing and ran, still clutching the brazier, leaving behind the fallen, and racing to save those I could.

31

I wondered how the beasts would get inside, since they didn't have arms to open the doors. As we rounded the corner, though, we saw the last two creatures squeezing through the crack between the doors.

"They're not solid," I said in relief. "They can't really—"

The last Hell-dog launched itself at me with a cougar-like scream. Pure reflex jerked the brazier up as the quite solid weight of the monster sent me sprawling to the ground. I screamed, too, as razor teeth hammered at the brass, trying to get through to my throat.

Justin kicked the beast aside. It immediately flung itself back at us, but I whacked the snarling thing with the brazier and it exploded in a cloud of infinitesimally small dropules of the primordial goo. Almost instantly they began to gloam together and rebuild themselves.

"Semisolid, I'd say." Justin pulled me up from the ground and away from the quickly growing Hell-blob. "Keep that weapon handy."

We each yanked open one of the glass doors. Terrified screams poured from the ballroom. By my quick and dirty reckoning, the monster-per-kid ratio lay in our favor; only it wasn't how many people they killed, but how much terror and pain they inflicted, feeding Azmael's hunger.

There was nothing to do but wade into the carnage. I swung my big brass bowl of kick-ass at a demon-dog that had pinned a boy from my chemistry class. The monster burst into a satisfying, if temporary, wet mist. Grabbing a napkin from the nearest table I handed it to the guy. "Keep pressure on the bleeding."

Justin grabbed a chair and smashed a creature savaging a girl's leg. She burst into hysterical tears, and he had to pry her loose before moving on to the next fight.

Three monsters down. Seventeen left. Eighteen, I amended, as the first re-formed beast leapt on a fleeing band geek. I quickly un-formed it again. At the end of the room, one of the light stands crashed to the floor in a shower of sparks. A speaker went next, conveniently squishing an eight-legged monster beneath it. Anything heavy, applied with enough force, could smash the things, but I noticed my brazier, perhaps because of its link to their master, made the smallest bits.

A few students tried to fight back. But the more the kids

screamed, the more blood that soaked the ugly carpet, the stronger the monsters became and the more quickly they remade themselves. Despite the numerical advantage, we were fighting uphill.

The demon-hounds herded and pushed with flashing teeth until the crowd stampeded like Irish fans at a soccer match; tables, chairs, and fallen students were only temporary impediments while the beasts picked off the stragglers. Feeding time at the watering hole, and survival of the fittest.

A heavy student, side-blocked by an even heavier dog-beast, crashed into the table in front of me. I jumped back as empty dishes and silverware catapulted into the air. I brought the brazier up like a shield; something clanged against it, and dropped at my feet.

I looked down. The salt shaker lay on the carpet, spraying my stocking-clad toes with white.

Something important lay in the memory of Azmael casually brushing aside the salt circle, something besides his new invulnerability to sodium chloride. It had cleared a path for the pack of minions, given them a clean way out.

So . . . what the Hell, to use a fitting phrase. I picked up the shaker, unscrewed the lid and climbed over the table to get to the student, who screamed as the beast teethed on his arm. "Close your eyes!" I shouted over the din, and dumped the entire shaker over them both.

The Hell-dog disappeared in a puff of black smoke. No tiny droplets, no wet mist. Just a dry, clean 'fffft!' and then nothing. Even the smell vanished.

"Dude!" I turned my head to see Backstage Guy, the one

I'd met at play practice, his tux spattered with blood and black demon-goo, a mike stand in his hand, heavy-side up. "Yo, Glowing-ass-girl! What did you do?"

"Salt," I said, clambering down from the table. In the wreckage of another setting I found two more shakers, handing both to Dude. "Unscrew and dump."

I ran through the tables, gathering as many shakers as I could. Professor Blackthorne was holding his own with one of the beasts, standing over it with a chair leg and splattering it apart every time it re-formed.

"You will not"—splat—"defy"—squish—"the laws"—scrunch—"of nature."

I dumped one of my saltshakers over the monster between squishings. The droplets fizzled out of existence, and Blackthorne looked at me, eyebrows shooting all the way up to his wildly askew hair.

"Supernatural creatures follow supernatural laws," I explained, grabbing ammunition off the nearest table.

"Of course they do," he said, smoothing white wisps out of his red face and regaining his sangfroid.

"Unscrew and dump." I dropped two shakers in his hand and left him to it. I saw other students getting the idea, and felt the tide turning with every *poof!* Just like magic.

Jessica Minor was perched on a table, defending the high ground from a snapping beast by whacking at it with a paper-seaweed centerpiece. It was tempting to let a Hell-dog take down the Hell-bitch, but a blast of white from behind me ended my moral dilemma and obliterated the demonette so quickly that its mad snarl hung in the empty air.

"Viva Maggie!" called the guerrilla of the Spanish Club. Don de Chiclet raised a fist full of salt. "Viva la revolucíon!"

The stampede had ended. Jocks, band geeks and brains, preps, ropers and stoners stanched each other's wounds and helped one another up. Thespica was sucking Backstage Dude's lungs out—in a good, nondemonic way—with a pile of salt at their feet. Good for you, Backstage Dude.

I saw Justin and hurried toward him, limping barefoot through the carnage. He was bleeding from some teeth marks on his arm, and his face was streaked with sooty demon residue. "I'm okay," he assured me, as the sound of sirens reached us.

"Come on." I pulled him toward the back door. "They won't let us leave once the authorities get here."

"Hang on, Maggie . . ."

Seeing Professor Blackthorne directing the first aid efforts, I stopped. "Professor, there are three more students out back. One of them is . . . he fell over the terrace wall."

The teacher gave me a level look. "That's what I'm supposed to tell the police?"

"I . . . I don't know." I was out of lies. "I have to go stop the . . . the thing that started all this."

Another stare, an instant's examination that seemed eternal. Finally, he said, "Go. I'll think of something. But your final grade is going to depend on your explaining the supernatural chemistry at work here."

"I will, I promise."

And if I live that long, I'll make good . . . somehow.

32

the Jeep raced along Beltline. I hoped all the cops were at the Marriott, because I was way past the speed limit.

"How do you know where they are?" Justin asked me, one hand clinging, white-knuckled, to the roll bar. The wind whipped my hair around my face and I had to drive with the skirt of my dress tucked tightly under my thighs. I never found my shoes.

"I just know. It's the way the quest always ends. Luke goes all over the galaxy, but he still has to come back to the Death Star to meet Darth Vader."

"You know this isn't a movie, right?"

"Yes. That ugly bastard has my best friend, and I have no idea how to fight it." I zipped through a yellow light. "Now think. Why did the salt work before, but not tonight?"

"It might have to do with its solid form." He shook his head. "All the supernatural traditions say it should have worked. Jewish folklore uses salt to bless a baby and keep the demons away. Chinese women take salt baths for the same reason . . ."

"So what do we use instead? Crosses? Holy water?"

"Azmael predates the birth of Christ. I don't think either of those would affect him."

I whipped onto the street that ran behind the school, my mind racing through the problem. If Azmael predated Christ, then he, it, also came way before Morton.

With a squeal of the tires I turned the Jeep in a tight U, changing directions as quickly as my thoughts. "We're using the wrong salt."

"What?"

"Azmael isn't going to be afraid of easy-pour, iodized, table salt. We need the real unprocessed thing."

"Where are you going to find sea-salt at this hour?"

I pulled up in front of a corrugated aluminum building and pulled the brake. "Landscaping shed. They keep fifty-pound bags for deicing the sidewalks in winter. Grab the bolt cutters in the back, will you?"

Justin stared at me, wasting precious moments on bewilderment and perhaps a little awe. "You were a Girl Scout, weren't you?"

"Nope. But Nancy Drew was *always* prepared."

✳   ✳   ✳

My bare feet met the cold tile of the natatorium with a quiet slap-slap; the diving board loomed above, and I saw the man-shaped darkness waiting there.

It was all about knowing the rules. Quests were circular; Azmael held to tradition, obviously. The accident at the pool had been the first time I'd glimpsed the Shadow. Even if the accident had misfired because Stanley wrote my name down wrong, it was still where the demon had come for me.

And of course, the deep water terrified me. Lisa knew, so Azmael knew; there was simply no other place they could be.

The smell confirmed this, faint but distinct. Chlorine and brimstone and rotting flesh. It was a good thing I had nothing but dread churning in my stomach.

Outside the gym, Justin had helped me shoulder my backpack and balance the weight. "Can you carry all this?" His paladin's face pinched with worry.

I grinned. "I've been in training for twelve grades." Then sobering, I went over our hastily constructed plan. "I have to go in by myself, but once I have him distracted—"

"I'll be there." His hands rested on my bare shoulders as he looked down at me, a riot of emotions in his eyes. If this were a movie, he might kiss me now, or tell me to stay alive, no matter what, or vow to rescue me. And I might be wearing shoes and have less mascara running down my face.

Though come to think of it, "I'll be there" had been the perfect thing to hear just then.

"Are you alone, Magdalena Quinn?" The demon's reedy voice echoed in the big, empty gym. The water in the pool beside me shivered, then returned to placid lapping.

"Yes, I am, oh great and powerful Az."

"You took your time. One would think you were leaving your friend to reap her own wickedness."

Judge not, lest you be judged. I remembered that much from Sunday school. Lisa would have to answer for her ancillary role in the events of the past two weeks, not to mention tonight's carnage. But not to me.

"Lisa is my friend. And I don't let jumped-up, minor demon jackasses take my friends."

The smell intensified with said jackass's anger. "Then come up and try to rescue her, mighty demon-hunter. I'm waiting."

I guess that was netherworld speak for "Nyah nyah nyah, I'd like to see you try it."

Ahead, the diving pool glimmered darkly; diffuse light reflected on the surface, but did not penetrate the inky blackness at all.

"Leave the backpack on the ground," Azmael said. "Do you think I'm a fool?"

An ominous growl rumbled out of the shadows. I saw the gleam of teeth. Great. Another doggie. We'd destroyed the ones at the prom, so the demon must have regained enough . . . power, mojo, whatever . . . to create more. Not the best news I'd had all evening.

"I'm leaving it," I shouted up at him. "Call off your dog."

"When you obey me, stubborn child."

I had to get my burden to the pool, so I walked forward, the beast shadowing me, its claws clicking on the tile. The growl deepened as I reached the base of the diving platform, the claws sped, leapt. In a practiced move, I slipped one shoulder from its strap, let the weight of the pack swing down, around, to meet the dog's attack. The monster sank its teeth through the nylon and *pffft!* disappeared without time to whimper.

Whoa. It had barely touched the salt inside, hadn't taken a dousing at all. I wish that had worked as well on the Jacobson's dog when it had chased me to school every morning of fifth grade. I began to think this insane plan might actually work.

I heard another growl, and figured a second minion had come to ensure my compliance. But hell-dog number one had done me a favor, ripping a large hole in the fabric. In the blind spot beneath the platform I set the pack on the edge of the pool and let the big crystals of the unprocessed rock salt pour into the water.

"Okay. I'm coming up. No backpack."

I hiked up my dress and began to climb the ladder to the high dive, another thing easily accomplished by heroines in movies, but a major pain in real life. In my next battle with a creature from Hell, I would definitely forgo the formal wear.

An eternity later, I crawled onto the wide platform, winded and trembling from fatigue and nerves. Turns out I like heights only slightly more than I like the depths. There's irony for you. I stayed on all fours as I fought off the vertigo and tried to catch my breath. I was one scary demon-fighter, all right.

Azmael stood in the center of the dais. Lisa lay unconscious near me. If we survived this, she was going to be pissed that she'd been cast in the helpless female stereotype, getting kidnapped and fainting.

"No quip, Maggie Quinn? No witty repartee?"

I stared at the creature's feet, as not-quite-right as the rest of its mistake of a body. "Just wondering if you shouldn't have cloven hooves."

"I am exactly as I should be!" Its voice rang against the steel beams and concrete. "Exactly as I have been for ten thousand years."

Slowly, I got my legs under me. Movie heroines never have to hitch up their tops, either, but I'd be darned if I'd give Azmael a thrill by falling out of my dress. "Ten thousand years, huh? No wonder you go around with the veil-o-stench. You must be pretty sorry to lose it."

The demon lurched toward me, angrily. I sidestepped, letting it drive me farther from the ladder. Live and die by the wisecrack. Sir Justin had a gift for prophecy.

"No matter." Old Smokey recovered its aplomb. "I'll rebuild my form quickly." Lidless yellow eyes burned more deeply with hunger. "How I love every neurotic, apprehensive, irrational member of your generation. I will feed on your kind until I have power to build an army of shadow hounds." It looked down at me with an eerily human expression of distain. "Then we will see who is the *minor* demon."

"Don't feel you have to prove yourself on my account."

"Insolent insect!"

Our dance of quip, lunge, and dodge drove me toward the pool. I thought I saw movement below, knew I heard a growl. But I couldn't warn Justin about the hell-dogs without drawing their master's attention to him.

"I feel your terror, Magdalena." It moved again, herding me. "It boils below the façade of your bravery."

"That's my acid indigestion." Prickles of sweat broke out on my skin as I reached the edge of the platform. I guess this is what they mean when they say "Between the devil and the deep blue sea."

"I can smell your fear." It drew a noisy breath through the two elongated ovals of its nose, and smacked its mis-shapen lips. "Your stubbornness hides a bounty of dread."

The balance tipped with my final step; the effect was tangible, an inevitable teeter-totter slide into the depths. Azmael's horrible mouth curved into something like a smile.

An updraft caught at the bell of my skirt. The familiar, irrational terror of the deep—of sinking into the abyss—crawled around in my brain like a parasite, and I gave it rein. I hung my heels over empty space, and opened my mind to my ravaging phobia.

The demon couldn't resist. It sprang at me with a voracious scream, like an animal, a feral, starving thing. I fell back, into the void, and the creature jumped after me.

Dear God, let this work.

I hit the water with that prayer, and then wished that I'd listened to Coach Milner's instructions on how not to die a horrible death coming off the high dive. She might not have covered the part with the Hell-born psychic vampire, but at least I might have known that surface tension was not my friend.

The impact felt like hitting a wall at five or ten miles an hour. As the water closed over my head my entire being, down to my cells, screamed in protest. Then I heard the demon splash down beside me. It sank, grabbed on to me with long, sinuous arms and pulled me deeper, drinking in my terror and my despair.

Part of the plan. I chanted it in my head as my skirt billowed up around me like a shroud. Part of the plan, a salt bath, a cleansing, a solution. But the Maggie that curled up in my brain, catatonic with fear, only knew the tentacles of a monster dragged me down.

Part of the plan. The creature's limbs had gone amorphous and pliable. The demon was losing substance, and its elongating fingers entwined my arms and legs like slimy, rotten vines. With a spark of hope, I started to kick.

My legs churned the water, sped the process as each molecule of NaCl bound to a demonic atom, making it inert. The snaky fingers that gripped me broke apart. I reached blindly out, stretched my arms into the water and grabbed double handfuls of the protoplasmic mess that remained of Azmael. Now that it was shadow-substance again, I could hear it in my head, flailing mentally in fury.

And then it disintegrated completely. My hands held nothing, and my mind was empty.

Numbing panic rushed to fill the void. I swirled my arms and legs through demon-free water, but I had no idea which way was up. The burning in my chest grew intolerable, and little dots of light jumped at the edges of vision.

A hand grabbed my arm, a solid, human hand, pulling at me insistently. I tried to kick, tried to move my arms, but it was like moving through Jell-O. My skirts wrapped around my legs, trapping them. I was so tired, and the dancing sparkles flooded the whole of my sight.

33

My head broke the surface of the water and I sucked in a greedy lungful of air. Something constricted my middle—Justin's arm, holding me afloat while I coughed and sputtered and reminded my body what oxygen felt like.

"Good to see you," I managed between gasps.

"Told you I'd be here." He swam to the ladder, pulling me along. "Can you climb up?"

"Maybe," I lied. My limbs were spaghetti.

He wrapped my arms around the railing. "Just hold on."

That, I might manage.

He climbed from the pool, then hooked his arms under

mine and hauled me out. I think I was heavier than he expected. I hoped he assumed it was my waterlogged dress. He fell back, and I sprawled on top of him like a big, soggy fish.

For a long time neither of us moved. I didn't think I could. Not one muscle in my body wanted to obey my commands. Truthfully, though, it felt good to rest there, Justin's chest rising and falling under my cheek as he caught his breath. There was another issue as well, but I hadn't figured out what to do about it.

"When I saw you dive from that board"—his hand stroked my back, almost absently—"and I use the word *dive* very loosely—I thought my heart would stop."

"You, too?" Mine still beat kind of erratically.

He looked at the pool, which rippled innocently against its concrete borders. "Is it—the demon—gone?"

"Yeah." It *felt* gone. The way it had disappeared from my head with a little pffft, just like its Hell-dog offspring, made me certain. Well, as certain as I could be, with my vast experience in matters mystical.

"Do you think you can get up?" he asked.

"No."

"Why not?"

"Because my dress slid down when you pulled me out of the water. I'm not decent."

"Oh." His cheeks flushed visibly in the dim light, which I thought was kind of cute, until I noticed a tinge of guilt in his blush, and it occurred to me he might not have been completely unaware of that fact.

Call me clueless. And slightly flattered.

He covered his eyes while I sat up and quickly tucked things back where they belonged. Collecting the dinner jacket crumpled on the tile nearby, he handed it to me, his head still turned.

"Thanks." I wrapped the fabric around my bare, wet shoulders, grateful for the warmth. "You can turn around now."

He offered a hand and pulled me to my feet. My knees buckled—no, really, they did—and Justin caught me tight against him.

"Thanks." I rested my hands on his shoulders, not quite able to meet his eyes. "For helping me save the world and all."

"Anytime." His crooked smile never looked better. If this were a movie . . .

The kiss couldn't possibly have felt so good. He bent his head and fit his lips to mine, as naturally as, well, breathing. But I'd never again take oxygen for granted. I slid my arms around his neck and kissed him like I might never kiss anyone again, ever. He kissed me as though I'd scared him to death, and he needed to tell me something important before I did something else foolhardy. I think I got the message.

A few blissful centuries later, he broke away and wrapped me tightly—tighter still—in his arms. "Maggie Quinn, when you take a leap of faith . . ."

"I knew it would work." I rested my cheek on his shoulder, very warm beneath his sodden shirt. "I just thought: water. The universal solvent."

He laughed. Even with the incredulous shake of his head, it was a wonderful sound.

"Hey!" I startled guiltily at the voice, calling from above. "Maggie? Is that you?"

"Lisa? Are you okay?" I saw her pale face at the edge of the diving platform.

"What the Hell am I doing way up here?"

"It's a long story," I said. "Can you make it down?"

"Yeah. If I made it up in this dress, I guess I can make it down." Her head disappeared.

Justin let his arms fall away from me, obviously reluctant. "I'll give her a hand." I wrapped his jacket close and watched Lisa's shaky descent; once on the ground, she stood for a moment, grasping the ladder and brushing off his assistance.

Then she looked at me, confusion knotting her forehead. "Why are you wet?"

Justin spoke, not coldly but not kindly, either. "She vanquished the demon with a trap in the water."

Her eyes widened. "The dive pool?" A dizzying jumble of emotions chased each other across her face. Shock, awe, relief . . . shame, grief, and regret. Finally she raised a shaking hand to her face. "I didn't understand what it was. A vengeance spirit, Stanley said. I didn't think it would . . ." She trailed off as we all remembered what it had done.

"Why did he come to you?" I asked.

She gave a bitter laugh. "I'm D and D Lisa. He thought I knew about sorcery and things."

"But you came up with the spell." Justin's tone clipped the damp air.

Lisa walked to a bench and sat, as if her legs wouldn't hold her any longer. "Research and improvisation. An academic exercise. I didn't really expect it to *work*."

I moved to her slowly, my arms folded. "Did you send the demon after me?"

"Of course not." That sounded more like Lisa, impatient with me for even thinking it. "Stanley made the list. It had to be written in the same ancient script as on the artifact, and he had his mother's books. I couldn't even read it. Fortunately, he thought your name was Margaret."

"Not so fortunate for Karen," I pointed out. "Was it just coincidence, that she was your closest competition for valedictorian?"

"I hoped so." She sank her face into her hands. "But it was like the thing was taking thoughts out of my head. I knew what would hurt the Jocks and the Jessicas, but I never wanted to *act* on those ideas, not seriously. Except maybe Brandon. And I would only want to beat Karen fairly."

I could sense the guilt that wracked her; I'm not sure how. Still as stone, she didn't ask for forgiveness. I suspected from the starkness of her voice, she didn't think she deserved it.

"We should go." Justin touched my arm. "I'm going to check the hall. Meet me at the door."

I nodded, understanding he was giving us privacy. I sat on the bench and took my friend's hand. "You forged the weapon, Lisa. You didn't wield it."

She raised her bleak gaze to mine. "But I didn't stop it, either."

"I'm not sure you could have, once it started." I looked away, at the rippling blackness of the pool. Curiosity, anger, arrogance, denial. I couldn't judge Lisa, because I'd been guilty of all those things at one time or another. Sometimes all at once.

And we would need each other. Azmael knew us. He was gone from this plane, but had he ceased to exist? Vanquished was not the same as destroyed.

I stood, decisively, and pulled her with me. "Come on. It's time to go."

34

"Hallucinogenic Drugs Suspected in Wild Dog Attack on Senior Prom"—that was the headline Saturday morning.

"Wild dogs?" I posed the incredulous question in our living room, full of family. "Who's going to believe that wild dogs attacked the Marriott?"

Dad settled on the couch, a fresh cup of coffee in his hand. "More people than will believe demon-spawn did it."

"I would rather believe in wild dogs," said my mom, warming her hands on a mug of tea. "I'm not sure I can handle the truth."

She might not believe it at all if I hadn't brought Justin

home to tend to his bite marks. The circumference was more like a shark than a dog, but fortunately it hadn't gone very deep. I couldn't say the same for Mom's denial.

Justin was still there—Mom had insisted he stay in the guest room. Lisa had stayed upstairs with me, but she was gone by the time I woke up.

Gran had arrived with doughnuts, just as the coffee was finished perking, of course. She stole a moment to tell me how proud she was, then pinched my ear, hard, for not keeping her in the loop. She couldn't have been too angry, though, because she brought blueberry-filled doughnuts, and no one likes those but me.

I stuffed the rest of a doughnut in my mouth and read the article. "Listen to this: 'When asked about strange reports of ghost dogs that couldn't be killed, Dr. Silas Blackthorne said, "Ridiculous. That would run counter to all natural laws of physics. Clearly someone must have spiked the punch with some kind of perception-altering drug. You would be amazed the effect that certain combinations of chemicals can have on the brain." ' "

Maybe Silas Blackthorne had a career in fiction after all.

"Well," said Justin, sounding very amused as he read the paper over my shoulder, "he did say he would make something up."

I looked up at him from the floor in front of his chair. "Do you think people are really going to buy that?"

"Your mom is right. No one wants to believe in demon-dogs. Even eyewitnesses search for a logical explanation, no matter how big a stretch."

A valid point. And really, there were few who knew the

whole truth. He, Lisa, Brian, and I. Brandon and Stanley weren't talking.

The doorbell rang. "I'll get it," I said, levering myself up from the floor. "Maybe it's Lisa."

I had seen no reason to go into details of either Lisa or Stanley's involvement. Stanley's parents were going to have enough to deal with. The EMTs had found him wandering the golf course, babbling about the snapping jaws of Hell. His condition backed up the "experimental mind-altering drug" theory, and he was undergoing psychiatric observation. Maybe he would recover, maybe not. My gut told me, though, that he'd been a victim of Azmael, too.

As for Lisa, she stood on my doorstep, the purple shadows under her eyes speaking to a sleepless night. "Hey, Mags."

"Hey. Where'd you go this morning?" I floated the question, not wanting to make it an accusation.

"The hospital." Running a tired hand over her face, she seemed to unravel a little as I watched. "He's not dead."

I knew she meant Brandon. His critical injuries were mentioned in the paper, but no death.

"He doesn't remember anything at all. And he's going to have months, maybe years of orthopedic therapy ahead of him. But he's not dead."

I pulled the front door closed, leaving us in privacy on the porch. "You talked to him?"

"Yeah. Sort of. I snuck in. He was on serious drugs."

"How . . ." I tried to think of a way to ask if she was all right, when she obviously wasn't. "How are you feeling?"

"I don't know." She shook her head. "I used to think I would do anything to get back at him for making me feel that way, so powerless." She looked up at the gabled roof, blinking hard. "But when the demon was tearing him up, I lost track of which one of us was the monster. It was an ugly place to find myself, Mags."

"I know." Except that I didn't, really.

"Nothing justifies that."

Possibly I could say something placating, like she didn't really know what she was letting loose, or he deserved it. Both those things were true but both were also too easy.

"I think you should talk to a counselor," I said.

She looked at me strangely. "About summoning a demon?"

"No. About what happened over Spring Break. You need to deal with that. Atonement can come after." I put my hand on the doorknob. "But first, you need to come inside and have a doughnut."

Somewhere behind her weariness, maybe there was a spark of hope, but she was still Lisa. "That's not going to fix things."

"No, but with a cup of coffee, it's a start."

We went in. The folks greeted her warmly, Justin with a reserve that made Gran glance at him curiously. Mom, oblivious, fussed and asked where she'd run off to.

"I went to see Brian in the hospital," Lisa said, surprising me. She'd mentioned only Brandon.

"How is he?"

"Good. Apparently having a remission as abrupt as his onset. And his room was already filling up with female visitors when I left." She snuck a look at me, which I ignored, because I wasn't anything but happy for him. I thought maybe Justin was looking my way, too, but I didn't turn to see.

"I'm going to Karen's house later," I said, not quite changing the subject. Brian's recovery made me hopeful for her own return to normal. "She called at the crack of eight a.m. to ask for the scoop."

Hesitancy seemed such a foreign expression on Lisa's face. "Maybe I could go with you?"

"I think that would be nice."

I understood what Lisa was doing. When you almost lose something, you have to touch it often to reassure yourself it's still there. None of these people had been that dear to her, but they stood for what she'd put in jeopardy by helping Stanley. They represented her soul, nearly sacrificed to vengeance.

Then I *knew* Justin's eyes were on me, sending a strong "I've got something to say about this" vibe. Not subtly at all, I looked down at my empty cup and said, "I need more coffee. Back in a sec."

I left them discussing whether wild dogs might really roam the thickly forested State Park near Avalon. Their voices hummed from the other room as I emptied the last of the coffee into my industrial-sized mug, and grabbed the milk from the fridge.

When I closed the door, Justin had joined me. "So everything's okay now? Everyone is chummy again?"

I gave him a tart look, because sarcasm didn't suit him at all. "No one was that chummy before. And it's not all okay. But it might be, someday."

He studied me a little longer, then unwound with a sigh. I liked that about him, that he could pick his battles and let other things go, at least for the moment. I'm not so good at that. But then lately, my battles seemed to pick me.

"What about you?" he asked. "Are you all right?"

"Why wouldn't I be all right?"

He leaned on the counter. "I don't know. You faced down the dark forces of the universe. And went to the prom."

"Don't ask me which was more traumatic." I stirred my coffee thoughtfully. "I feel . . . different."

"A lot has happened."

"I'm never going to be able to ignore my dreams again. I'm always going to wonder what is a hunch and what is, you know . . . the freakitude."

"Maybe it'll get easier with practice. You could talk to your gran about it."

I watched the whirlpool in my cup. "You know what the weirdest thing is? I have to go to school on Monday. Shouldn't I get special dispensation for saving the world?"

"From wild dogs?" He grinned. "Probably not."

"Gee, thanks." Mug in hand, I started to breeze past him. He caught the back of my T-shirt.

"Listen. What do you say we go on a date that doesn't involve ghostbusting or demon hunting?"

A shy sort of smile crept to the corner of my mouth. "Just you, me, and a basket of chicken fingers?"

"Maybe even a movie."

I pretended to think about it. "Okay. But not a horror one."

"No? I was thinking about *Prom Night*."

"Very funny."

"What about *Carrie*?"

"Don't make me hurt you. I'm a demon slayer now, you know."

"Look out, Buffy."

✳   ✳   ✳

And that was how I survived the senior prom. I had faced down a demon, saved the senior class, and even managed to snag a date in the bargain. Now all I had to do was survive the three weeks to graduation.

But that's a story for another day.

ACKNOWLEDGMENTS

There's an axiom among authors that you have to write a million words of crap before you can produce publishable prose. Here's to everyone who suffered through mine.

But especially I'd like to thank . . .

My agent, Lucienne Diver, who answers my newbie questions with good humor, and Krista Marino, who has spoiled me for all other editors. What a great way to start.

Candace Havens, Britta Coleman, Shannon Cannard, and all the Divas. But especially Candy and Britta, for recognizing greatness underneath the stark terror.

The Dallas–Fort Worth Writers' Workshop and the after-hours IHOP Irregulars, especially Shawn and Dan. Rachel Caine, the LJ crew, and the Old Guard: Carole, Jennifer, et al. You may not even realize the little things you said that kept me coming back to the keyboard.

The young thespians of Victoria Community Theatre. There's something of each of you in this book. Hopefully you'll never figure out which parts.

Haley M. Schmidt, who wanted a manuscript for her graduation present.

My husband, Tim, because you've seen "better" and you've seen "worse" and you love me anyway.

And all my family, Mom, Peter, and Cheryl Smyth, sister of my heart. You all believed in me, even during the times when I didn't believe in myself.

ROSEMARY CLEMENT-MOORE has been writing stories her whole life, even when she should have been doing other things, like algebra homework. Despite this inauspicious beginning, she managed to acquire a master's degree in communications, along with an eclectic résumé: telephone operator, Chuck E. Cheese costume character, ranch hand, teacher, actress, stagehand, director, and playwright.

A recovering thespian, she writes full-time, a job that combines all the things she loves best: playing with words, researching weird subjects, entertaining people, and working in her pajamas. She lives in Texas with her husband and too many pets, none of whom really understand why the best working hours are between ten at night and two in the morning, but all of whom let her sleep late anyway. *Prom Dates from Hell* is her first book for young readers. Visit Rosemary at www.rosemaryclementmoore.com.

falling
is never easy.

ROSEMARY CLEMENT-MOORE

the
splendor
falls

When Sylvie Davis's dance career is ended
by a broken leg, her mother ships her off
to Alabama to spend some time with her father's
family. Suddenly, there are two guys she can't
stop thinking about, a house that just might
be haunted, and a question:
who is worth falling for?

And Maggie thought the cheerleaders were bad. . . .

Look for Maggie Quinn's next showdown with evil in

Hell Week

Coming in fall 2008